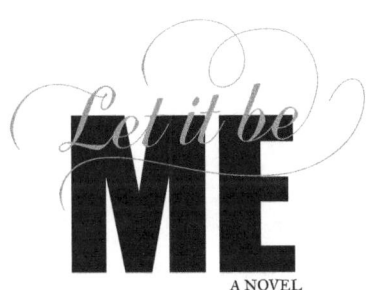

Let it be
ME

A NOVEL

Let it be
ME
A NOVEL

toni aleo

This is for my mom, Patricia Ortiz.
I love you & miss you so much.

Prologue

See that woman there?

The one with beautiful long wavy blond hair cascading down her shoulders, her arms up protecting her eyes and face?

That's me. Violet Moore.

I've always loved my big blue eyes, hence the reason I'm balled up trying to protect them, along with the nose I received from my mother and the defiant chin I got from my father. Before, Rob used to say my eyes could light up a room. Now he says they annoy him. Everything I do annoys him. I think even when I breathe, he's annoyed, which is why he hits me.

Like now, his booted foot connects with my gut with a force strong enough to obliterate any breath I thought I had. A strangled cry pitches from deep within my diaphragm, scorching my throat, and he ignores it. He always ignores me. In some ways, I think it makes it worse. His kicks get harder, more frantic and violent when I scream or cry, but I can't help it. His broad, 5'11 frame towers over my own willowy 5'6 build. He is stronger, much stronger, and Lord knows I'm scared of him. Like now, he lets loose a string of obscenities about how I'm the world's biggest piece of shit when, not two years ago, I was his world. Before, I used to be the most amazing woman and he was the luckiest man on earth to have me. He promised me the world, and all I've received in the last two years is pain and heartache.

Why the hell do I stay? Why do I take this and why do I allow this to happen?

I've asked myself those same questions for the last seven hundred and thirty days, but for some reason I still stay. Even through the horrible honeymoon where I learned that the way I eat has driven him half past mad a dozen times. I spent most of our trip with sunglasses covering my bruised eyes, trying to hide from the stares of bystanders. Or when he took me away from my family in Colorado to Tennessee, so they would stop asking questions about my injuries. Or when he kicked me so hard, I lost my child.

Is it love? Hell, I sure don't think so because his voice makes my skin crawl. Even with his dark hair and even darker eyes, his olive skin, and the thick scruff that used to turn me on, I can't stand the sight of him. I hate him. Am I scared to leave? Yes. Do I feel like I'll never find someone to love me? Definitely. I'm scared shitless and it doesn't help that Rob tells me daily that no one will ever love me. Have I lost all faith? Am I at the bottom of all bottoms? Fuck yes.

I know it's horrible, and I know I shouldn't believe him, that I should love myself before anything. There used to be a day when I did, but Rob sucked it out of me. I'm aware that I could be classified as a weak person, but don't give up on me yet, because, look, do you see that? Do you see the way I am getting up? Look, I'm grabbing his grandmother's ugly vase and looking at my face. See the way my chin is going up, the way my tears have stopped? How my shoulders are squaring up? See how my grip on the vase has tightened? And look, do you see the shocked look on his face?

Because I do.

With my hands cupped over my face, I tense and wait for the blow, the one that tells me it's going to be a long night and he's had too much to drink. I don't want to lie down and give him an even bigger advantage than he already has, but as his booted foot cracks into my sternum, I know it's all over. My ragdoll body flies back a few feet and my hip slams into the cold linoleum of our kitchen floor. I used to love the swirling pattern of the tiny, cerulean flowers, but now I avoid this room for fear of gagging.

I let my body sag down until my temple hits the floor, the stars in my eyes and heave in my chest threatening bile or worst: blood. His foot connects again and a strangled cry pitches forth, straight from my diaphragm, ripping apart my throat. I can't help but scream, even though I know it'll only get worse.

It always does.

His kicks become harder and more frantic, and I long for the warm detachment of unconsciousness, willing it to take me away.

It's amazing that Rob – the tall, dark and handsome stranger I fell in love with years ago, the one who carried me down the beach so I could snap my own "Footprints" photo, who stayed up with me late at night to tell stories and draw endless circles in the soft flesh of my back with his fingertips – could change so completely that he's nothing more than a distorted image, a blurry memory of what could have been.

I should have run the first time I heard "I'm sorry" while hiding my black-and-blue eyes behind dark sunglasses. I should have known better when he packed up our home and took me away from my family in Colorado to move to Tennessee, a place I'd never been, after my mom questioned the fingerprints on my forearms.

He lets loose a string of obscenities about how I've ruined his life as his foot cracks into my sternum again, and any breath I thought I had whooshes away and leaves me empty inside. I wrap my shaking fingers around my long blond hair, holding it close to me so that he has nothing to grab on to.

Letting out a maniacal laugh that makes my blood curdle and congeal instantly in my veins, he takes a few steps back to look at the mess he's made. The small pool of blood from my nose, and my supine, willowy form with slim arms that cradle the stomach in which a baby had been growing before he kicked that away mere months ago. His eyes are distant, cold, and I know he's not looking at me anymore. For once I feel the strength that has been hiding inside me for the last two years, the kind that converges under my skin until it manifests itself into something I can use. I'm going to beat the shit out of Rob for once. I am going to fight back. I have to or he may very well kill me.

Why am I doing this now, you may ask?

Why hadn't I done this way before I married him, lost a child, and became so weak that I hate myself?

Well. Get a blanket and maybe a glass of wine, you're going to need it, because my story isn't a happy one. Well no, I take that back. It can be happy, I can be happy; I just have to get there. I have to fight for it. So sit back and let me explain how the fight was woken inside me.

It all starts with Tucker McCloud

Chapter **ONE**

I used to be freakishly in love with Rob Moore.
I thought of him from the first moment I woke, and he was the last thing I thought of before I went to sleep. His smile made my world shine and his eyes could bring me to my knees, so blue that they reminded me of the ocean. I loved him, and I thought he loved me.

Things started between us three years ago, when I was in my finishing my last year of college to be a registered nurse. He was a nurse at the hospital at which I was interning. He stunned me with his angular face and square jaw, the muscles that rippled under his scrubs, the way of his dark hair. I remember how shy and fidgety I used to be when he was around. How his velvety-smooth voice sent cascades of gooseflesh across my skin like the angels were singing and I had to listen. I was completely and utterly mesmerized by him.

It didn't take long for the attraction between us to blossom. He worked long hours and I only interned four times a week, so I treasured the time I had with him. He had a sly way of captivating me with stories of the hospital. He was funny, and Lord, could he make me squirm in my scrubs. I wanted him. Desperately. At all hours of the day, it was mind blowing. Never before had I just wanted a man, but boy, did I want Rob Moore.

When I was a teenager, I thought that reality TV shows depicting inter-office relationships between nurses in hospitals – the kind that happened behind the closed doors of supply closets – were all fake, but I was wrong. Before Rob, I didn't consider myself one of *those* girls, the ones who'd hook up without any real romantic ties, but I found myself rapidly becoming that girl.

He had me.

I was his, and I wasn't looking back. I had never been in love before, and when Rob came into my life, I felt like he was it. He was my ocean, and I was drowning in him.

Another big mistake on my part.

Once we slept together, over and over again, I found myself so in love with him that I could hardly breathe. When I told him I loved him, he smiled and said, "I have loved you since the moment I set eyes on you, Vi. The word *love* doesn't even express what my feelings are for you. I am and always will be completely and utterly yours."

For the next year, everything I did involved Rob. I didn't notice then but slowly I lost all contact with my friends, the ones I thought were in it for the long haul. I stopped calling, stopped answering, and soon all I did was love Rob. He was everything to me. I was completely consumed by him. The only thing I didn't seem to let go of, despite Rob's trying, was my mom. I talked to my mother everyday, we went to dinner with her, and I knew she loved Rob as much as I did.

On my wedding day, my mom told me that Rob had asked for my hand before asking me. Now, I wonder if he promised to love and care for me. To always protect me. I wonder how he could have looked my mother in the eyes and told a bold-faced lie because, for the last two years, he has not loved or taken care of me. Protect me? Please. It's been hell, and instead of calling my mother and telling her, I've taken the abuse.

Disgusting, I know.

After the honeymoon from hell, I remember being home and reaching for the phone so many times to call and tell my mom or even the friends I had let go. But every time I got to the last number to make the call, I'd hang up. I still don't understand what I was thinking. Did I think it was a one-time thing? Did I believe the sob story of how bad his family treated him and how he had all this pent-up anger inside him from having his father hit him? Or was it that he promised he'd never do it again? Or maybe it was my own fucked-up issues of needing to be loved by a man? Did not having a father to love me when I was growing up fuck me up so bad that instead of walking away and picking up the pieces, I decided to stay and take the abuse? I guess so because, after two years, I'm still here.

I know, I'm shaking my head too, but remember how I asked you not to give up on me yet? Well, please, don't. Not yet. Give me a little longer because this is just the beginning of my story, and I still have tons to tell you.

When I graduated from nursing school, I immediately got a job at the hospital that Rob worked at. On the surface, we were the golden couple. He wasn't one to hide public displays of affection. Nope, he'd grab me and kiss me for the world to see before telling me how much I meant to him. I know, I was confused by it too. Because once we got home, if I didn't cook or clean something the way he wanted, he'd hit me before begging me to forgive him. Saying that he didn't mean it, that if I'd just do as he asked, we wouldn't have a problem. For some stupid fucking reason, I soon was walking on eggshells trying to please him. He started to control everything – what I wore, who I talked to, and even how long I talked to my mom.

It was sad and ridiculous, but I allowed him to do it.

I was used to it and for a while, no harm came my way, but then a new doctor started working my floor and Rob *hated* him. I mean, despised the man, and every night after our shift all Rob did was bitch and moan about how much he hated him. I, for one, thought that Dr. Reeves was a nice guy. He was a young and an eager doctor who loved his patients and treated his nurses well. This was good because not all doctors are like that, some can be real assholes. I was thankful to work with a good one, but that all changed when Dr. Reeves hugged me one day.

It had been a tough day. I had lost one of my favorite patients to lung cancer and even though this was part of my job, death happened daily, it affected me more. Mr. Ralph and I were buddies. There is and always will be a special place in my heart for that man. He was the grandfather I never had since my mom lost her father at a young age. Still to this day, I go to his grave once a month to put flowers on his headstone. I cared for him deeply, and it honestly broke me to lose him.

I remember breaking down after getting him ready for the morgue to come get him. I cried so hard that my body shook with the sobs. I hadn't cried like that in months, and I guess Dr. Reeves heard me and came in to comfort me. He told me that we have to have a thick skin working the cancer unit but that he understood my grief since he too, cared for Mr. Ralph. Hell, everyone did.

I covered my face with my hands and the next thing I knew, he had me in his arms, telling me that it would be alright, that Mr. Ralph was in a better place, and was not feeling any pain. It helped and when I parted from him, I smiled because he was absolutely right. I whispered thank you to him but then out the corner of my eye, I saw Rob standing there. It was easy to tell that he was beyond pissed, and I knew I was in for it. When Dr. Reeves cupped my face and asked if I was going to be all right, Rob lost it. The next thing I knew, he was beating Dr. Reeves to an inch of his life. I couldn't believe it, I had never seen him get physical with anyone but me, and it scared me shitless. It took three people to pull him off the doctor and when his eyes met mine, I knew I was fucked even though I had no romantic feelings whatsoever for the good doctor.

Needless to say, Rob was fired that day, and I'm pretty sure he'll do time as soon as he goes to court for it later this year. But that's beside the point because when I got home that night, he beat me to a bloody pulp. He broke my arm in two places, busted my lip, broke my nose, and even killed the child I was carrying after repeatedly kicking me in the stomach. Want to know what I told the hospital though? That I fell down the stone stairs of our apartment. Hey, it's better than saying I ran into a doorknob, right?

But even with my wonderful lie, my mom didn't believe it. She begged me to tell her the truth. I wasn't a clumsy person and it wasn't raining that day, so how did I fall? I was so close to telling her what had happen, crying about how I lost the child that I was already in love with when Rob ripped the phone from my hands and hung up. He then informed me that we were moving back to his hometown of Maplewood, Tennessee. I tried to convince him not to move me from the only place I knew and loved. He told me that he'd kill me before he'd live without me, and he was going, so I was too.

Did you swoon that time? Or maybe you are shaking under your covers? I know you're thinking, 'don't go, it's that easy!' But if you'd had been there and had seen the way he said it, you would know that I had no choice. He had nothing but hatred and anger in his eyes. After watching him beat up Dr. Reeves, I decided that he wasn't messing around. For some reason I wanted to live, so I agreed and went with him.

Even despite my mother's pleas and tears, despite my grandmother begging me to stay with them, I followed my husband across the country to a place I didn't know or want to live in. I played the wife, setting up our home in the house Rob grew up. I did what was asked of me through pure fear of Rob actually going through with his threats and killing me. I even stopped calling my mom everyday because being slapped in the back of the head each time begins to wear on the soul.

He was sucking everything out of me, and I let him, like a complete idiot.

Chapter
TWO

I know Rob's going to be pissed when I get home, but for the next eight hours I get to sit in the quiet comfort of Dr. McCloud's office filing paperwork. There's something almost cathartic about finally being able to get out of bed in the morning and having something to look forward to. I even managed to dress myself and conceal the fading, greenish-yellow bruise on my cheek. My long blond hair is in waves falling over my shoulders and framing my face, and I'm happy in a way I haven't been in a long time. I even took the time to brush on some lip gloss this morning. Ignore the bruise on my collarbone though. I tried to cover it with makeup, but apparently it didn't work well.

My desk is organized and personalized with zebra print office supplies and a framed picture of me, my mom, and my grandmother. Rob would have a fit if he saw my desk – he hates anything ostentatious – but I love it, and I finally have something that's mine. I'm starting to feel like an adult again.

Leaning back in my plush-back chair, I smile as I looked around my little office. It isn't as big as Dr. McCloud's, but to me, it's perfect. The old office manager, Dr. McCloud's wife, and I had spent the last week training. Thankfully, I'm a fast learner, and we hit it off quickly. She's a lovely woman, and I loved working with her, but the rush I'm feeling right now is unreal. For once I'll be in control of something, and that alone makes me shiver with anticipation. I know I'll be the best damn office manager ever and even with Rob in the back of my head telling me I'm going to fail, I can't help the smile spreading across my face.

I actually feel alive.

Just as I'm about to reach to turn on my new Mac, my door opens and in comes Dr. McCloud.

"Morning, Violet."

I smile. "Good morning, Dr. McCloud, how are you?"

"Wonderful, and you? Are you settled?"

"Yes sir, I'm great," I say, my grin growing by the second.

He lets out a hearty laugh and I swear my face is going to break from the smile that's been there so long it could crystalize. He reminds me of Harrison Ford with his strong facial features and light brown eyes. He is a good looking guy for his age and most of the nurses have a slight crush on him. I wouldn't go that far as to crush on him, but I know I will love working for him. He's built his small practice from the ground up, and I couldn't be more excited about the new possibilities.

"I must say, Violet, you look great behind that desk. I'm glad I picked you for this position. It's time we had some spring chickens in this office and, with my beautiful wife retiring, even she agreed we needed someone that would be long term. I feel I'll have you until you retire."

I nod like a bobble head, still completely shocked that he did give a twenty-three-year-old woman with little experience a position that should have been given to someone with more experience and age. But I understand his reasoning and I thank sweet baby Jesus he picked me, because I need this. I need this chance to see what I can do.

"I won't let you down, sir," I say with a surge of confidence I didn't know I had.

He nods before he says, "I know you won't. Come on, we're having a meeting."

"We are?" I didn't have a meeting written down. I look down at my appointment book, kicking myself for forgetting this. My first day and I miss a meeting!? *Damn* it.

"Yup, it wasn't planned; I got some news I need to share with the office."

Oh, thank God. "Oh, okay! I'm right behind you," I say, scrambling out of my seat to catch up with him since he was already halfway out the door. I follow behind him and smile when we reach our staff lounge. Last week, I got to meet my staff. We have three nurses who work with patients, two receptionists, and four floating nurses. They help with patients, file, and do anything else I assign. I love my team. Each one has different things at which they excel, and I know I'm going to enjoy them. The only thing that makes me nervous is that I'm the youngest person employed here; everyone else is in their thirties.

But they seem to like me. I hope.

Everyone returns my smile, and one of our nurses, Tammy, scoots over so I can sit beside her. Leaning back on the couch, I look up just as Dr. McCloud claps his hands together and says, "Morning, team. I hope all is well with everyone. Did everyone have a good weekend?"

Everyone answers back with smiles and one by one tells him about their weekend. It blows my mind how he is so concerned and even asks more questions about everyone's family life. He is so in tune with his staff and it makes me nervous. It isn't like I'll be doing this. I'm not going to share my home life. I won't even bring up it up, so all I'll have to talk to him about is work. I hope that's enough.

After everyone's finished with their weekends, attention returns to Dr. McCloud as he says, "Well, I'm glad everyone had a good weekend and well, mine was eventful. As lot of you know, my wife is retiring, and I've been entertaining the idea of doing the same thing for some time. After this weekend, I've decided that I'm going to leave the practice."

I gasp, along with everyone else. What the hell does he mean!? I just started here, just became comfortable in my new position. How could he leave? I know everyone is thinking the same. Even Ms. Lynda is crying and Tammy looks as if she is on the verge of tears. We love this guy! He can't leave!

"Calm down everyone, it's okay. You all know me, I'm not going to leave you unless I have the best replacement and, to my delight, my son has finally accepted the task of taking over for me."

His son? What? I don't want to deal with the son; I want Dr. McCloud.

"So, help me welcome my son, Tucker McCloud, to our practice."

Oh, he's here? I glance back up. Everyone starts to clap but my arms stop mid-air when my eyes fall on Tucker McCloud. For the first time in three years, I'm completely stunned by a man before me. My insides are clenching, and I don't think I could form a word if someone asked me something. Especially if *he* did. He's beautiful. Light brown hair that looks like he spent most of the day running his fingers through it, and whiskey-colored brown eyes like quicksand. He has dark brown scruff on his chin and a little along his upper lip and oh Lord, his lips. They're full, a light-peach color, and curved up in a way that makes my heart pound a little faster. He's gorgeous and the mere act of gazing at him is turning me inside out.

He is wearing black slacks that hug every inch of his long legs, showing off the curvature of his rippling muscle, along with a white dress shirt that hugs his chest and arms. The sleeves are rolled up to his elbows, his forearms thick and hard. He looks around the room, his smile intoxicating, as Dr. McCloud introduces each of us. I'm last and when his whiskey-colored eyes land on me, the room fades away until we're the only two people in the room.

His smile falls, his eyes darken, and everything inside me flashes white hot. I have never – and I mean NEVER – seen such a gorgeous man. Not even Rob stunned me like this fine doctor, and he never ever made me feel this, even before the abuse started. It's insane and freaks me out because this doctor is turning me on. No one and I mean no one has done that in a very long time. Not even my husband.

After losing my baby, something went wrong inside me and when Rob would try to penetrate me, he couldn't get in. I went to the doctor, not for his sake but for mine because I was tired of getting the shit beat out of me for not pleasing him, plus it scared me. Why couldn't he get in? Was I broken down there? Had he done more damage than I thought when he caused me to lose the baby?

In the end, I found out that I am suffering from vaginismus. I know what you are thinking: What the hell is that? I thought the same thing, but it's basically where I am too scared to have sex. The walls of my vagina contract whenever anything tries to enter me and it is basically like hitting a wall, which is the reason it hurts anytime he tries. Of course the doctor asked me a whole bunch of questions about being sexually abused but I was able to deflect them and get the hell out of there. When I told Rob what was wrong, he told me I was stupid and worthless, not even a real woman since I can't even please my husband. Told me no man would ever want my broken body. It sucked and I know he's probably getting it somewhere else but to be honest with you, I don't care as long as he stays off me. I have had no desire to have sex in months. I haven't even been turned on but right now, that is all changing.

And that scares me.

"This beautiful young lady will be your office manager,

son," Dr. McCloud says, slapping Tucker on the shoulder as he reaches out to shake my hand. I take it as his father says, "Violet Moore, this is my son, and he'll be replacing me. He'll take good care of you."

If only.

"Violet, it's a pleasure to meet you."

Oh. My. God. His voice is velvety smooth and deep and my name trickles from his lips slowly, deliberately

Good. Lord. Almighty.

Clearing my throat, I manage, "The pleasure is all mine, Dr. McCloud. I look forward to working with you." My voice is shaky and high-pitched, and it sounds strange even to me.

Tucker's mouth curves up as he slowly nods. "As do I."

His eyes continue to hold mine, and all I can do is stare back. I have no clue what's happening, but as he slowly drops my hand, and steps back from me, his eyes say more than words ever could. My body reacts, contracting, closing in on itself. And that's bad. Very bad. I am married to an abusive psycho; what the hell do I think I'm doing lusting after my new boss? Do I want to die? Do I want him to die?

But sweet Jesus, he is beautiful.

No!

I need to get these intense feelings under control before they blossom into something dangerous. The only problem is I don't think I can.

Chapter
THREE

After scattering away from the meeting, I fall into my chair and take in deep breaths. My heart is still racing, my palms are sweaty, and I'm having a hard time forming coherent thoughts. What the hell is wrong with me? I've encountered men before; I've seen them naked; I've healed their wounds; I've nursed them back to health. What the hell is so different about Tucker McCloud?

My reaction to him is baffling. I've never been this worked up.

Violet.

The way he said my name was sensual and smooth. He has an accent, a down home one that I swear was designed to talk girls out of their panties and, for the love of Christ, it works. I'm not sure if mine were going to stay on much longer if I didn't get away from him when I did. Oh fuck, what am I going to do? I have to work with this man!

A gentle knock sounds at my door and when I glance up,

Dr. Sexy Pants is standing in my doorway equipped with one hell of a grin.

"Hey, are you busy?"

If fantasizing about stripping you down and licking every inch of you is busy, then, yes, yes I am. I'm so screwed. How the hell am I going to work here when I've only known of Tucker's existence for maybe thirty minutes, and I've already had sex with him in my head? And it isn't normal sex, it's hang off the chandeliers, smack my ass, sex. Hot sex. The kind of sex I've been deprived of for far too long.

I swallow loudly before slowly shaking my head. "No, what can I do for you?"

I swear I see him bite into his lip before he comes in but maybe I'm imagining it. I don't know, but he sits in the chair in front of my desk, his elbows on his knees, leaning toward me as he looks straight into my eyes.

"I just wanted to come in and talk. We're going to be working very closely over the next couple of months, and I want to make sure we're on the same page."

Closely? How close because I'm not sure how close I can get and still keep my panties intact. Telling myself to shut up, I nod as he goes on.

"With my dad only being here for another month before the practice is fully mine, I want to start making changes so that we can better this practice. Right now, it's good, but together we can make it great."

"I agree," I manage to say, which causes his grin to grow.

Oh, please don't do that. I can't take it.

"Great. I've looked through your resume, called your references back in Colorado, and I think my dad was completely right hiring you. I feel great about our partnership. We're going to do really great things and by the time my dad gets back from his vacation with my mom, he'll see that leaving this practice in our hands was the best choice."

His grin is contagious, and I'm grinning just as hard as I

nod like a fool.

"I'm excited for the future."

"Me too," Tucker says as he stands up. "So let's get started. I would like you to make a list of things you want to change around here. Ask the staff, get feedback from patients, and we'll discuss everything next week."

I watch as he walks, my jaw dropping at his firm and perfect ass. Jeez. Before he reaches the door, he turns to look at me and says, "Do you like sushi?"

I like his ass more but still I nod. "Sure."

"Cool, I'll order in, and we'll eat as we talk."

My heart flutters. Alone? Eating food, with this Adonis of a man? Oh. Shit.

"Sounds great."

"Awesome," he says but stops before he goes out my door. His brow comes together before he asks, "What happened to your clavicle?"

I blink. "What?"

"You have a bruise on your clavicle, what happened? That's a odd place to get a bruise."

I look down. I don't know why because all I can see is my boobs, but I need to figure out what to say. Thankfully, when you've been the victim of abuse as long as I have you can come up with stuff quickly.

"I got hit with a ball in the chest when I was playing basketball with my friends."

Oh, good one, even though I've never played basketball a day in my life.

"Oh, really?" he asked, concern lighting up his angular face. He closes the distance between us and starts probing my collarbone. My skin is on fire under his soft touch, and I'm sure he can feel my heart pounding under his fingers. Keep. Breathing.

"It's not broken," he informs me.

I look up slowly. His eyes are bright shining beacons and

I'm the dumbass bug drawn to them. I glance down at his lips and take in a sharp breath. He is doing that naughty lip-biting thing that I know I didn't imagine earlier. When my eyes meet his again, he's looking at me with wonder. I know I need to get away from him, but I can't will my body to move away. I want him. So bad, it hurts. I want to lean toward him. Meet his delicious mouth with my own. I want to run my fingers in his hair and allow him to tangle his own in mine.

Oh, how I want him, but I know that I can't have him. Instead, I say, "I know, but thank you, Dr. McCloud."

His grin is back, and being this close to him, I see that he has a little scar below his bottom lip. I want to ask what happened but before I can, he says in his deep drawl, "Call me Tucker, Violet."

I think I just died.

If I thought it was hot and sexy when he said my name, hearing him say his own name is downright sinful.

"So how is my dream team?"

Taking in a deep breath, I look toward the door and see Dr. McCloud smiling at us.

"We're great, Dad," Tucker says then stands up and heads toward his dad. "Violet has a bruise on her collarbone, I was making sure it wasn't broken or anything."

Just like his had, his father's face fills with the same concern. "You alright there, Violet?"

I smile at his concern. "Yes, sir, I am fine. Thank you."

"Good," he says with nod. "Are you happy with her, Tuck? I told you, she's a keeper."

Tucker looks back at me and nods. "Yeah, Dad, she sure is."

I smile, my cheeks growing warm and burning scarlet as they both send me one last grin before leaving my office. Once my door is closed, I slither down in my chair and hold my face in my hands. Oh my God, I am in so much trouble. My body is still on fire from where he touched me. What am I going to do? How am I supposed to come to work every day and act like that man doesn't make me want to take off all my clothes? How am I supposed to go home and act like I've never met Tucker McCloud? That my whole day hasn't brightened from looking into his eyes? I'm so screwed it isn't even funny and even though I'm trembling in my seat from my unknown future, I can't help but be glad I met Tucker.

When Rob comes into the kitchen, I'm working on the questionnaire I plan to give all my staff tomorrow. I don't glance up at him, but my eyes watch his feet as he moves through the kitchen. I always do this, I always want to know where he is, just in case he suddenly moves toward me. Unlike the way my heart raced when Tucker was around me today, my heart is thrashing with fear. I'm scared Rob will suspect something and internally I'm freaking the fuck out.

When a crash happens behind me, I jump in my seat with a cry. His laughter is like nails on a chalkboard. He picks up the pot off the ground and moves to the sink, filling it with water.

I know his eyes are on me.

"Why are you so jumpy?" he asks.

"I'm not," I say simply, trying to focus on what I'm writing.

"Hmm."

I take in a deep breath, trying to pay attention to what I'm doing, but I'm keeping my eyes on him. His movements are slow and lithe, and I'm just waiting for the telltale pivot. I don't want to be sitting down if he attacks. Did he see the smile on my face when I got home? Did he hear me singing in the kitchen when I made dinner? Does he know that my job just got ten times better when my old boss introduced me to my new boss?

"So, I heard that old fart you are working for is retiring."

I freeze. I don't dare look at him as I say, "Yeah, he's going to travel with his wife."

"Yeah, that's what I heard, and his son is taking over. Heard he's a dick, though."

Really? He seemed dreamy and hot to me.

"I only spoke with him a little today."

Rob doesn't say anything else as he moves through the kitchen, making himself a plate of the dinner I cooked for him. Rob works nights – he wakes up around six, gets ready for work, and eats before leaving for the night. I love his new schedule; it's perfect. I don't have to deal with him much, and my life is much better because of it.

When he falls into the seat beside me, I move away but without him knowing. Or at least I don't think he knows, he doesn't say anything about it and I feel like I'm in the clear, but then he says, "Stay away from him."

I feel his stare on me but I still don't look up as I write the same word twice, my hand shaking while sweat drips down my back.

"Rob, I work with him. How am I supposed to stay away from him?" I force myself not to cringe as I wait for a backhanded slap.

"I told you I don't want you working there. There's a position at the hospital. Come there."

I shake my head, finally looking up at him. He has let the scruff on his face grow out and it's patchy. He looks gross, like a crack head or something. His dark brown eyes are glued to mine and his lips are in a straight line. I'm sickened looking into his eyes but I know I can't look away or he'll know something is up. I count the flecks around his pupils to distract myself.

"I don't want to work there and I like where I am."

"Because of this guy?"

He's insanely jealous, and I don't understand why. He beats me, treats me like dirt, and is probably fucking all the stupid nurses at the hospital. I'm obviously not going anywhere, no matter how much looking into Tucker's eyes makes me want to pack up and run. I know I won't. I'm stuck, no matter what. I don't have the strength to leave him.

"No, Rob, I like the office. I have a lot of control, and they think I'm going to help the practice strive."

He laughs, slapping the table and making me jump in the process. "You can't do shit for them. You're worthless so what makes you think they're going to keep you? As soon as this guy sees that, he'll turn you loose and by then the job at the hospital will probably be filled and I'll be the only fucking paycheck."

With a shake of his head, he looks back down at his food as he picks up his fork and at that moment I hate him so much that I want to rip the fork from his fingers and stab him in the eye. But I don't, instead I say, "Then why do you care? If I'm going to fail, then let me fail."

I don't know why I said that. I don't know what has gotten into me and when his eyes dart up to mine, I wish I had kept my mouth shut. Dropping his fork, he glares at me. I try to look away but soon he is out of his chair, kicking it back sending it crashing into the ground before gripping my chin, making me look into his hate-filled eyes. Pain shoots up my face from his grip, his thumbnail digging into my skin as he holds my gaze.

"I care because you are mine. You are fucking lucky I let you out of this fucking house, or better yet, let you work at some practice that I'm not at. You are fucking stupid if you think I'm going to sit back and let you whore yourself off to this fucking doctor."

"I'm not whoring anywhere," I cry out, trying to get out of his grip, but he isn't letting go. His hand tangles in my hair, squeezing so hard that tears spring to my eyes. I scream but stop moving, hoping to relief some from the pain. It doesn't work. He pulls harder.

"Not now you aren't, but I know you. You're a hot little thing, ready to fuck anything except me."

"I can't have sex; I've told you this!"

He pulls hard, making my head fall back. "That's right

and don't make me make sure that you never have sex again, because I will. Let me get word that you're trying to get with this doctor and I swear, Vi. I swear it will not be good. Don't fucking do anything stupid."

Tears are rushing down my face and my face is burning from where he has his thumbnail. "I'm not. I won't."

He shoves me away and I fall back into the counter, holding my face as the tears continue to fall.

"That's right. Now sit down."

I don't want to move. I want to fall into the fetal position and pray he goes away, but when he cuts me a look, I take the steps to the chair, and fall into it without looking at him. Taking in a shuddered breath, I wipe my face as he says, "Stop crying. I didn't even hurt you. I wouldn't do this if you'd just fucking listen. You make me so fucking mad, Vi. Shit. Don't you know how much I love you? I don't want anyone to have you but me."

Looking down, my tears fall on the paper in front of me. My tears mix with the ink, creating purple-black pools and running down the page as my heart pounds against my chest. I don't know what I'm going to do. Maybe I should quit but as soon as I think that, I know that I can't quit my job. I love the people I work with, I love the position I have, and most of all, I want to see more of Tucker. I need to see more of him. I want to know who he is. I want to know things about him. Is he married? Does he have kids? Is he single? I have to know. I don't know why because more than likely curiosity is going to get me in trouble, but something inside me is pushing me to know. It's pushing me past my fear of Rob, and I have no clue what that means.

I feel Rob's eyes on me, and when I look up, he is moving his dark-as-night hair out of his eyes. He is waiting, and I know what I'm supposed to say.

"I'm sorry."

But I'm not.

Not in the least.

Chapter
FOUR

For the most part, I was able to keep my distance from Rob and Tucker for the next three days. It involved me staying in my room or in the living room – when Rob was in our room – but I managed. He, of course, tried to talk to me, and act like he didn't almost rip off my chin but I wasn't having it. I answered what I needed to and ignored everything else. Usually after one of our altercations, he tries to suck up to me, showing his old affections and telling me everything I needed him to say three years ago. I usually let him, but not this time. I keep my distance, something I've never done before. I'm pretty sure he noticed, but I don't care. Another thing I've never done. Usually I'm so scared and worried about pleasing him, I do what he asks, but not this time. I'm pissed, and my fucking face hurts, dammit.

It may have been easy to ignore Rob, but with Tucker, I'm surprised that I can hold myself together at work. The last three days have been hell on me, but I've managed to keep my lust-filled thoughts under control. Mostly because he was very busy following his father around and winning over his new patients. Not that he had to try hard. From what I've noticed, it was easy for him. He's a people person. He's charming and sweet, just like his father. When he unleashes that smile, the big one that shows his deep dimples, I swear everyone in the office swoons while I just try to breathe.

I'm fanning myself at this very moment just thinking of those sexy dimples.

I've done well keeping my lusty thoughts to myself but some of the office staff don't know how to do the same.

"Did you see his ass in those slacks? He said earlier he was hot and took off his jacket and good Lord Almighty I wanted to burn that jacket so he never wears it again!" Tammy gushes while the other nurses giggle.

We're having a small meeting during lunch, going over the questionnaire I have for everyone while the doctors are out. The fact that Tucker is gone for these hours each day is bittersweet. On one hand, I can actually breathe, but on the other, I just want to stare at him. His office is across from mine and when he is in there with his legs on his desk doing things on his laptop, I can't help but steal glances. His strong legs crossed at the ankles and propped up on his desk, eyes downturned in consternation as he reviews a patient's chart. When he bites down on that sexy bottom lip of his, my whole body catches on fire, and I have to fight off the gooseflesh that spreads its way across my skin.

Of course, I'm disgusted in myself afterwards because really, what would someone as gorgeous as Tucker McCloud want with me? There is no way I'm up to Tucker's standards. He's probably married to some gorgeous model with the longest legs he's ever seen, and has little model babies, but I can fantasize, right? The image of me on my desk with him between my legs is one hell of a fantasy.

One. Long. Hot. Sexy. Fantasy.

"I know, right? He is so sexy, if I was twenty years younger and maybe fifty pounds thinner, I swear I'd be on him like white on rice," Ms. Yolanda says, snapping me from my daydream. She has everyone laughing, even me. Ms. Yolanda is our oldest staff member at fifty-four, and she is crazy, obviously.

"He'd be in a world of trouble, Ms. Yolanda, if you had your sights on him," I say with a smile, my hand on her shoulder.

She laughs as she nods. "Damn right, he would. You know, honey," she says, looking at me so intently I feel like she can see the fantasy behind my eyes not mere seconds ago, "you two would be cute together. Maybe you should get with him. You know he's single, darling, so go after him. Share all the juicy details so we all can live vicariously through you."

Everyone laughs and my mind whirls.

He's single? Oh. My. But that doesn't matter. Right?

I slowly shake my head, my cheeks red as a tomato. "Sorry ladies, I'm married."

Unfortunately.

I'm beside myself but I look up when I notice all the laughing has stopped.

"You are?" Tammy asks, her face scrunched up in confusion.

"I didn't know that," Ms. Yolanda says with her brows to her hairline.

"You're so young, though," Annabelle, our receptionist, says. "What are you, like twenty-one?"

I shrug, hating all the attention on me. "I'm twenty-three. I got married when I was twenty."

The conversation stops, but all eyes are still on me. I start to squirm in my seat. I hate when all the attention is on me. I feel weird and self-conscious, so I quickly clear my throat and say, "Anyway, so back to the reason we're here. What are some thing you guys would like to change around here?"

When Ms. Yolanda's hand comes up, I smile. "Yes, ma'am."

Everyone's attention goes to her, thankfully, and with the straightest face ever, she says, "I think clothing should be optional for Doctor McCloud Jr."

Peals of laughter bubble up and out of my chest and I snort from the force.

The only thing my nutty staff could come up with was a clothing allowance and maybe raises and more vacation time. All of these are understandable, and I had already written them down before I had the meeting. When I left the meeting, I had the biggest smile on my face. I'm excited to have some control here, to be able to relay all the ideas I've come up with to Tucker, but once I get to my office, my smile falters. I've missed a call from my mother, and since she called during my working hours, I know she isn't calling just to chat. Reaching for my phone, I dial my mother's number and wait until she answers.

"Mom?"

"Violet, baby, things are bad."

I take in a deep breath, my heart picking up speed from my mother's words. "Grandma?"

"Yes, she isn't doing well. I think you may need to come up here and spend some time with her. I'm not sure how much longer she'll be here with us." Her voice cracks in a silent sob.

My heart drops and tears rush to my eyes. My chest feels like it's caving in and I swallow a lump at the base of my throat. Not my grandma. I love her. She's the person who stepped up and was the father I never had but needed. Tears rush down my cheeks and I want nothing more than to be there with them, but I don't know if I can be.

"I'll call Rob. Hopefully we have the money."

My mother pauses and I know she is counting to ten. "You don't know if you have the money?"

"You know Rob controls our finances," and has since the day I married him, "and I've just started working again. I've just received my first paycheck." I lie a little because my checks go directly into Rob's bank account. He gives me a weekly allowance, but it's not enough to buy a plane ticket anywhere, let alone to Colorado.

"Fine, Violet. Honey, I'll pay. See if you can get the time off. I know you just started this job, but surely they'll understand."

I let out a breath, trying to suck in air around my sobs. It isn't my job I'm worried about; it's Rob. "Let me call Rob, and see if we have the money first. If not, then I'll need you to pay, but I need to make sure I can get the time off. I'll call you this afternoon, okay?"

"Alright, sweetheart, talk to you soon."

I disconnect and cover my face with my hands. The last thing I want to do is call Rob, but I have to. It isn't even about the money. I make a decent amount a week and so does he, and Lord knows I don't get to spend any money so I know we have it. But will he let me go?

Dialing his number, I wait until he answers, and I know by his voice that I've woken him up.

"What?"

"Sorry, I woke you. I'll call back."

"Well, yeah you woke me. I worked all night, Vi. I'm asleep during the day," he spits.

"I know, I'm sorry. I call you later."

"No, it's fine. What do you want?"

I pause. I know the answer so why am I even wasting my time?

"My grandmother is dying."

"That sucks," he says passively. He won't even pretend to care.

"She wants me to come up and see her before she passes. Do we have the money for a ticket?" I ask softly.

He doesn't even pause. "Nope."

I know we do, so instead of asking where the money is, I say, "Oh, well my mom offered to pay, so I just need to work it out with my work and I'll be good."

"No."

"No?"

"No, you're not going."

"Why? It's my grandmother, Rob. She's like my second mom. I love her and want to say goodbye," I say, the tears streaming down my face. I don't know what I expected; I knew he wasn't going to say yes.

"I don't care. Call and say bye. You're not going back home so that your mom can talk you into leaving me."

"She won't. Come with me, you'll see that," I plead. The last thing I want is for him to go, but I'll bring him to see my grandmother if it's the only way around this. I have to see her.

"Fuck no," he says with a scoff. "I don't want to see those people. You're staying here, and that's all there is to it."

The phone goes dead in my hand.

I drop the phone on my desk, curling up in my seat as I let the tears fall down my cheeks. Taking in a shuddering breath, I curse Rob Moore to the fiery depths of hell. I hate him so much, it hurts. Why couldn't he just let me go? Why is he so controlling and such a fucking prick that I am stuck here, under his fucking thumb.

Because I fucking let him.

I put myself in this position, I allowed him to do this to me, and now I have no way out. I am too scared to leave and even when I do, where will I go? I have no money to get me anywhere and then, if I even get there, he'll probably come along and kill me. God, I'm so fucked.

When a knock sounds on my door, I hurry to wipe my face before saying, "Come in."

I silently pray it's anyone but Tucker. Fate is not being kind today.

Not looking at me but at a piece of paper in his hands, he starts, "Hey, did the insurance company call you because I don't understand what the heck they're – whoa, what's wrong?"

I guess I didn't clean my face well enough. With a shrug, I say, "Nothing, what's up?"

"No, you're crying," he says, coming toward me with his hands out, like he's trying to figure out how to help.

"What's wrong?"

My lips quivers and soon I'm crying so hard I can't see. I hear the door shut and then I feel him beside me. His hand on my shoulder, his other resting on the arm of my chair as he slowly rubs my back, whispering to tell him what's wrong, to let him help. I'm not only crying because I'm married to a fucking jerk, but because I won't see my grandma before she leaves this earth for good. It kills me inside and I wish I had to strength to say fuck him and leave, but knowing him he'll call off work and stay home, watching everything I do. He'll fuck with my car again so that he has to drive me everywhere.

I'm stuck.

"Violet, tell me what's wrong?" Tucker says, his voice is deep and breathy, soothing and velvet. I want to sink into him.

Taking in a deep breath, I clean off my face as I whisper, "My grandmother is dying."

"Oh, I'm so sorry."

He takes my hand in his, rubbing it with his thumb as tears continue to fall down my cheeks.

"What can I do to help?" he asks. "Do you need time off?"

I shake my head. "No, I don't have the money to fly out there right now."

Without even thinking, he says, "I'll pay for you to go, and I can man things here till you get back. We can make this work."

God, he is a saint. I slowly shake my head again before looking up in his beautiful eyes. He is looking at me, like I'm the last person in this world and he is Superman, ready to save me. I want to let him save me, but I know he can't.

"No, I couldn't ask that of you."

"I insist, Violet."

"No, Dr. McCloud—"

"Tucker," he corrects.

I smile. "Tucker, thank you, but I need to work and I can't take a handout. I'll just save my money and when she does pass I'll fly out then to be with my mom."

I know he wants to keep insisting but thankfully, he just nods and asks, "Are you sure?"

"Yes," I say with a strained smile. "As much as I want to be there, I know she'd understand."

Man, what a lie. She hates Rob and if she were well, she'd probably kill him if she knew the extent of what he's done to me. What he continues to do.

"Okay, well if anything changes let me know. I'll fly you out there in a second."

Looking up at his exquisite face, I smile. "Thank you, Tucker."

"Anytime. We're a team, remember? You and me. I'm here for you."

Why? He hasn't known me but a couple of days. How can he just want to help and be there for me like that? How did I get so lucky to get a job where I am basically family to these people when before I was just a number at the hospital? It's mind blowing and as much as I want to question it, I can't because I like the way it makes me feel.

It makes me feel like I'm worth it.

"Thank you," I whisper.

"You're welcome, Violet."

I take in a deep breath, cleaning my face again with a smile. I then take the paper from him and ask, "Now, what about the insurance company?"

After answering his question, he leaves my office, sending me one last grin before shutting my door. My heart is still racing and my shoulder and hand are still tingling from his touch. Something inside me is warm and I can't believe how loyal he is to me. My husband, the one man who's supposed to love me unconditionally, can't stand the sight of me, but Tucker knows me for five minutes and he's a better man than Rob will ever be. Mr. and Mrs. McCloud did a great job with that guy and the woman he ends up with will be one hell of a lucky lady.

I want that woman to be me, even though I know it never will be.

Shaking my head, I know that I might as well get this phone call over with and stop worrying about who Tucker will pick to make the luckiest girl on earth.

He isn't my concern.

So I pick up my phone again and I dial my mother's number slowly, wishing I didn't have to do this. When she answers, the tears are hot and fast down my face as I say, "I'm sorry mom, but I can't come out there."

I know she doesn't believe my lie about my work not letting me off but what else am I supposed to say?

That Rob beats me, has all my money, and will kill me if I leave?

I can't tell her that. Instead, I let her voice her disappointment while I cry.

Chapter FIVE

I lay watching the sun fill my room. It warms my face causing me to slowly close my eyes. I know I need to get up, but I don't want to move. Rolling to my side, I feel a little flutter of nervousness in my stomach and a small smile pulls at my lips.

Today is the meeting with Tucker.

I have been preparing myself for this meeting for the last week but the little flutter and the tightness in my stomach won't stop. I don't know if I'll even make it through this meeting in one piece, but I'm going to damn well try. I have to. I have to ignore these feelings, this desire. It's a waste of time, but it's so hard to ignore him. All week Tucker has been sweet and thoughtful. Checking on the status of my grandmother, asking if I need anything, offering to give me time off, everything. He's been perfect.

And it's not just Tucker. Everyone in the office has been the same. Never have I been around more caring people. Word of my grandmother's health was soon all over the office and everyone I work with offered whatever help I may need. It feels good to have people there if I need them. For so long I've felt alone, but I'm starting not to feel that way anymore. I feel more at home and loved at the office than I do in my own home.

Kicking the blankets off of me, I get out of bed and head for the shower with a little pep to my step. After showering, I get dressed in a pair of nice black slacks and a light blue, long sleeved, wrap shirt that show just a hint of cleavage. I usually don't wear this shirt but I want to today. It's nice and used to be one of my favorite shirts. I blow dry my hair before curling the ends and making sure my blond curls fall nicely down my shoulders. After spending a little longer on my makeup than I usually do, I smile at the final product.

It's not every day that I think I'm pretty, but looking at myself, my blue eyes shining, I can't help the well of confidence today. Tears rush to my eyes but I hold them back. I can't let them go, I've polished myself up to find this girl and I can't let her go, not yet. As my eyes travel over my rosy cheeks, my sweet nose, and beautifully done up lips, I can't help but ask myself, where did this girl run off too? Why has she been hiding and when did I stop caring about the way I looked?

Sliding into my only pair of heels, I head into the kitchen for some cereal. Sitting down with my bowl, I'm about to dig in when the door opens.

Oh shit.

Rob looks tired and irritated, looking every one of his thirty-six years. My heart instantly speeds up as my palms go all clammy and I can't seem to swallow around the lump in my throat. What the hell is he doing home already? I usually don't see him in the morning, since I leave before he gets home, and I sure as hell don't want to see him this morning. Not this one. I need this one to start off well and dealing with Rob Moore causes one thing.

Hell.

When he turns to look at me, it's only for a second before he looks away. But, just as quickly, he looks right back, his brows knotting together as his head cocks to the side.

I'm busted.

I never get dressed up, hardly ever wear makeup or heels. I expect him to say something but he doesn't as he storms into the kitchen, his eyes raking up and down my body. I don't dare look him in the eyes. Will he suspect something? Will he know that I'm dressing up to impress a man that I'll never have the chance to touch or kiss?

"Where you going?"

I shrug. "To work."

"Like that?"

I look down at my outfit and then nod. "Yeah, what's wrong?"

"You look like a painted whore. Go change and wash your face."

I shake my head, still not looking at him as I say, "I do not. I look nice. I'm the manager of the office, Rob. I have a meeting today and I have to look nice."

I feel his eyes on me as I stand. I've lost my appetite and I need to get out of here. I don't trust him and I'm not changing or washing my face. I look amazing, I know I do. Moving past him to the sink, I feel his eyes still on me, and for a split second I think I'm going to get away but just as fast as the thought came, his hand latches around my arm, squeezing it before he pulls me back toward him, causing the milk from my bowl to slosh onto the floor and all over his pants.

Ah, crap.

His face turns red. My heart starts to pound and I want to run.

"Fuck!"

"I'm sorry, I wasn't holding the bowl right," I say quickly, moving away and grabbing a towel.

He snatches it from me and wipes his legs before sneering up at me. "I told you, you look like a slut. Go fucking wash your face."

"And I said I don't," I automatically say. "Please, let me be Rob. I have to get to work. I have a big meeting today."

His eyes narrow as he holds my gaze. I wish that the guy who I fell in love with would look back at me. That Rob would never tell me I looked like a slut. He was controlling, but he had always thought I was beautiful. What happened? What had I done to change him into this monster?

"I don't like you working there."

I try to move away but he's holding me hostage with his dark eyes. I don't know what to say, so I don't say anything and finally will my legs to move. Reaching for my bag and purse off the couch, I go to the door, but his words stop me.

"What has gotten into you?"

I turn and look at him. His face is set in a sneer. His body is taut, his fists balled up at his sides. My chest tightens with fear of what he might do next. I might not make it out of this house unscathed if I don't play this right.

Fidgeting with the strap to my purse, I ask, "What do you mean?"

"You are deliberately ignoring what I told you to do, and I don't fucking like it."

I want to say is 'fuck off' but I know that won't go over well, plus I don't have the guts to ever say that. If I did, I'd more than likely be reapplying makeup since I'd have a black eye to cover up. Looking up at him, I meet his eyes. I hate the way he looks at me, as if I'm covered in skunks. Like the sight of me actually hurts him or something. I feel horrible and my confidence falters as I slowly take in a breath. Maybe I'm not as beautiful as I felt twenty minutes ago.

"I'm sorry, it's only for the meeting. I'll wash it off once I'm done. I just want to look nice."

Rob eyes me before running his hand through his hair. I hate being under his scrutiny like this. It makes my heart beat so hard and loud that I'm sure it's cracking ribs, ready to explode from my chest. I fear that he's going to start screaming, maybe grab for me again, and force me to wash my face and change. I should have just kept going, shut the door, and run to my car; but then again, knowing him, he'd chase me down.

Swallowing loudly, I squeeze the straps to my bag, preparing myself for the worst when he says, "You're lucky I'm tired or this would have ended differently."

I don't doubt that one bit, but I'm not telling him that.

Reaching for the door, I leave without even saying goodbye. Once in my car and on my way to the office, my eyes suddenly fill with tears. I don't want to go to work, or better yet, the meeting with Tucker. I want to run inside and wash my face, change into something that covers every inch of me. I want to run and hide.

But, more than that, I want to feel like I did when I saw the gorgeous girl I miss more than anything staring back at me in my bathroom mirror earlier this morning. I fear that in that short ten-minute interaction with Rob, she may be lost again.

I spend most of the day in my office. Usually, I go out and mingle with my co-workers, make sure they're doing well, but today I want to be alone. Every time I look at the clock on my computer, I cringe. It seems that the day is flying by, something that never happens when I want it to, and soon, it will be time for my meeting with Tucker. I'm dreading it. I washed my face once I got here, and even safety pinned my shirt closed. I can't believe I did it either, but I did, and I feel even worse than I did when I left my house.

Moving my hands through my hair, I pull it up into a bun before reaching for the file of the case I'm working on. I'm well into my work when I hear a knock at my door.

Tucker stands in the doorway and my breathing picks up at the sight of him. The yellow button up shirt, tie hanging loosely at his neck, is a stark contrast to his tan, and the fitted khakis don't leave much to the imagination. One hand holds files, while the other holds a white bag. His grin is unstoppable, and his eyes are on me as he enters my office.

Tearing my eyes away from his gorgeous body, I glance at the time and I can't believe that my day is gone and it's time for this meeting. How did this happen? I didn't even have time to freshen up or anything. Just fucking great.

"Did I catch you at a bad time?"

I shake my head before saying, "No, sorry, I lost track of time."

"No worries. I'll set up our food while you get what you need," he says.

I shake my head again. "Actually, I'm not hungry. Can we just do the meeting?"

As much as I want to eat with him, I know it's a bad idea. I'm lusting after a man I can't have, or better yet, one who has no interest in me. I need to stop feeling like this. I had no right to get all jazzed up this morning. Not only was it stupid but it almost got me in a world of shit with Rob. I need to be careful and I need to bury these feelings. I married Rob and until I can get the balls to leave him or something, I need to stay clear of Tucker. He has the power to get me in trouble and that is the last thing I need.

So dinner is a no-go, this meeting will be quick, and then I can go back to my personal hell. Back to being Rob's wife, and not the girl I want to be.

With just that thought I want to cry. I want to change things. I want Rob to stop hitting me. I want him to love me like he once did and if he can't fucking do that, then I want to leave. I want to not be scared anymore. I want to feel pretty. But I've been wanting these things for a long time now, and still haven't done anything about it.

When am I going to do what's right for me?

"Oh, okay," Tucker says, as a flash of hurts fills his face. It's brief but I see it and before I can say or do anything, he smiles as he lays the bag on the edge of my desk and sits in the empty chair in front of my desk. He lays his files on the other chair before looking back at me. "What did you come up with?"

I look down, grabbing my file and opening it to the three-page proposal I had for him. When I glance up, I am stunned to find that his eyes are glued to mine. I feel like I've stopped breathing and my mouth slowly falls open. I can tell he notices because his mouth is curving up, his dimples singing to me as I try to catch my breath. I have conveniently forgotten everything I was going to say, and I try to look away but I can't.

My skin is on fire and it feels like he knows me, inside and out, peeling away every layer of me until I'm bared in front of him. Utterly naked. Finally, I look away; I have to. Crimson flames lick the edges of my body and I feel exposed, even though I know every piece of me is covered. My heart races. He is lethal with that grin and it's unfair for him to release it on a girl like me. I don't know how to handle this

NO! I can't! I have to bottle these feelings; I cannot let this man affect me!

Taking in a deep breath, I close my eyes and muster up everything inside me before looking down at my file. When I open my mouth to say the first word, I squeak.

Mortified. I drop my head to my desk and want to die. I'm supposed to be exhibiting the aura of great office manager and I can't even get out a single word!

"What's wrong?" he drawls in his sexy southern accent.

I shake my head. Why am I so nervous around this guy?

"I squeaked."

His chuckles fill the room, curling my toes. I quickly lock my ankles, squeezing my legs tight as my heart continues to pound in my chest. Why the hell do I want this man so much?

I have never been like this. Not since Rob, and it's not like he's kept me locked in the basement. Not yet at least. If I sleep with this man though, I'll have a one way ticket there, and I don't want that. I also don't want anything to happen to Tucker.

"It's endearing."

I pause before looking up at him. He is grinning at me and all I can say is, "It's embarrassing."

"No, it's cute. Now come on, show me what you got."

Even though I know he's talking about the proposal sitting in front of me, his whiskey-colored eyes are telling me that he wants something totally different.

I pick up the file with shaking hands and clear my throat before reading my proposal to him. I'm nervous, my chest feels like it is seizing up but every time I look up, Tucker is looking right at me, his rippling arms crossed over his chest, listening intently to me. I have his undivided attention and I feel my confidence building inside me.

When I'm done, I look up and he's nodding.

"I agree. I think a clothing allowance for the staff is reasonable and vacation time too, but we need to make sure that people put in their requests in a timely manner."

"I agree, also I want to get new dental insurance for the practice. We're paying out the yin yang and I found a great premium." I hand him the paperwork I had laid out for him.

He reads it quickly before nodding again. "Sounds good. Get that done too, please."

"Alright, I will first thing in the morning," I say, making myself a note.

"Also, I've talked this over with my father and we feel that we want to give everyone in the office a dollar raise."

I nod as I write a note about sending out a letter to the whole office about the raise. A smile plays on my lips because I know the office will love that news and love Tucker even more.

"Sounds great."

"Also we want to give you a raise too; my dad is still

working the numbers and I'll have that to you by tomorrow. It won't go in affect till your probation is over, but I feel you'll be happy with it."

With a strained smile, I say, "Thank you. I know I will."

It's a complete lie though. I'll never see that money and it makes me sick to my stomach when I think about it. When I look up, Tucker is watching me. His gaze makes me nervous, like he can see my soul, a place that hasn't been happy in a very long time and I wish he would stop looking at me because I know he doesn't see the woman I used to be. He sees the broken one in front of him, the one scrubbed free of makeup with pins in her shirt. The one that wants a good man to look at her for once with something other than sheer hatred in his eyes.

Now the only feeling I ever have is fear. Fear is the only friend I have. One that I don't want but is constantly around me. Fear constantly reminds me that Rob is watching. He always knows what I'm doing and where I am. He's the reason I can't enjoy a meal with my boss or even take the time to get to know him. I have never wanted to be with someone so much but at the same time want to get as far away as I can. I'm scared of my feelings for him, but most of all, I'm scared of the man I call my husband.

Clearing my throat, I say, "Okay, so that's everything, anything else on your end?"

"Yes."

I look up from my notes. "Yes?"

His eyes hold mine making it hard for me to breathe.

"I want you to eat with me, Violet. I want to get to know you. I bought dinner, and I don't want to eat it alone. I want to eat it with you."

Looking away, I say, "I don't know."

"Why?"

"I really should get home."

"And do what?"

I look up. "I don't know."

He laughs as he opens the bag and I can't help it. I smile.

"Well, since you don't know what you're going to do once you get home, why don't you stay here and eat with me? It sounds like a way better idea than just going home."

It's not a good idea in the least. The best thing for me to do is to go home. I know that's what I need to do but instead, without even realizing I'm doing it, I'm nodding.

"Okay."

Chapter SIX

"**S**o then, he just pushed me!"

I dissolve in giggles as Tucker tries to hold in his own laughter. I haven't laughed as much as I have in the last thirty minutes in the past three years and it's all because of the gorgeous man sitting in front of me. We're well into our dinner and I don't think I'll ever know enough about this man. I want to know everything and anything about him.

Tucker has been to almost every country. Mind blowing! I've been to only two states. And he's been everywhere. His favorite place is Spain. He says the food there is fantastic but the people are better and apparently, I have to go there or my life will never be complete.

I wish.

He's also fluent in four languages. I swoon at just the mere mention of him saying he can speak Spanish, French, German, and Japanese. And when he started to speak French, I had to look down to make sure my clothes were still there. I am completely enraptured with this man and I love listening to his stories. Not only did he graduate a year early but he backpacked through all of Europe for a year. After that, he went to college and graduated at the top of his class before going straight to med school. When he was done, instead of getting a job, he backpacked more, this time through South America before going to China and Japan.

Dr. McCloud was livid with him, but Blaine, his brother, talked him into seeing the world before following in his father's footsteps. I hadn't even realized there was another McCloud and yes, I wonder if he is just as gorgeous as his brother. This fact is still unknown, but give me time ladies. What I do know is that Blaine is two years older than Tucker, making him thirty-one. He's a chef and is traveling to broaden his horizons and improve his skills in cuisine all over the world. From what Tucker has told me, they're very close and I find myself jealous of their relationship. I didn't have a constant companion like that growing up.

Like right now, Tucker is telling me about the first time he went skydiving and I honestly don't remember the last time my face hurt from smiling, or the last time my stomach hurt from laughing, but it feels amazing.

"He just pushed you?!"

"Yes, my own brother, pushed me right out of the plane cause I wasn't moving fast enough for his liking."

I continue to laugh. "Did you scream?"

"Like a girl. Blaine said I was still screaming even when we landed on the ground. I'm pretty sure I had a heart attack. I have a tick in my eye now, do you see it?" he ask, leaning close to me but his eye is just fine. All I see is the gorgeous whiskey color that stands out against his tanned skin. Instead of letting him know how much his close proximity affects me, I push him away, before holding myself. I'm laughing so hard, it's unbelievable.

"That's crazy," I say between peals of laughter.

"I know, but it was the best experience of my life. I've never felt so free, so alive," he says with a grin on his face.

"I'll take your word for it; I'm scared of heights," I say with a shake of my head. I'm not entirely sure that's true, but since I've never been in the air, I'm going to stick with that statement.

"I'm telling you, you'd love it," he says, so sure of himself.

His confidence is intoxicating and I feel it radiating from me, lighting a spark in my own. He's so sure of himself, so comfortable in his own skin. It's refreshing. I'm so used to dealing with Rob, who's arrogant and selfish, that to deal with such a laidback, genuinely happy person is such a change of pace. Grinning over at him, I say, "I would scream so loud, someone would think I was being murdered."

Tucker laughs at that, but then his eyes meet mine and my laughter stops. His eyes are light, playful, and sweet. I want to reach over, touch his face with my fingers, feel the scruff on his chin, but instead, he says, "You know, we could scream together. I'd love to take you. It would be fun."

I look away, my cheeks burning scarlet. I feel horrible because I wish I could. What does that say about me? About my marriage? But I can't help but want to go with him. Get lost in the air with him, to feel him hold me once we're on the ground. It would be perfect. But the perfection would be ruined as soon as it started. Rob would kill me, or maybe even Tucker. Not that I would go anyway.

"What, are you scared?" he teases but I am. Just for a different reason than he's expecting.

"Yeah," I say with a strained laugh, "I wouldn't make it."

"Sure you would. I'd protect you."

I can feel his eyes on me, but I can't look at him. If I did, he'd see how much I want that. How being in his arms, having his protection, would make me the happiest person on earth.

Nothing is said for a moment as I pick at the top of my sushi roll. It has nasty raw fish in it and as much as I want to like it, just to make him happy, I can't. It's gross, and you know what I did, I told him that. I even covered my mouth, in complete shock when those words left my mouth, but he just laughed. He didn't care. I expected him to get mad, but he did the opposite; he told me next time I get to pick dinner.

Insane right?

"It's not as if I'm making you go, I was just picking at you."

I look up at him to find him watching me. "What?"

"You got quiet on me. Don't worry, I'm not going to make it mandatory that you go," he says with a laugh.

I laugh, but it's fake. I don't know what to say, and then, out of nowhere, I say, "I'm married."

When I look up, his brows are up into his hairline. His mouth is parted and he is looking at me as if I told him I like to steal food from the homeless. His eyes are so dark and I can tell he is genuinely stunned. Instantly, I feel disgusting and I look away, my heart hammering in my chest.

"What?"

I swallow loudly. "I'm married and I don't think my husband would like to go skydiving, and I doubt he would let me go without him."

Really, he would never let me go with Tucker, or any man for that case, but I leave that out. I won't look at him even though I can feel his eyes boring a hole in my head.

"But you don't have a ring."

I look down at my bare hand. Rob took my rings two years ago because he says I don't deserve to wear them. It doesn't bother me because I don't care. I don't want the rings, but I hate when people ask me this. It happens a lot and my lie is kind of stupid.

"I lost the ring in the ocean, and I don't have the money to buy another." I've never even been to the ocean.

When I look up to gauge his reaction, he looks away. I can still see the shock on his face, and I feel horrible for leading him on. I guess that's what I've done. How disgusting of me. How could I do that to such a great guy? I should have never flirted with him. Wait, did I flirt? Shit, I don't know but I feel like I've done something wrong and I want to fix it, but how?

A heartbeat later, he looks up at me and the shock I saw before is gone.

"Oh, that sucks he won't let you go. I'm sure my girlfriend would have liked to have someone to hang out with."

Girlfriend? Whoa, what?

"Oh, I didn't realize you have a girlfriend."

"Yeah, been together a while. How long have you been married?"

His face is like stone, and I hate it. His eyes are dark and he isn't looking at me anymore but at the same time I notice that his chest is rising and falling quickly. I don't know what to think, what to do, or even how to feel. Really though, why do I care? Nothing was going to happen between us anyway. Nothing. So why am I worried about his feelings or how he feels about me?

Stupidity. I'm so freaking stupid.

"Three years," I answer, looking down at my fingers.

"You married young."

I shrug. I hate when people say that. "When you know, you know."

"I guess so."

I watch him, my heart pounding in my chest as he moves his fingers along his leg, still not looking at me. I can't stand the silence, and so I ask, "How long have you and your girlfriend been together?"

"Not long," he said with a wave. Before I can ask why he said 'a long time' before, he gets up and starts gathering his stuff. "I got to go. I have to call my dad and stuff. This was good, Violet. I'm happy with everything."

I watch as he quickly picks up the trash, not letting me help before he throws everything away.

"Me too," I say after he is almost out my door. "Thank you for a wonderful dinner."

He stops. Looking over his shoulder at me. He smiles before he says, "It was great. See you tomorrow."

I smile back as he closes my door but then he opens it again. "Are you ready to go?"

I nod. "I am closing everything down and then I'll be ready."

"Okay, I'm going to do the same and I'll meet you out front to walk you out to your car."

Something inside me flutters as I nod again. "Thank you."

I rush to get everything put up because I don't want to keep him waiting but after locking up, I'm the one waiting for him. Finally, after what seems like forever, Tucker emerges from his office and, like before, he won't look at me. He motions for me to go first and once the office is locked we walk to our cars. I feel like I need to say something, like I need to apologize. For the last twenty minutes I've been trying to come up with a reason to apologize, but I can't think of a reason. I don't want to apologize for leading him on, when really I did. Or did I? I'm confused and my heart is beating so damn hard my chest hurts; I have no clue how to make this right. Tucker is never this quiet and he always looks at me, but now he is doing neither and I hate the way it makes me feel.

Letting out a breath, I reach for my keys before we reach my SUV. It's an old beat up Ford Explorer, nothing sexy like his BMW, and I'm embarrassed to be getting in it in front of him. I wish that things were different, that I wasn't married and that instead of looking at Tucker and wishing him goodnight, I could smother him with kisses before going home and dreaming happy dreams.

But that's not my life.

My life belongs to Rob.

Opening my car door, I look over my shoulder to find Tucker watching me. The look of melancholy on his face twists my stomach into knots, and my mouth is moving before I even think about what I'm about to say.

"I'm sorry."

God, I'm so stupid!

I want to slam the door and drive away but I know he heard me. His eyes bore into mine as he takes in a labored breath. He runs his fingers through the hair I so desperately want to touch and I can't believe I'm jealous of his own fingers. It's disgusting but before I can scold myself, he says, "Sorry?"

I shake my head.

"Ignore me. Goodnight, Tucker," I say quickly but as I go to slam my door, he stops me, putting his body between me and the car door. Even with the height of my SUV, I still have to look up at him. Staring up into his angular face, eyes curious and probing, has me breathless.

"No, why are you sorry?"

I look down and close my eyes. Really? I really had to say that? Jeez. Knowing I have no out, I decide that honesty is the best way to go about this.

"I feel like I led you on. I'm sorry."

"Led me on?" He shakes his head before a smile replaces his troubled face. He chuckles before shrugging his shoulders. "No, Violet, you didn't lead me on. I should have asked. Instead, I just jumped in like I always do. It's not your fault; it's mine, but it's fine. No worries, have a goodnight. See you tomorrow."

He sends me one last grin but it doesn't reach his eyes. He then slowly shuts my door and I watch his form retreat before heading home.

I didn't sleep at all last night.

All I did was replay the dinner I had with Tucker the night before. Especially the part when he told me it was his fault. What the hell was *his* fault? I don't get it and I am so confused it isn't funny! It's driving me crazy, but I have work to do.

Plus, why does it matter? Tucker McCloud means nothing to me.

So why does he feel like everything?

Moving a window to the side on my computer, I lean on my hand as I click through boring insurance paperwork. I'd rather be out in the office staring at Tucker, but not today. I have too much work, and of course, that's a horrible idea. Staring at him will not cure me of my insane crush. It would probably make it worse.

When my phone rings, I see that it's Rob.

Shit.

"Hello?" I ask.

"Hey, your mom keeps calling the house phone. She said something about not liking to call you at work, and she wants to talk to me but I'm walking out the door. Call her."

He's such a liar. He doesn't want to talk to her because he knows she will cuss him out for not letting me come home but instead of pointing that out, I say, "Thanks, I'll call her now."

"Whatever. Remember you're not going."

"I know," I say and then hang up. I'll probably hear it later that I didn't say 'bye' but whatever. Dialing my mom's number, she answers on the third ring.

"Hey sweetie," she says.

"Hey, Rob said you were calling. Is everything okay? How's Grandma?"

She lets out an annoyed breath. "I was trying to get a hold of that husband of yours to talk some sense in him. You need to be here. This is such bull-Oh-wait, grandma wants to talk to you."

An ache starts in my chest as my grandma's lilting voice rings over the line.

"Hey, ladybug."

Tears gather in my eyes. I miss her so much and hate that I'm not there.

"Hi, grandma, how're you feeling?"

"Alright today. I miss you, ladybug, you know that right?"

"I know, I miss you too, and I'm so sorry I'm not there," I say around the lump in my throat.

"It's fine, you're in my heart. You'll always be there."

"And you'll always be in mine."

Suddenly she is coughing, a deep cough that rattles in her chest, and my heart breaks at the sound. I close my eyes, tears leaking down my cheeks from the horrible noise. I want to be there. I wish I was holding her in my arms the way she did when I was a child. Hate burns inside me and I would give anything not to be married to the monster I'm married to. How could he keep me away from her? Why is he doing this to me?

When the coughing subsides, she gasps for breath. My mom's hushed voice comes over the line in the background. She's trying to take the phone but my grandma won't let her. She still wants to talk to me.

"Promise me something," she says once she is able to speak.

I wipe my face, taking in a deep breath before saying, "Anything."

She pauses for only a second, taking in a wheezing breath before she whispers, "Be happy."

That breaks me and I put the phone down as I silently sob. How the fuck can I promise something like that? Happiness is unattainable to me. I am constantly walking on eggshells, watching my back, and I never know if I'll make it to the next day. So how in the world can I promise that? Do I lie? Do I tell her the truth – that I'll never be happy and that I'm sorry? That I did the opposite of what they raised me to do? Instead of finding a man to love and cherish me, I found one who beats the shit out of me and hates me?

I want to tell her everything, but I know that she'll tell my mom and my mom can't handle this right now. She has enough to deal with. So I do what I've been doing for the last three years.

I lie.

"I promise, grandma."

"That's my girl. I love you, ladybug."

"I love you."

I hear the exchange of the phone and soon my mom is on the line.

"I am so disgusted with Rob, Violet June," my mother says in a hush whisper.

"Mom, I told you, it's my work. I can't leave right now. I have so much going on –"

"Stop!" she yells, and I jump in surprise. "I know that asshole isn't letting you come and I could kill him, Violet, I could, and I will if you aren't here for the funeral. I need you."

Her voice breaks and I slump to my desk, laying my forehead on the cool wood. I want to run to my car, go to the airport and leave, but with what money? I can't even drive because Rob fills up my tank when it needs it and all I have on me is thirty-six bucks. It wouldn't even get me halfway there. I don't know what to do. I know I could get the money from Tucker, or even my mom, but I'm too scared to do it, and I can honestly say I hate Rob. I want to kill him, just like my mom wants to, but I know I won't. I know I'll stay where I am and never attain what my grandmother made me promise to do.

I'm stuck, and I hate myself for it.

"Mom, I'm sorry I'm not there. I promise if I could, I would be and I will try my hardest to be there for the funeral."

My mom pauses before taking in a deep breath and letting it out. I can tell that she wants to say more, but she won't. I won't listen. I won't do what she wants. I will continue to disappoint her, and I don't know how to change that. Or I do, I'm just too scared to do it.

In a strained voice, my mother says, "I hope so."

I move my fingers along my cheeks, catching my tears. I want to guarantee her I'll be there, but I can't. All I can do is hope, but in all reality, why?

Hoping has never done anything before and I doubt it will now.

Chapter
SEVEN

The rest of my week didn't get better. All I did was miss my grandma and hate myself for not having the strength to do what she wished. I couldn't help but be disgusted in myself for staying, for letting someone completely control me. Why did I allow this to happen? Is there a way out? Every scenario I come up with always leads to Rob stopping me. I can't ask for a divorce; he'd kill me. I can't run; he'd find me and then kill me. I can't kill him because I don't want to go to jail and more than likely he'll kill me before I can kill him. I could tell my mom. Maybe she could help, but what if Rob killed us both? I've seen Rob overreact and it's scary as hell. I don't know what I can do, and it scares me to the core that I have no other options. How did I let this happen?

Leaning against the wall in the office, watching as my staff works, I can't help but be jealous of them all. I bet they all have great lives. Loving husband or boyfriend. I know that Tonya is a single mom but she's happy. She tells me all the time how much she loves her children and her life. I yearn to be happy, to be loved, and to be cherished. I just wish I had it in me to fight for what I want.

When a exam room door opens and Tucker comes out, I can't help but stare. His dark slacks and light purple shirt with a silver tie make him look like a businessman straight out of some magazine. His stark white jacket tells everyone to call him Dr. T and it makes me smile. I don't understand it since I think Dr. McCloud sounds a lot more professional, but he said he isn't old yet. He's young and wants to stay that way. I watch as he walks out with one of our elderly patients, his hand on his shoulder as they discuss the weather. His eyes only meet mine for a second and it only takes that one second for my skin to break out in gooseflesh and for my heart to flutter in my chest. It has been like that all week. He won't look at me for long and it's driving me insane. I don't think I've been hit with the full force of his grin in four days. Four days! It's horrible and I miss it, despite the fact that I shouldn't miss or want anything from that man.

But I still do.

Tucker shakes hands with the patient and I smile when his face breaks into a huge grin.

"My daughter is single, Dr. T. She's a gorgeous thing, too, and needs a good man," the patient says.

Everyone around them giggles, including me. All our elderly patients try to fix Tucker up with someone. Even Dr. McCloud has tried. My heart always falls into my stomach, though, because I don't want him to be fixed up with anyone. It shouldn't matter.

I'm married.

"I might fit the bill, Mr. Edwards, but I'm sorry. I have my eyes set on someone else," Tucker says and I swear to God, his eyes flickered to mine. I want to ask everyone if they saw it, or even what he means, but I don't. Instead I continue to watch him while acting as if I am working something on the tablet

I'm holding. I don't know if I look convincing, but I can't help but stare at him.

"You know, Violet, I think he's talking about you."

I jump in surprise and look to my left to find Ms. Yolanda smiling at me.

"Excuse me?" I ask, even though I heard her just fine.

She leans in, her voice in a whisper as she repeats herself. "Tucker. I think he only has eyes for you."

She adds a wink, and I can't help but laugh.

"I'm married," I say with a wave of my hand.

She smiles. "Married or not, that boy has a crush on you."

My body tingles at the thought of him having a crush on me. I mean, I know it isn't true, but wouldn't it be great? It would also be great if I could leave Rob, and skydive into the sunset with Tucker.

Yeah, that would be just fucking grand, but oh well. Enough daydreaming. Back to work.

Later that afternoon, I glance at the clock to see that I only have thirty minutes before my day is over and it will be time for me to go home. I groan at the thought. I don't want to go home. I'd rather work but I do need to get the house clean, and cook something before getting in my tub and relaxing until my fingers and toes turn to prunes. Rob is on his four nights, so I won't see him until Monday which is just fine with me, but I still need to have food waiting for him in the morning. I'll hear about it later if I don't. Leaning on my hand, I click through emails but stop when a knock sounds at my door.

Looking up, I find Tucker entering, his arms full of files. He stops in front of my desk and looks at me with worried eyes.

"Please tell me you can stay late tonight and help get these insurance forms in the computer."

I nod. "Sure, but why? Everything is done for the month; I finished the last of it yesterday morning."

He shakes his head, the frantic look in his eyes making me frazzled. "No, my dad had these under his desk, and I can't do it all myself. It's over two hundred claims."

I take in a sharp breath. "There is no way."

He drops the files on my desk and runs his hand though his hair before looking at me. "Way. Tomorrow is the beginning of the month. It has to be done tonight. Please tell me you can stay tonight."

I look up and down all the files and slowly shake my head in surprise. I can't believe this. Dr. McCloud is always on top of things, this is so unlike him. "Sure, but I can't believe he let this happened."

"Neither can I, but I guess things were a little crazy with him retiring and all."

"Yeah," I agree as I reach for a file and open it up. "Well, I guess I've got my work cut out for me."

"Cool, I'll grab my laptop and we can get started."

I should point out that he could take half the files to his office and I'll do the other half, but before I can even utter the words, he's across the hall getting his laptop. He sits in the seat in front of my desk and opens his laptop before reaching for the first file. I watch him for a moment but quickly look away when he looks up, hoping he didn't catch me staring at him.

I try to engross myself in my work, but it's hard when this beautiful man is distracting me. Every time he makes a move, I notice. When he bites his lower lip, I'm watching and wish I could do the same. When he moves his hands through his hair, I'm tingling I want to touch him so bad, but I know I can't and it's starting to weigh on me.

I know I need to distance myself from this man, but I don't think I can. I mean, why do I even feel like this? I have never, not once, been attracted to another man until Tucker McCloud walked into the office. Never. I was so obsessed with Rob that I believed his lies, his abuse, but now? Now I fucking hate him, and I want to leave so bad but I don't know how. I wish it were easy. I wish it was a simple break with the knowledge that I'll never see Rob again –but it never will be.

I want to be able to say I'm leaving and fuck you. I want to hit him back, and never see him again but I'm scared I never will and I hate that.

"So does your family live in Colorado?"

I look up to find Tucker still working, but I know he asked.

I nod, even though he isn't watching me. "Yeah, my mom and grandma do."

"Is your father not in your life?"

"No, I never knew him."

"That sucks."

"Yeah," I say with a nod.

"Do you have any siblings?"

"Nope, only child," I say and smile when I look up to see him looking at me. "I'm really boring."

A grin pulls at the side of his mouth. "I doubt that."

A smile is still on my face as I look back down and go back to work. Silence fills the room as we work, but it's a comfortable silence. One that I like. I'm almost halfway through when Tucker clears his throat.

"I'm starving."

I nod. "Me too."

"We'll, let's order something."

"Okay."

I need to finish so I can go home and gets things done but I don't want to. I want to stay here and eat and finish work. Everything else can wait. More than likely, I'm making a horrible mistake staying and spending more time with Tucker. I'll pay for this later but I can't stop myself and I don't know what that means. Am I stupid? Do I not care anymore? Have I finally had enough of Rob that I'm going to do what I want? I'm not sure but being with Tucker makes me smile, and I like the way that he makes me feel, so I'm going to stay right here.

"I don't know what I would do without Blaine."

I look up from my file, a piece of pepperoni on my lips from the pizza that sits in front of me. We haven't said anything for the last hour. We worked while we waited and then stuffed our faces once the pizza arrived, so it's easy to say I'm confused. "Huh?"

He laughs. "Sorry, I mean from earlier, you saying you have no siblings."

I smile. "Oh, okay, yeah, I always wanted a sibling but I had my mom and grandma. I was okay."

"That's good. I bet they miss you and you miss them."

I nod as the tingling of tears hit my eyes. "Yeah, I never expected to leave but Rob wanted to come here. His family is here."

"Did you want to come here?"

I shake my head. "Nope, but I had –" I stop myself and look away. I can't believe I almost told him I had no choice. Clearing my throat, I say, "But I don't mind it now."

I glance up and can tell that he knows that's not what I was going to say but he doesn't pry. Instead, he says, "That's good. I've lived here my whole life."

"I don't believe you," I tease, "Everyone who grew up in this town dresses like a cowboy and you don't."

He laughs and I smile as I look back at my computer. "Not everyone does, but I do, just not to work. I even wear Wranglers. I'm a country boy at heart."

I slap a hand over my mouth to stop the bite of pizza trying to force its way out through the laughter spilling from me. I have never seen him in anything but slacks and dress shoes. The vision of Dr. Tucker McCloud in tight Wranglers and boots has me gasping for breath. I picture him in his jeans and boots, shirtless of course, sitting on a horse, and asking me if I want to take a ride. I would say yes, but I wouldn't be talking about riding the horse.

"Don't you think so?"

I blink before looking back over to Tucker. Shit, he's talking to me.

"Sorry what?" I ask.

He smiles. "I was thinking we should have a casual Friday. Then I can wear my boots to show you I have real country roots."

"Yeah," I say, even though I know that's a bad idea. I'll pass out when I set eyes on him. The nurses would go crazy, too, and more than likely, no work would get done. I laugh, and he looks at me questionably.

"What?" he ask, a smile pulling at his lips.

"Nothing," I say but then I can't help it. "Just don't expect work to get done on Fridays."

His brows go up in confusion. "Why?"

I giggle. "Because all the girls will be checking you out in your jeans and boots."

He smiles and his cheeks flush crimson. "No, they won't."

"Yes, they will. Everyone crushes on you."

He eyes meet mine, and I know my face is bright red. I can't believe I said that! He probably thinks I crush on him! I do, but he doesn't need to know that.

"Everyone?" he asked, wagging his brows at me.

"You did *not* just wag your eyebrows at me."

That has us both laughing and I shake my head, reaching for my soda as my laughter subsides.

"You know you like it," he teases as I take a drink.

I look over to find him smiling at me, his brows going up and down and with that, soda promptly shoots out of my nose. Tucker dissolves into a fit of laughter and one would think that soda coming out of my nose is the funniest thing in the world, but I beg to differ. Wiping my nose, I send him a dirty look as he continues to laugh.

"I do not like your wagging eyebrows, Dr. T," I snap at him playfully but even I can't help but laugh, too. His laugh is contagious.

"You do," he says as his laughter finally slows down. "God, that was funny."

"I'm glad I amuse you," I say with a roll of my eyes before

picking up another file.

I'm well into entering the data for the next file when Tucker asks, "You're not mad are you?"

I look up in surprise at his question. "No, not at all."

"Oh good, I thought I pissed you off," he says with a smirk.

I grin back. "No way, just trying to get done."

"Tired of me?"

I laugh. "No, just need to get home and get stuff done."

His mouth forms a straight line. "Your husband is waiting for you?"

I shake my head. "No, he's on his four nights at the hospital."

"Oh, he's a doctor?"

"No, a nurse."

His eyes light up and the corner of his mouth twitches. "That's how y'all met?"

I don't want to talk about Rob. Not at all.

"Y'all?" I tease. "The more time I spend with you, the more your country roots shine."

"Yeah, I love sweet tea and sitting on my front porch playing my banjo."

I stop what I'm doing. "You play the banjo?"

He laughs again. "No, I'm kidding."

"Crap, I was so going to ask you to teach me," I joke before looking back down at my file. His laughter continues and I just love the sound of it: loud, hearty, from the gut. I like that I make him laugh. Rob never laughs. Well, I take that back, he laughs at me but never with me. Not like he used to.

Sad thought, huh?

Hours pass and I swear my eyes are going cross-eyed staring at this damn screen. I squeeze my eyes shut and run my hands down my face. I have about thirty files left but I swear it feels like three hundred. Looking over at Tucker, I find him with his face on the desk beside his computer.

"You okay?"

"I want to kill my father," he mutters against the desk.

I smile. "I've killed Dr. McCloud at least twice in my head in the last hour."

Tucker sits up and grins. His eyes are the bright whiskey color that causes butterflies to go nuts in my stomach.

"We're almost done."

"We are," I agree.

"We can do it!" he says throwing a fist in the air.

I laugh and throw my own fist in the air. "Yes, we can!"

Through his laughter, he says, "We sound like Bob the Builder."

"Who's that?" I ask with a smile on my face.

"Nicky, my nephew, watches this show called *Bob the Builder* and when he's about to take on a task, he says, 'Can we do it? Yes we can!'"

"Sounds like a great show."

Tucker laughs. "It's horrible, but Nicky loves it."

I smile. "I didn't know you had a nephew."

"Yup, he's four and the coolest kid I know. We don't get to see him much. Blaine and his ex don't get along."

"That sucks."

"Yeah. Thankfully, she loves me so I get to steal Nicky away sometimes but it's tough on Blaine."

"I bet," I say. I don't know Blaine but my heart hurts for him. I know what it's like to grow up without a father.

"Which reminds me, the conference we're going to is in Georgia. We can take him to get ice cream or something."

Huh? "Conference?"

"Yeah, I sent you an email. I already paid for it. You are free that weekend right?"

"I thought that email was junk," I say embarrassed. "I deleted it."

I thought that he would be mad, but I'm starting to think he's a laidback person because all he ever does is laugh off situations where Rob would blow a gasket.

"Good thing I mentioned it then. But yeah, we're going to

see about the benefits to going completely digital for the office. My dad would never do it, but I think it would be best for us."

I nod while my insides cringe. Rob won't let me go; he'll freak. "You need me to go?"

"Uh yeah, you're my manager. You need to be there."

"Oh, okay, I'll figure something out," I say and I wish I hadn't.

"Can you not go?"

I shrug. "I'm not sure."

"Oh, okay, well let me know. It'll be fun."

"Yeah," I say before reaching for another file.

Neither of us say anything else and get back to work. I try to pay attention to what I'm doing but it's hard when all I can think about is how I'm going to go to this conference. Rob is going to flip the fuck out, no matter if I lie or if I tell him the truth. It's frustrating but I know I need to go.

I want to go.

It's another hour or so before I'm finally done. Glancing at the clock, I see that it's almost ten. I'm so tired but I still have to get stuff done and I know I should be mad that I had to stay late but I'm not. I enjoyed my time with Tucker. More than I probably should have. When I look over at him, Tucker still has a few files by his laptop. I reach over and grab some and start his. He smiles at me, and I smile back before getting to work.

The next time I look at the clock, it's eleven fifteen and I groan. I'm going to be a zombie tomorrow.

"Man, I'm beat," he says reaching up in the air to stretch. I try not to watch him, but it's hard. His long, lean arms reach above his head, accentuating the rippling torso beneath his button-down shirt.

"Me too," I say as I shut down my computer.

He stands up and gets his computer before heading to his office. After shutting everything down and deciding I can give those file to one of the girls tomorrow to put away, I lock my office up and wait for Tucker as he finishes what he's doing. Once he's done, we head for the door and then to our cars after everything is locked up.

"Thanks so much for staying, Violet."

I smile up at him. "No problem. It went quick."

"That's 'cause we're a great team," he says with a wink.

I nod before looking down so he doesn't see the flush of crimson spreading across my cheeks. "I agree." When I glance back up to say more, I see that his hand is coming toward my face and I jerk back away from him. Was he about to hit me? Heat fills my face, my neck and my chest hurt from my heart banging against it. Tucker is frozen, his hand still reaching for me while his eyes widen in confusion. I take in a quick breath, and I cannot believe that I just did that.

Without a word, not even a second glance, I'm making my way to my car, quickly.

"Violet? Violet, what's wrong?" Tucker calls after me, but I have to get out of here.

Now.

Reaching for my car, still ignoring him, I get in and slam the door. Quickly, I suck in a deep breath and clench my shaking hands. What the hell is wrong with me? Tucker is not Rob. I have no clue why I thought he was going to hit me, but I did. I don't know what he was doing or what he was reaching for, but it looked like he was about to hit me. Am I really that fucked up? Is this the way my life will always be? Any kind of quick movement will make me think I'm going to be harmed? Why am I doing this to myself?

I slam my hand into the steering wheel and I have no clue how the hell I'm going to face him tomorrow.

Fuck.

Chapter EIGHT

"Where is my dinner?"

I roll my eyes, moving my hand down my face. I'm so tired, I can't even keep my eyes open, and dealing with Rob is not what I want to do right now. After rushing away from Tucker last night, I went straight home and to bed, where I cried most of the night from embarrassment. I don't know what my deal was last night but I've been in my office with my door shut, ignoring Tucker all day. I can't face him. I know he'll have questions, and I don't know how I'm going to answer them.

"I had to work late and I went to bed."

"Work late? Why?"

"I had files that had to be done last night, last-minute stuff."

"So when did you eat?"

"I ordered pizza."

"Couldn't bring me any?" he asks, and I let out a breath.

"I ate it all."

He scoffs. "Better watch out. You'll get chubbier than you already are, eating like that."

"Thanks," I scoff back as I look over at my computer.

"What's wrong with you? You've been really mouthy lately. It's pissing me off."

"Sorry," I say but I don't mean it, and I think he knows I don't.

He pauses and I'm sure he is trying to decide if he wants to yell at me or not.

"Whatever. Next time don't hog all the pizza. Have a little consideration for your husband."

The line goes dead, and I drop my phone to the desk. God, he drives me insane. He wants me to have consideration for him when he has none for me. How is that fair? And why does he always hang up on me? I should start screaming and then hang up on him. He wouldn't know what to do with himself. He'd know what to do to me, but it would stun him, that's for sure. I won't do it, though. I only think it and then I'm mad at myself for not saying it. It's a sad, ugly thing, my life has become.

Moving to my computer, I open my email because it is blinking but before I can click on the first email, a message comes up.

Dr. T: I think we need to talk about what happened last night.

I drop my head to the desk. Of course, he wants to talk and that's the last thing I want to do. I know I can't ignore him though and I do owe him some kind of explanation.

Violet M: Sorry about that, I don't know what was going on. I freaked out for no reason. No big deal.

I wait for him to write me back, but then my door opens and he's coming through it, shutting it softly before turning to look at me. He looks worried, stricken, and I hate that I'm the reason he's so concerned. I'm the fucked-up one, and I can't understand why he's worried about me. I'm not worth his time.

"I hate typing what I have to say because you can't see me say it," he says as he walks toward my desk. Once there, he places his hands on the edge of my desk and looks right into my eyes. My breath quickens and my palms start to sweat from the close proximity.

"The thing is, Violet, last night, I felt like you thought I was going to hurt you, and I can't express how far from the true that is. I would never hurt you, and I need you to know that. You should always feel comfortable around me because in no way, shape, or form do I want to cause any harm to you. I'm sorry if I scared you or made you feel like that. It was never my intention, and I hope you can accept my apology."

My heart is beating out of control and I want nothing more than to wrap my arms around this man's middle and just stay there. Looking up into his eyes I want to tell him that it isn't his fault. That it's my husband's fault because instead of loving me the way a man should, he hurts me, causes me pain, and scares the living shit out of me.

I don't know why I want to tell him those things, but I do. With a smile, I say, "No apology needed, Dr. T. It was no big deal, like I said. I don't know what was wrong with me. I thought I saw a bug or something coming toward me, and it freaked me out. I should be the one apologizing."

"A bug?" he asked incredulously.

"Sure, or something," I say with a wave of my hand. "It's no big deal, I promise."

He stands up to his full six feet of glory before running his hand through his hair, his other hand on his hip. Looking down at me, he says, "I feel like there is more here that you're not telling me."

I shrug. "I don't know why. I'm great." I'm surprised I can say it with a straight face. I'm nowhere near great, but he doesn't need to know that. I need to protect him because if I let him in, he'll get hurt. Physically and emotionally. I swear I can see, in vivid detail, Rob getting a hold of Tucker, and it scares me to the core. I can't ever let that happen. I care too much for Tucker—I know that is stupid on my part, but I do. How can I not? He is amazing, sweet, and an all-around great guy. Gorgeous, too.

He's still watching me and as much as I like how he looks, I don't want to be under his scrutiny right now. I feel like he's finding cracks in the walls I've built up around myself that hides the shit I go through at home, and it makes me nervous what will happen if he finds out or if he even suspects something. I've only known him for a month, but I know he's a fixer. He'll do anything and everything to help people, and I don't think he'll understand that he can't help me.

I'm not fixable.

"You can talk to me," he softly says, "I'm here for you."

See? Fixer.

"Thank you, but really, don't worry about me, I'm fine," I say, and I even add a smile for good measure. I've gotten so good at this lie, it's scary.

Tucker eyes me for another minute, his eyes peering straight through mine like he can see every ragged, bloodied piece of me.

"It's hard not to worry when I care, Violet. Just remember I'm here."

I can only blink before he lets out a breath and then turns to leave. When the door shuts, I lean back in my chair and close my eyes, covering them with my hands. Even if he had given me a chance to respond, I wouldn't know what to say. I don't want to lie to him anymore than I have but I'm going to have to. He knows something is up and I'm not sure if I should be worried or relieved.

"I don't know why we're going to this. It's stupid."

I let out an annoyed breath as I walked through the house.

"I told you, you didn't have to go."

"And I said I'm going 'cause I don't trust your ass."

I roll my eyes before sliding into my heels. Rob going to the office Christmas party was not what I had planned, but he invited himself when I told him I was going. I never expected that. I expected him to throw a fit and tell me I wasn't going, so it's easy to say I'm a little surprised.

"I don't understand why you don't trust me to go to my office party but okay, that's fine. Let's go, I don't want to be late."

When a remote breaks by my head, I whip around to see Rob glaring at me. My heart jumps up into my throat and my hands start to shake from the icy look on his face.

"Don't fucking rush me."

I reach down, collecting the broken pieces of remote. "Sorry," I mutter as I walk past him to throw away the pieces.

"You're buying a new remote since you made me break it."

Like you, I wonder how I made him break it, but whatever. I don't have the time to argue or fight with him. I just need to get to the party, wish everyone a Merry Christmas, and then get the hell out of there. I don't want anyone around Rob, and I especially don't want him around Tucker. I wish I could just say the hell with it and stay home, but it's mandatory that everyone is there. My co-workers are bringing their families. I was excited about meeting everyone, but now that Rob is going, I'm freaking out that he'll embarrass me or something.

"Are you ready?" I ask, looking back at him. He's wearing a pair of slim-fitting boot-cut jeans and cornflower blue button up shirt. His dark hair is falling in his even darker eyes, and I wish that I could muster up some kind of desire for this man, but nothing is there. When his eyes meet mine, I look away, nervous that he's going to yell at me.

"Yeah, let's go."

I tense up as he walks by me and once he's passed, I let out a breath. As I watch him walk to the car, all I can think is that this is going to be a blast.

Not.

"Oh my goodness, it's so nice to meet you, Rob, we just love Violet. She is a doll!" Ms. Tonya gushed. I'm smiling ear to ear, but when I look up at Rob, my smile falls. He has had the same look the whole time we've been there. The look is somewhere between stinking cheese and seeing an outbreak of herpes. I'm not sure what anyone thinks about him, but I know I'm ready to leave. Like now.

"That's nice," Rob says before taking a sip of his beer.

I want to smack him. He's being an ass but apparently Ms. Tonya doesn't notice.

"Are y'all going anywhere for Christmas?"

I shake my head. "No, we're staying here."

"That's too bad, I would think you'd go home to see your grandmother," she says before taking my hand. "How is she?"

Rob lets out an annoyed breath, but I ignore him and say, "She's hanging on. She's a strong lady."

"Of course she is, having raised such a sweet and strong woman like you. I've been praying for her."

I smile and I don't miss the scoff that comes from my husband. "Thank you. That means a lot to me."

"Of course. Oh, Tucker is finally here."

I follow her gaze and find him walking in with his arms full of presents and the biggest grin on his magnificent face. Like the rest of the staff, Ms. Tonya starts for him, leaving me with Rob. I try not to watch as everyone gushes and fusses over Tucker, but it's hard not to. He looks sexy as hell in a black expensive tailored suit that hugs every inch of him. His tie is a festive gold and his eyes shine as he looks out into the office. I hope to catch a glimpse of his 'girlfriend'. I still don't believe she exists and I'm starting to think I'm right because he stands alone. Wouldn't she have come to the party? Yeah, I think so, too.

When his eyes land on me, his smile grows but then it is

gone just as quick as it came and I know it's because of Rob.

"Is that your boss?"

"Yeah," I say turning away from Tucker to look up at Rob. "He's a good boss. You'll like him."

"I doubt it, I hate him already."

"Why?" I ask with my face scrunched up. "You don't know him."

"I don't like the way he just looked at you. Actually, I don't like the way any of these fucking people look or act around you. They think you're such a great person, it pisses me off," he spits out before taking a long pull of his beer.

"But I am," I manage to say but I quickly stop talking when he sets me with a look.

A scary one.

"No, you're not," he says with a shake of his head. "See, this is why I don't want you working here."

"Why? Because I work with nice people who like me?"

"No, because they'll make you think you're something you're not. You are not a great person, you're not even a good person. You're worthless and a pain in my ass," he sneers. Rob then gets closer to my face and in a hush whisper says, "And if you don't stop talking back to me, I'm gonna make you regret it."

I flinch back, but it doesn't matter. He is right there, digging his fingers into my arm. "I am tired of it," he says harshly, spitting on the side of my face with every word.

"Hey, you must be Violet's husband."

Rob lets me go and I look up to see Tucker looking down at me. I know he can see the tears welling up in my eyes and even the way my hand comes up to cover where Rob's fingers dug into my skin. I look down at the ground, trying to compose myself as Rob says, "Yes, I am."

"It's nice to meet you. I'm Tucker McCloud, the doctor here."

"I know."

When I glance up, Tucker's hand is held out for a handshake but Rob has no intention of taking his hand.

Asshole.

"This is my husband, Rob Moore."

Tucker's lips are in a straight line as he tucks his hands in his pockets and an awkward silence falls between us. I won't look at him, but I can feel his eyes on me. I don't want to give Rob anything else to bitch about but I can't just stand here. I have to talk or Tucker will know for sure that something is wrong. Looking up, I meet his eyes and force myself to swallow the breath at the back my throat. Concern is shining in his eyes and it's as if he's trying to ask me if I'm okay without speaking. Looking up at Rob, I see that he's looking out at the party, ignoring the situation completely like the asshole he is.

"Are your parents going to be home for Christmas, Tucker?" I ask looking back at him.

He nods. "Yeah, they're leaving afterwards, though. I think my dad might go to the convention with us."

I freeze. Shit. Shit. Shit.

"Convention?"

I look over at Rob. He's looking right at Tucker, his brows together and I can see the white of his knuckles, fingers wrapped around the cold glass in his hand.

"Yes, I haven't gotten to talk to you about that yet. We're going to Georgia, as an office, for a digital convention," I say quickly, my heart pounding in my chest. His gaze slowly leaves Tucker and lands on me.

"You're going to Georgia? With him?"

"With everyone," I say. "It's for the office."

"Who's paying? You don't have any money to go."

"I'm paying, for everyone," Tucker says, and I spare him a glance. His eyes are glued to Rob, and I feel like I can't breathe. You can cut the tension with a knife right now, and it's freaking me the hell out.

"Hmm," is all Rob says before walking away to get more

beer. I watch as he leaves and I dread going home with him. I don't know why he didn't freak out or tell Tucker he can kiss his ass, and it can't be good. The deadly silence is almost worse than the rage. It seethes under his skin, and I never know what to expect. I want to run, I want to hide, but it would be a waste of time. It would only prolong the inevitable. I know I shouldn't look at Tucker but I do. He's watching me.

We stare at each for a long time before I look away and say, "Sorry, he doesn't really like people much."

"Don't apologize for him, Violet."

I bite into my lip, running my finger along the rim of my cup. "Sorry."

"What are you sorry for? You've done nothing wrong." He pauses, letting out a breath. "Will you look at me please?"

I bite harder into my lip until it hurts before I look up to meet his gaze. A smile sits on his lips, but it doesn't reach his eyes at all. I hate that he's pitying me right now. I know he wants to say more, and I'm scared what will happen when he does.

"Thank you," he says. "Now, how are you?"

"Good and you?"

"Well, thanks," he says. "How is your grandma? I haven't asked lately."

"She's doing fine, thank you."

"Good, I'm glad to hear that. Hopefully she'll pull through until you can go see her."

A smile fills my face. "Fingers crossed."

Tucker nods before taking a pull of his drink. "Where is your girlfriend? I was hoping to meet her tonight."

He coughs before covering his mouth, his cheeks filling with color. Looking away, a smile comes over his mouth before looking back at me. "I have a confession."

"Okay?" I ask cautiously.

He laughs again before shaking his head. "Okay, see, well, I lied."

"You lied?"

"Yeah, I was embarrassed that I hit on you when you're married and I made up a girlfriend to make it look like I wasn't a loser."

Tucker McCloud hitting on me? It seems outrageous, but he's standing in front of me, admitting just that. Why does this elate me? Am I wrong for liking that he hit on me? Ugh, what is wrong with me?

"You were hitting on me?" I ask because I still don't believe it.

He lets out a breath and nods. "Yeah, I'm attracted to you, Violet."

He pauses as he looks away, running his hand through his hair. His face is full of color and when he looks at me, I just want to hug him. Smiling he adds, "But I promise it won't happen again. It was wrong on my part."

I want to say that it wasn't, that please, do it more! But that is wrong. I'm married and until I can leave him, I can't utter those words. No matter how much I want to. Silence settles around us and I don't know what to say, what to do but when I look up and meet his eyes with my own, I say, "It's okay. No worries."

"I shouldn't have lied," he reiterates.

"It's okay, it doesn't change how I think of you."

He smiles. "That's good. Maybe one day you can tell me what you think about me."

I blush as I look away. "Maybe."

We're flirting with each other, and I know it needs to stop. I look up and smile at him before looking away again. When I look off toward the left I catch Rob staring at me and my heart stops in my chest. His eyes are cold and flat and I know I'm fucked even before he starts for me. Reaching me, he stands in front of Tucker and faces me.

"I'm ready to go."

"But we haven't done the presents or anything. Can you

give me another half hour please? Then we can leave."

He shakes his head. "No."

"I can bring her home," Tucker says, and I wish he hadn't. Rob's face reddens before he turns to face Tucker.

"She's good. We're leaving."

Taking my hand in his, he gives me a look that says we're leaving—I can go willingly or he will drag me out. I look around the room quickly to see that everyone is watching me, and I have to handle this quietly. Putting a wide smile on my face, I say, "I told you, he isn't good with crowds. We're going to go."

"Are you sure?" Tucker asked.

"Yes, she's sure. She said it, didn't she? Who the hell do you think you are?"

I reach out, putting my hand on Rob's chest but he knocks it away, and I flinch.

"Hey now," Tucker says coming closer.

"What?" Rob sneers. "This is my wife, buddy."

"I understand that, but she's trying to calm you down. So take the hint my friend."

"I'm not your friend, ass—"

"Let's go, Rob," I say, starting for the door. I look back and Rob is giving Tucker one last look that could kill before heading for me. Once he passes me, I look back out at my friends and co-workers. I try to smile but it's hard because I really want to cry, I'm so embarrassed. "Have a nice night everyone, I'll see you guys tomorrow."

"But you'll miss the presents and food," Ms. Tonya says.

"I know, I'm sorry, but I need to leave. Goodnight everyone."

Everyone wishes me goodnight as Tucker walks toward me, running his hand through his hair. I know he's frustrated. I am too and I wish I could do something, but I don't know what that something is.

"Are you okay, Violet?"

I nod as I plaster a huge smile on my face. "Fine. He's

drunk, and I told you he doesn't like crowds. It's no big deal. Don't worry about me."

"You keep saying that, you know, and it only makes me worry more," he says quietly before looking up at the ceiling. "You don't deserve to be treated like that."

I look down and nod. I know I don't but I won't do anything to change it. It's my fault I'm treated this way and always will be until I do something about it.

"I'll see you tomorrow."

With that I turn and leave without waiting for him to say anything back. When I reach the car and open the door, Rob is waiting for me. Dread fills me because I can tell with one look that this is not going to be a quiet ride home.

Chapter
NINE

"Who the fuck does that guy think he is? I'm about to fucking lose my mind, Violet! I told you I want you to quit."

I shake my head, leaning close to the passenger door in the hopes he can't reach me even though I know he can. "No, I'm not quitting. I love my job, I love my co-workers. I am learning so much and this is a great opportunity."

"For what?" he yells.

"To better myself!" I yell back but wish I wouldn't have. His eyes are dark, cold and he is squeezing the steering wheel so tight his knuckles are white.

"Why the fuck are you yelling at me, and why the fuck do you need to better yourself? You're never going to be anything more than my wife. You don't need to work, I take care of you!"

I shake my head and I have no clue where this is coming from but I have to say it. "I am yelling because you won't listen!

I need to work. I need to better myself for *me*. I don't want you taking care of me. I want to be able to take care of myself."

When his hand comes crashing into my chest, knocking the breath out of me, I bend over, clutching my chest as I try to catch my breath. Tears instantly come to my eyes and threaten to fall. When his hand connects with the back of my head, I cry out, covering my head with one hand as I try to get away from him, but I can't, the car is too compact. Grabbing a fistful of my hair, he lifts up my head and when I look out, I see that we're on the side of the road. Tears rush down my face as he squeezes my hair, bringing my face right in front of his.

"Why do you want to better yourself? For what? That doctor? Do you want his cock, Violet?"

I try to shake my head but I can't move. "No, I don't want him. I just want to make money and be successful."

"Why? I don't need you to be successful to fuck you."

"Please, Rob, let me go," I cry, trying to get away, but his grip tightens.

"Let me tell you something, you bitch. You are mine and you are going to start doing things the way I want them or you're gonna get it," he sneers. His breath reeks of beer and I want to gag from the smell. I need to get away. I don't know why I did it, but I push into his chest, trying to get away and the next thing I know, my forehead slams into the dashboard causing pain to shoot to the back of my skull. I cry out but he ignores me, bringing my face close to his again.

"Do you hear me? I own you."

Blood is coming from my nose and running into my mouth. The salt taste make my tears come faster down my cheeks and I want to hit him. I want to get away but I'm not strong enough. Looking into his eyes, seeing the pure hate and anger in them, I'm scared but I can't do this. He can't own me. I deserve better.

"I'm not quitting."

His head cocks to the side, his eyes narrowing as he looks at me. "Is that right?"

"Yes," I say pulling back and to my surprise he lets me move back some but he is still holding my hair tight. "I take a lot from you and if you want me to stay then you need to treat me right."

He scoffs. "Or what?"

I swallow loudly, my heart beating so hard I swear it's about to explode from my sternum. "Or I'm leaving."

His laughter fills the cab as he lets my hair go. I reach up, rubbing the spot where he was holding me as I trying to scoot away. When he looks up at me, I feel rooted in place. I want to scream but I hold it in as his eyes narrow. I don't even see it coming until everything goes black. My head is ringing, my face aches, and I can feel my eye swelling shut. Covering my face, I coward away from him as sobs rip from me. When he takes my chin in his hand, I try to fight him off but he hits me in chest again, knocking the air out of me. I can't focus or even breathe but it doesn't matter. He has me by my chin, his face only inches from mine.

"Look at me," he says as he squeezes my chin.

I try but it so hard and it hurts to move my face. I can only see him from one eye, my other already swollen shut.

"Does it hurt? Good. Because this is nothing compared to what I'll do to you if you leave me. Do you understand me? I'll let you work but it's only because I feel like you'll get fired anyway. They won't want you for long. You are shit. Pure shit and that fucking asshole doctor will see it soon enough."

I can feel my tears landing on my chest along with my blood. I want to scream for help but who would hear me? Who would help me even if I did? I try to pull back but his grip tightens before he says, "And if I find out anything is going on between you two, I'll kill him and then you, so don't fuck with me. Do you understand me?"

I nod.

"That's right, now sit back and shut up."

I do as he says, and cover my face, crying as my body

shakes with fear.

See? This is why I can't leave. This is why I can't fight back. I try to and what does it get me? A black eye. How the hell am I supposed to go to work tomorrow? How am I supposed to face people who saw that my husband is an asshole? I'm so fucked it isn't even funny, and there is nothing I can do about it.

"Make sure when we get home you put ice on that. I hate when you make me hurt you like this. Just act right. I hate when your face is fucked up. Fuck."

My lip quivers as I try to catch my breath. I didn't do anything but try to defend myself and it got me nothing.

Why do I try?

Why am I even living?

What for?

Why?

I just feel defeated.

So fucking defeated.

"Hey, Tucker, sorry to call so early, I just need to let you know I need to miss for the next couple days. I think I got the flu or something," I say before I go into a fake coughing fit. "I'm so sorry, I'll try to do some things here but everything else will have to wait."

Tucker pauses, and I know he knows I'm lying. Closing my eyes, a tear leaks out, rolling down my cheek to my lips. I wipe it away and cringe when my hand grazes my eye.

"You seemed okay last night?"

"I know, it's crazy. It hit me so bad this morning. I can't hold anything down, I'm so sorry."

He pauses again. My heart is going crazy in my chest and I hate this. I want to tell him the truth but I can't. I won't.

"Are you sure you're okay, Violet?"

"Yes," I say before fake coughing. "Just sick."

I can tell he wants to say more. I know he does. "Take as much time as you need."

"I'll be fine in a couple days, I promise."

"I hope so. I'm here if you need anything."

"Thank you. Bye."

Slamming the phone down, I crumble to the floor as the sobs bubble out of me. Holding my midsection I look up into the full-length mirror in my bedroom and hate what I see. My left eye is black and blue, a little cut below my eye. My lip is busted and there is a bruise on my forehead. My eye doesn't look as bad as some have looked but it will need time before it is light enough to cover with makeup which is the reason I called out.

I wipe my face and I am disgusted with the person who is staring back at me. Why didn't I see through Rob's bullshit so long ago? Why did I think this was how someone should be loved? Why did I allow it to go so far and how the fuck do I get out?

Shaking my head, I lay down on the floor, the coolness of the hardwood soothing the pain.

"What did your work say?"

I looked up at Rob and shrug my shoulders. "They're fine with it."

"Whatever. How's your face?"

"It hurts," I say.

"I bet. Oh well, you'll be alright."

No, I won't be. Not until I get the fuck away from him.

The snow is falling so quickly that I can't even see outside my office window. I hope that it lets up a bit. My SUV's tires aren't the best, and I'd hate to be stuck here for the night. I shouldn't have come in, but I have to get payroll done. It has been four days since the incident with Rob, and my eye is not fully healed. It is still a little dark, but I was able to cover it with makeup just in case someone was here. Luckily though, no one was.

Sighing, I glance down at the payroll and get back to work. Tucker told me not to worry about it, that he would do it, but it's my job and I've already missed enough work. Putting in the numbers for taxes and hours and general stuff like that, I try to work quickly. I don't want to get stuck here but every time I look up the snow seems to be falling harder. I feel as if I made a mistake. Maybe I should have just waited until tomorrow to come in but then someone might have seen me and the last thing I need is someone looking too closely.

When my phone starts to ring, I let out a frustrated breath when I see the name, Rob. I know why he is calling and it is to bitch.

"Hello?"

"Are you done?"

"Not yet, maybe another hour."

"Do you think you can make it home?"

"I'm not sure yet, why?"

"I don't want you driving in this shit. I don't want to pay to replace the truck when you crash it. I'll come get you."

"Fine, give me an hour. I have to go, bye," I say and then I hit end call.

I'm surprise how great that felt but I know the feeling won't last long. Fear will creep back in when it's time for me to ride home with him. I should have given him a chance to say something. I'm just so tired of it. I'm at my wit's end and honestly the only way out I see is to end it all.

How sad is that?

When I hear a door open and then the alarm code being entered, I freeze. What the hell? Who would be here? Oh fuck, was Rob outside waiting on me? I hop out from behind my desk and look out down the hall. At the end is a tall figure, in a thick coat, with their back to me while they punch in the code. When the person turns around, I have no clue who it is since the face is covered with a scarf.

"Violet? What are you doing here?"

Tucker. Shit.

"I was about to ask you the same thing to you. I'm doing payroll," I say as he walks down the hall toward me, removing his coat. When he stops in front of me, all he has on is a grey long-sleeved Henley and a pair of jeans. I'd love to stare at him, but instead I turn away and head into my office. There needs to be distance between us. Not only because of my eye, but because nothing can happen with him. The problem is that my feelings for Tucker have been getting stronger—I know that can't happen, but it has. I want so many things. I want to leave Rob, I want to explore something with Tucker, and I want to be happy again. But until I can find a way away from Rob, I won't have those things.

The night before, I had been online, looking at battered women websites. It was the first time I had ever looked at sites like that. All of them said to call or email if you need help but what if I did and then something happened to the person who was trying to help me? I can't let something happen to someone for trying to help me, and the way Rob is, he will hurt everyone just to make sure I don't go anywhere. That is the main reason I tend to keep what my mother says to myself. I don't want Rob going after her. I don't know what to do but I honestly don't know how much more I can take. I'm tired of hurting, I'm tired of hiding, and I'm tired of being treated this way.

I worry that I'm getting depressed. After looking at those sites, reading some of the things the women have been through, all I could do is envy their strength. They left, they fought back, and it had me wondering where my strength was. Where is my fight? How do I find it? I want it. I want to better my life, but I feel like I can't. I have no options, and I'm too scared to find them. I'm scared that I'm giving up. Or maybe I already have. But I need to find an out, and every time I look at Tucker, I feel that he may be able to help me. I feel like if I was just to tell him what is going on he could help me but I can't risk telling him. If I did, Rob would go after him, and that scares me.

Going behind my desk, I sit down and open my file, ignoring that he is standing in my office.

"I was coming in to do it."

I look up real quick and then back down. "I left you a message on your phone saying I was coming in."

"I didn't get it."

"Oh, I'm sorry. I'm almost done here."

Without looking up, I watch as he comes toward my desk and sits down. Why won't he leave? What is he doing? Doesn't he have something else to do?

"You seem better."

I nod before letting out a little cough. "Yup, almost better. I should be back Monday."

"Good. We miss you around here."

I smile. "Same here."

"I hate being sick. I always get so bored at home without anything to do."

"Yeah, I've been so bored," I say moving quickly to get everything done. My knee is bouncing out of control from my nerves and my palms are soaked. I can't let him get a good look at me, but I feel like he's watching my every move. Sweat drips down the back of my neck, and I feel restless, like I need to run.

"You don't need to wait, Tucker, I'm almost done," I manage to say.

"It's okay. I want to make sure you get out of here okay."

"Rob said he is going to come get me in an hour."

He pauses for a second before saying, "Okay, I'll just wait a minute, maybe the snow will let up."

"I hope it does," I say as I move a file to the side and start my second to last file. I'm almost done and the faster I get done, the faster I can get away from him.

"Hey," he says but I don't look up.

"Yeah?"

"Violet, look at me."

"Huh?" I ask looking up for only a second before looking back done. "I'm trying to get this done."

He doesn't say anything for a moment but then he asks the one thing I don't want to him to ask. "What happened to your eye?"

My hands stop moving on my keyboard, and I look over at him, hoping he doesn't see through my lie.

"Oh, my eye?" I ask touching it softly with my hand as I laugh. "I was cleaning out the closet the other day and a box slammed down into my face. Busted my lip and even caused a cut below my eye. Stupid ass box."

I laugh a little longer before looking back at the computer.

"You were cleaning a closet when you were sick?"

I pause, biting down on my lip and cringing in pain since my lip is busted. I nod before looking over at him. "I couldn't find my thermometer and Rob thought it was in the closet."

"Shouldn't he have looked for it? You're sick."

"Yeah," I say with a wave of my hand. "He would have if he was home, but he was at work."

He doesn't say anything, and I'm thankful for the silence. I'm not sure what else I could have said to make my lie any more believable. Finishing the last of the paystubs, I hit print and then get up to get them off the printer. I can feel him watching me, and I wish he wouldn't. I don't want to get him involved. I have to do this all by myself. Taking the stubs off the printer, I count each one, making sure they are all here. When I turn to go back to go back to my desk, I run right into Tucker. He takes a hold of my arms, steading me but when I try to move back, he won't let me go. I look up into his eyes and freeze. He is examining my eye, my face, my everything.

It's as if he is looking into my soul and I know he knows I'm lying. I can see it all over his face.

Fuck.

"Tucker?"

"I'm sorry, Violet, but are you sure that's what happened to your eye?"

I nod. "Yes."

"You can tell me, Violet. I can help you."

"Tell you what?" I ask, and I hope to God he doesn't ask again because I'm not sure I can lie anymore.

His eyes are glued to mine. My breathing quickens and my heart pounds in my chest. I don't want to move and really I'm not sure I can. I'm completely frozen in place. And I think he is too. His breathing matches mine and I bet if I laid my head on his chest, I could feel his heart beating just as fast as mine. Suddenly his hand is moving away from my arm. Slowly, I watch as it comes up and he runs his finger softly across the bottom of my eye. With his eyes locked on mine, he slowly cups my jaw and runs his thumb along my bottom lip.

I don't know what the hell is happening. His eyes are boring into mine and I swear they're asking permission. If I want him to kiss me, and the answer is yes. Yes, please kiss the stuffing out of me and take me away from the hell my life has become. But he can't. As much as I want it, he can't do it, I can't let him, but I'm not moving and neither is he.

"You are so beautiful, Violet. Let me help you." His voice is deep and breathy, falling on my skin in wisps and turning my skin to gooseflesh. Then his head is dropping toward mine. My breath catches and oh fuck, I'm going to kiss him and I don't care how wrong it is or what will happen after because I need to feel his lips. Closing my eyes, I feel his breath on my lips and I turn up, giving him better access, but nothing happens.

Opening my eyes, I see that he's pulled completely away from me. He looks back at me and says, "Did you hear that?"

I'm breathless but I still manage to squeak out, "Hear

what?"

He drops his hand and I yearn for it back. Watching as he walks away, my breathing is still labored and my heart feels like it's about to explode. I hear footsteps coming down the hall and I don't know what I'm going to say to him. What will he say to me? This can't happen, and I need to reiterate that, I have to. I can't play with his heart, I can't hurt him. I need to think harder. I need to get help. I need to do something because I don't want Rob. I want my life back and I can't help but think that maybe Tucker can help. He said so, didn't he?

Placing my hand on my chest I look up and I'm going to tell him. I'm going to ask for help, but when I look at the doorway, the person standing there is not Tucker.

It's Rob.

"You ready?" he asks.

I feel like I can't breathe. His eyes are on me, waiting for an answer, and all I can do is stare at him.

"What's wrong with you?" he then asks as I continue to stare at him.

Putting my hand on my forehead, I look away. "Sorry, my head is killing me. Not yet. I need to sign these and then we can leave."

I go to my desk and start to sign each paycheck. My hands are shaking and when I see a hand reach over to take a check I have already signed, I look up to see that Tucker looking at me. His eyes are dark and I can't read the expression on his face. I wonder if it matches mine. I don't feel guilty but I feel like we almost got caught and that's not good. Maybe it was a sign from God. Maybe it's his way of telling me I shouldn't get Tucker involved. That I need to figure this out on my own.

"Sucks about her eye, huh, Rob?"

I look up quickly to find that Tucker is looking back at Rob.

"Yup," he says, looking at Tucker as if he's a piece of shit.

Tucker is glaring at Rob so intently that fire seems to roll off him in waves. Before he can say anything else, I say, "Okay,

I'm done."

"Good, let's go," Rob says.

I stand up and grab my purse and jacket. As I put them on, Tucker says, "Next time you need to get something out of a closet, Violet, ask your husband to do it. I know he doesn't want any harm coming to you, right, Rob?"

Rob looks back at me and then Tucker. "Yeah."

I can tell Rob is getting madder by the moment. I need to get him the hell out of here. Nodding my head, I say, "Will do. Goodnight, Tucker. I'll hopefully be able to come in tomorrow."

Tucker nods. "Yeah, I hope you can."

"Let's go, Violet," Rob says and I start for him. As we leave, I look back to see Tucker watching me and I want nothing more than to run back to him. Hold him in my arms, press my lips to his, but I can't. So I turn and go home with my husband.

Chapter
TEN

Grandma died at 9:32am the next morning.

Even though I knew it was going to happen, I still feel as if someone has ripped out my heart and stomped on it. My insides have been ravaged, torn apart until I'm nothing more than an empty husk. I'm numb and I don't know what to do. What I want to do is ball up and cry but I can't. Not now, not with my staff and doctor only feet away from me.

When my mom called, I couldn't even understand her. She just kept saying she needed me to come home. She needed me. Now. Then she just dissolved in sobs. It was heart wrenching and all I want is to hold her and make it better. It's been thirty minutes since she hung up and I am still holding the phone in my hand. My body is still in the same position, and I don't know what to do. I feel like a part of me is missing. It's gone. It died with my grandma.

My hands are shaking and I think it's because of the number I'm dialing or maybe it's the grief, I'm not sure. All I know is

I'm about to break down if Rob says I can't go.

When he doesn't answer, I call again and again until finally he answers.

"Seriously? I'm sleeping."

I hold in my tears as I say, "My grandma passed."

"Okay?"

My lip quivers and I try to hold in the rage that has hit me full force. How can he say that with no care in the world? He knows how much she means to me. Or meant. Damn it, this sucks.

"I need to buy a ticket to go home. My mom needs me."

"Okay, why are you calling me about this?"

I know that I need to keep my cool. I can't lose my mind and tell this man that he is the biggest piece of shit in this world. I need to keep calm, but fuck it's hard.

Taking in a deep breath, I say, "I need you to buy it; I don't have a bank card."

He laughs and my fingers dig into the cushion of my chair.

"I don't have money for that."

"I just got paid."

"Yeah, and I paid bills, Violet," he says with a hint of annoyance in his voice. "We're broke plus you don't need to go."

Fuck being calm. "Are you kidding me?" I shriek. "Where the fuck is the money that my grandpa left me?"

"Oh, I spent that last year when I bought my car."

"What?!"

He pauses and I swear the heart I thought was dead a second ago is pounding against my chest in overtime. I'm about to scream. How dare he? That was my money and he spent it? Seriously?

"Okay, listen here. You got one more time to fucking yell at me before I shut you the fuck up. Now stop calling me."

The line goes dead and I am stunned. Utterly and completely stunned. He spent my money. I had over twenty thousand dollars and he spent it? Oh my God, I am so fucked. I can't call my mom and tell her I have no money to come, she'll freak and she doesn't need that. Oh my God, what am I going to do? I only have thirty eight bucks, that's not enough for anything.

Covering my face, I let out the first sob since finding out. My body shakes as the tears gush down my face. I can't believe this. I move my fingers along my cheeks to catch my tears while my mind reels. I just don't understand. How could I allow this to happen? Why didn't I listen to my mom and grandma back then? I would not be going through this. I would already be home, I would have been there to help, but now it's too late.

I always thought I had the chance to get my money back. In my head, I thought that when I left and divorced Rob, I would have half the money to build my new life, but how can I if there is no money? Now, I won't have anything. I'll be starting from the bottom, and that's scares me. I've always had a cushion. That's what my grandpa left it for, but I allowed this man to take it. I've allowed him to take me and completely ruin me.

How did I let this happen?

Without even realize what I'm doing, I move out from behind my desk and then across my office to my door. Throwing it open, I look across the hall and meet Tucker's eyes. He is sitting behind his desk, his glasses sitting on the end of his nose as he looks up at me. I don't know what I'm doing but soon I am crossing the hall and shutting his door.

He removes his glasses before asking, "Violet? What's wrong?"

I can't hold it in and soon I am crying so hard, I can't breathe. I hold my stomach as the tears roll down my cheeks while my other hand covers my face. I hate that I came in here to do this. What was I thinking I'd accomplish by coming across the hall to my boss's office and crying my eyes out? I usually try to hide my feelings but not this time. This time, I'm losing it, and when his arms come around me, bringing me in close to his chest, I know why I came here.

I need the comfort.

I need him.

Sobbing, I wrap my arms around his middle, crying into his strong chest. His arms hold me so tenderly, so tightly and it's been so long since I've been held like this. I take in a deep breath and instantly feel safe. I want to stay in his arms forever. He smells so good — woodsy but with a hint of fruits and herbs. It's intoxicating and for only a second I forget that my life is complete shit. For that second I'm wrapped in the arms of a man who smells fantastic and can protect me. But just as fast as that second came, it's gone, and I'm back to the reality of my fucked-up life.

He holds me for a long time, not saying anything as I cry until finally, he asks, "Can you tell me what's wrong, Violet?"

I nod and glance up at him. He looks down at me with the same caring eyes I have grown so fond of. I should feel like shit that this guy is always worried about me, but it feels good to be cared about. Looking up into his eyes, my walls crack, my heart speeds up and all I want is for everything to go away. I want to completely forget about the world around me and just stay here.

In Tucker's arms.

"My grandma died."

His face fills with compassion as he says, "Violet, I'm so sorry."

"Thank you."

He reaches up before slowly moving my hair out of my face. "When are you flying out? Don't worry. We'll manage around here until you get back."

My forehead falls into his chest as my body starts to shake with a sob. I feel his arms tighten around me before he rests his head on top of mine. He is holding me like I am his, and God, how I wish that were true. I know I need to pull away and put some distance between us, but I don't want too. I need what he is giving me.

"I'm not flying out," I whispered against his chest, blinking the tears out of my eyes.

"What?"

I pull away some and look up at him. "I don't have any money to fly out there and I can't ask my mom because she'll flip. All her money is tied up in the arrangements and it's such a mess, Tucker. I can't believe it at all. I just got paid yesterday and Rob says it's all gone. My savings, my everything."

"He says?"

I pull away until I am completely out of his arms. He's watching me but I won't look him in the eyes. I can't. And I can't believe I'm about to admit this. I feel so ashamed but I need to tell him. I need to tell someone, and right now, Tucker is the person I'm going to tell.

"He controls everything. I have nothing."

His head falls to the side as he watches me. "Seriously?"

I nod as I look away. He probably thinks I'm worthless, stupid, and everything else Rob calls me. Maybe I am. Maybe I deserve what is happening to me because I have been so stupid about it all, believing, hoping that maybe one day Rob would change. Really, though, our relationship was doomed from the beginning, and I was too blind and stupid to believe it.

"That needs to change, Violet. You need to set up your own account or ask for a card of your own. You can't be blind through all this."

I shake my head quickly, still not looking at him. "He'll flip if I ask for a card or if I set up my own account. He watches for my money."

He pauses for a moment. "Okay, then just transfer some into your account and then his. You need money."

"I understand that, but I don't want the hassle that comes with it."

He pauses for a moment. "You can't live like that."

"Easy for you to say," I say, and I can't believe I did. Hell, why don't I tell him everything while I'm at it.

Shaking my head, I look away as I fight back the tears. When I see his feet move, I look up to see him walk behind his desk. Sitting in his chair, he slides his glasses back on before clicking something and then typing.

"I'm booking you a flight home," he announces, and I take a step toward him.

"No, Tucker. That's not why I came in here and told you all that."

He looks up at with his brows drawn together. "I didn't say it was."

"I know but it just feels like that. I don't need a handout."

He shakes his head before he says, "It's not a handout. You're my friend, and I want to help."

"But Rob will flip if I go and—"

Tucker puts his hand up to stop me. "If _Rob_," the name drips from his lips like it's hemlock, "has a problem with it, send him to me. You just lost someone who was basically your second mom. You need to be there for her and for your mom. _Rob_ will be okay."

Do you hear the way he says Rob's name? Doesn't it make you cringe? He says it like it is the most disgusting name in the world, which really it is. At least to me.

I watch as he types with a little more force than needed before looking over at me. "They have a flight leaving in three hours. That gives you time to go home and pack before getting to the airport. Here is some money for anything else you might need," he says before he gets up, taking his wallet out. He then comes toward me with some bills in his hand but I shake my head, moving away from his outreached hand.

"I can't take it."

He gives me a look before taking my hand and putting the money in it. "Yes, you can."

I glance at the money before looking back up into his strong face. His eyes are dark and beautiful, glued to mine as he waits for me to say something. He looks at me like I'm something desirable, his gaze penetrating through my flesh and warming me from the inside out. Even though this is a shitty time in my life, I still feel special—like I matter—but I hate that he is giving me money. I don't like handouts.

"But I don't know when I can pay you back."

"Don't. It's my gift to you."

"Tucker," I whispered.

"Please," he says softly, laying his hand on mine. "I want to help you, but promise me you'll be a little smarter with your money. You control that. You decide what account it goes in. Fix that. Don't let this happen anymore."

I nod. He is right. I can figure out something. Tell Rob my pay got cut for missing so many days or something. Maybe he won't even notice. I can fix this and then after I save enough money, I can leave. Start a new life once I figure out how to get away without anyone getting hurt. There has to be a way, I just have to figure it out. But the thing is, every time I look at Tucker, I feel like he's the one who can help me. Take this moment, for example, he didn't have to help me, but he did. He took a shitty situation and not only helped me but guided me through it. It's as if the answer to all my problems is standing in front of me but the fear inside me is trying to push him away. Trying to hide and not allow him in.

My stupid fear is keeping me from telling him everything. From accepting the help I need to get me out of the situation I'm in and I'm completely disgusted by it. How much more am I going to have to take before I get past my fear and allow this man in? Or anyone for that matter?

With a nod, I say, "I promise."

He smiles before cupping my shoulder. "See, that's payment enough."

I wrap my arms around his middle and hug him tightly. He hugs me back, squeezing me just as tight, placing his head on mine. It's inappropriate, the way he is holding me, but I don't give a damn. I love the way it feels to be in his arms, and

I never want it to end. I know it's about to, though. I have a plane to catch and this man is not my husband, so I slowly pull away and smile up at him. "Thank you."

He smiles back and looks deep into my eyes. "Anytime, Violet. I'm here for you, always remember that."

I hope I do.

The funeral was one of the saddest and hardest things I have ever been through.

After leaving work, I went straight to the airport, figuring I could just buy the clothes I need. I didn't want to chance going home and Rob getting a hold of me. I know that's ridiculous, but I have no doubt in my mind that he would have kept me from getting on that flight. Going straight to the airport was the easiest way. Or at least I thought it was until I got here. I forgot how pricey clothes were and I'm down to my last twenty bucks but it's okay. I wouldn't change any of it. I need to be here for my mom even if it has put me in a clusterfuck with Rob. When I talked to him two nights ago, he called me a stupid bitch and hung up on me. I haven't talked to him since and even though I'm freaking out about going home, it's been nice not to deal with him at all.

Being back home has been nice, too. I grew up in this house, and I'd love to stay here forever. It's small, only three bedrooms with one bath, but it homed my family just fine. There isn't a single bad memory in this house. My grandma and mom loved me unconditionally, but unfortunately I still yearned for a father. I hate admitting that. I feel bad because they tried so hard, but I always wondered what it would have been like to have a daddy. Someone to cry to when the boys were mean to me. Someone to throw a ball around with. A man to show me how to be loved and treated by a man. It would have been nice, but Mom and Grandma did their best with me. Or at least they did until Rob got a hold of me.

Standing in the kitchen, I look out into the living room where my mom sits. I swear she is holding on by a thread, and it's killing me. She won't talk to anyone but me, and she doesn't even do that much. She mainly sits in my grandma's chair and watches the snow fall, like she is right now. She's thinned down considerably and her skin is waxen and hollow, like someone took out her bones.

Everyone says we look a lot alike. Same blond hair, the same thin nose, and wide blue eyes. She used to be my best friend, but the last three years have been hard on our relationship. I didn't want to listen to her when she said Rob was a bad guy. And when things went really bad, I put this huge wall between us, not allowing her to look in to see what I was going through. I wish I would have listened back then. I wish I would have stayed here. I wish I never would have married him. Maybe then I would know what to do right now. What to say to comfort my mother. But then again, what do you say to a person who has lost her best friend? Who lost a piece of herself? That kind of pain sucks. It's the kind that hits you like a tornado, only to leave you breathless and aching, longing for the crumbled pieces to knit themselves back together, but knowing that no matter how hard you try, you'll never be the same. I know because I'm feeling it, too.

When my phone goes off, I pick it up to see that it's a text message from Tucker. I smile as I read his text.

Just checking on you and your mom. Did you get the flowers from the office and me?

Yes, thank you so much, Tucker. Things are rough right now. My mom is hurting; so am I.

I understand that. I'm sorry again for your loss. Let me know if y'all need anything.

I will. Thank you. :)

Goodnight, Violet :)

Goodnight.

I lay down my phone and lean against the counter as I wait for the water to boil for tea. Everyday Tucker has texted to check on me, and I couldn't be more thankful. He has been the light through this dark time and I really don't know how to thank him.

When the pot starts to scream, I make two cups for me and mom. Carrying the cups of tea into the living, I sit down beside her and hand her a cup before sipping my own. She leans against me, and I wrap an arm around her, holding her close.

"I couldn't have done today without you."

I nod, a lump in my throat before I kiss her forehead. She sits back up, sipping her tea as she looks out the window.

"Has he called?"

"Who?"

"Rob."

I shake my head. "Not since Friday."

She nods. "Why didn't he come?"

"I didn't ask him to. I just left."

She nods again before sipping her tea. Nothing is said for a long time. I'm watching the snow fall too, and I'm surprised how soothing it is. The snow here is breathtaking—big, puffy, and white. The kind of snow that you see in movies. I love it here. I love this place, and I miss it so much.

"Stay here, Violet."

I look over at my mom, surprised by her statement. She is looking at me with hopeful eyes and I hate what I'm about to say, but I have no choice.

"Mom, I can't. You know that."

"We could move," she says taking my hands in hers. "We

could find somewhere where he would never find you."

"I can't leave him. He loves Tennessee, and it's okay. I don't mind it. I have a great job. I don't want to leave that."

She looks up at me and holds my gaze for a long time before saying, "I know what he does to you Violet. I know why he took you away from here. Please, baby. This is your chance to get away, to start a new life."

I don't want to lie to her, but I know she worries about me and I can't have that. Shaking my head, I say, "Mom, he doesn't do anything to me. Everything is fine. I'm fine."

"No, you're not Violet. I know you're not. Please, please leave him."

I let out a long breath and look away. "Mom, I can't. I just can't."

"Yes, baby, please. You can. You don't deserve this. You're better than this. Don't let him hurt and control you any longer, sweetheart. Let me help you."

Tears rush to my eyes because that is what I want. I want my mom to help me, but I can't risk anything happening to her. She may act like she could kill someone but she can't. She couldn't protect us. She's small, like me, and I couldn't live with myself if something happened to her when she was the one to tell me not to trust him in the beginning. Maybe it's pride, but I need to do this. I need to get myself out of this mess.

I can't look at her as I say, "I can't. Not yet."

She squeezes my hands and I look up at her. "Yes, you can."

I shake my head. "No, Mom, I can't. I've let him control everything. I have to get my money straight. I get paid great at the job I'm at right now. Let me save, let me figure things out. He doesn't do anything bad to me, he just yells and throws things. I can handle it, but I promise I'm going to leave."

"How dare you lie to me like that? You don't think I can see that black eye, Violet? What, did you run into a doorknob?"

I cover my eye in shock. I thought I had covered it perfectly.

I look away as a tear escapes down my cheek. Her hand reaches up and wipes my tear away before cupping my face. She then turns my face to look at her before she says, "I can't be quiet anymore. I was quiet before because my mother said you'd fight your way out but you aren't. You're allowing him to control you, to hurt you, and I can't take it anymore. I can help. Just let me. Let me help you, baby."

"It's nothing, Mom. I dropped a box on my face. He doesn't do anything to me."

A look of disappointment comes over her face and it kills me. "Oh, Violet. Please stop lying to me."

"I'm not, Mom. Please, I'm fine. I'm getting out of the situation, I just need time. I can handle it all. It's not that bad, I promise."

You're probably screaming at me, asking why I'm lying to my mom like this, but I have too. She's mourning and I can't have her worrying about me any more than she already is. If I admit what's going on, she'll flip, fly down to Tennessee, and then my mom will go to jail. I know that you think that is probably best, but I beg to differ. I plan to get out of this situation and, like I told her, I just need time. I need to get my money straight. I can't depend on her when I come home. She has enough to worry about. Plus, I need to figure out how I'm going to get away from him with a clean break. I need to be able to leave and not have to look behind my back every second of the day.

When she drops her hand from my face, I take a hold of it and say, "Except for Rob, I have it good in Tennessee. Just give me some time, Mom. I'm figuring it out, but I need you to believe in me, to hold tight. I got myself in this mess. Let me get out of it."

She looks down at our hands as a tear slowly rolls down her cheek. "I can't lose you, Violet."

I wrap my arms around her shoulders and kiss her cheek. "You're not, Mom. You won't."

She leans her forehead against mine, and we stay like that for a long time, just holding each other until she says, "Okay, I'll let you handle it, but I hope that you're telling me the truth, Violet, that you're leaving him. He doesn't deserve you and I'd hate to come to Tennessee and kill that bastard, 'cause I will."

I want to smile. My mom is so strong, so beautiful, and I know that is in me. I just have to find it.

"I promise."

She doesn't say anything to me as she looks out the window before letting out a long breath. As I watch her, I'm not sure she believes me. But then again, I don't even believe myself.

Chapter ELEVEN

Tomorrow is here and I'm nervous as hell.

My plane came in too late for me to go to work so I have to go home and that's the last place I want to be. It takes me two tries to get my door open because my hands are shaking so bad. Just the sight of Rob's car has me both terrified—because I don't know what I'm about to walk into—and pissed off because that stupid car took my savings. I would give anything to go slash his tires, to kick the bumper, but what the hell would that accomplish?

Nothing, unfortunately.

I finally get my key in the door and open it. Stepping inside, he is the first thing I see. He's sitting in his chair watching TV, a bowl of something in his lap and a tall glass of milk in his hand. He's wearing his scrub bottoms but no shirt. His dark hair falls in his eyes and when he looks over at me, I look away quickly before going to the kitchen to lay down my keys and phone along with my purse that holds some of the clothes I bought in Colorado. I fidget as I take my clothes out of my purse and throw them in the back room to be washed. With shaking hands, I grab a bottle of water before going back to the counter to lean against it. Watching him.

I don't know what to do. I don't know how to act. It's as if I'm walking on eggshells, waiting for something to happen. I know it's coming, and I just want it to happen so it can be over. I close my eyes as I take in a deep breath. I'm so nervous that I'm sick to my stomach and I don't think that feeling will ever go away. Even if I knew what to say, I'm pretty sure it won't help the situation, but then again, maybe I'm overreacting. He isn't getting up; he hasn't said anything to me. Maybe he doesn't care. But that doesn't feel right. The tension is thick in this room, and it's freaking the hell out of me.

Looking down at the counter, I try to gather my wits but then I see an opened letter with a well-known Colorado lawyer's letterhead. Picking it up, I read the letter. There's a case against Rob for the assault and battery of Dr. Reeves. The letter is a subpoena for Rob to appear in court back in Colorado next week and failure to appear can result in a warrant.

I jump when he snatches the letter from my hands. When I look up, Rob is glaring at me before he throws the paper in the trash. He dumps his bowl in the sink before turning to look at me.

"Are you going to go back to Colorado?" I ask trying to act as if I'm not scared shitless of him.

"Nope, I can't get off of work. Don't you worry your little head about it though, it doesn't concern you," he says before crossing his arms across his chest. "What I want to know is how you got back to Colorado? Did your mom pay for it?"

"Yes," I say without hesitation. I'm not stupid — I know you may think differently, but I'm not.

"Didn't I tell you that you couldn't go?"

I shake my head. "No, you said you didn't have any money and then hung up on me. Not once did you say I couldn't go.

I wasn't going to miss my grandma's funeral so I asked my mom."

"I'm pretty sure I said you couldn't."

"You didn't," I say.

"Whatever, she didn't love you anyway. I don't know why you wasted your time or your mom's money."

Rage rips through me, and I swear I can only see red as I sneer out, "That's a fucking lie and you know it."

He laughs looking off to the side. When he comes off the counter, I take a step back but the way the kitchen is set up, the counter makes an L shape and I am stuck in the corner with nowhere to go. When he reaches for my face, I smack away his hands and I guess that surprises him because he stops, his eyes wide as he glares down at me.

"Did you just hit me?"

"I don't want you grabbing on to me," I say, my voice breaking as I look up at him.

"What the fuck is your problem?" he yells, making me jump.

I try to act like he doesn't faze me, but I know it isn't working. My hands are up, trying to protect my face, and my chest is rapidly rising and falling. Swallowing loudly, I say, "You have to stop hitting me. It isn't right and I don't deserve it. People are starting to notice, people are asking questions."

He glares before saying, "Do I look like I fucking care about the people asking questions or if they notice? You are mine."

"You don't own me, Rob," I whisper, shaking my head.

Why I said that is beyond me. I should have just agreed, walked away, but instead I say that. Within second his face is red, his hands are shaking, and he towers over me. He smacks away my hands, wraps his fingers around my throat and starts to squeeze. I reach up, trying to pull his hand away but he presses his body against mine, holding one of my hands up as he continues to squeeze. I can't breathe, my vision is spotty, and I know this is it.

He is going to kill me.

But then he lets go and I gasp for breath, holding on to the counter for support as tears fall from my eyes. He then takes me by my chin and says, "The fuck I don't. I own you, I tell you what to do, and you do as I say or you will get what you deserve. You deserve to be knocked around 'cause you don't fucking listen. It's as simple as that."

I take in lungful of air as I slide down the back of the counter to the floor, balling up and holding myself tight. My body is shaking and my head is throbbing. I feel him looking at me, I feel his body heat and when I open my eyes, I find him crouched down, his hands resting on his knees as he looks at me.

"I don't understand why you do this. Why do you talk back to me, Violet? Surely by now, you know how things go? You know that I am the man, the one who runs things, and you are the one who does as I say. You've been so disrespectful lately, sort of like you were at the beginning of our relationship. And just like then, I will beat the living fuck out of you until you break and submit to me. I will control every aspect of you or else."

Tear gush down my face as I look into his eyes. There is so much hate, so much anger, and I don't understand why.

"Why do you do this to me? It's obvious you don't love me. Just let me go."

He shakes his head. "Love has nothing to do with it, Violet. This is about what is mine. I do this because you don't listen, you don't do as I say. When I married you, you were the perfect little wife, but over the years you have become worthless. Sometimes I can't stand the sight of you, but I'm not giving up. My perfect little wife is in there."

"No, she's not," I whispered. "This is me, and I can't keep taking this."

"What are you going to do? Leave?"

When I don't say anything, he just laughs. "That's right,

you won't. You can't really, 'cause if you do, I'll kill you. It's that simple."

I shake my head. I don't know what I'm doing, I don't know why I am fighting back but I am. I have too.

"No, it's not," I say causing his eyes to narrow.

"No?"

"No, it's not simple at all."

"How do you figure?"

"Because I don't deserve this."

Nothing is said as he holds me in his intense hate filled gaze. "You don't think so? Who told you that? Your fucking mom? Maybe that dickhead of a doctor you work with?"

My voice is shattered and dry as I say, "No, this is me. I don't want to be hurt by you anymore. I can't take it."

He opens his mouth to say something but his phone rings. Standing up, he takes his phone out his pocket and then checks the screen before answering it. I've never seen him answer the phone so quickly. I want to ask who it is, but I don't want to give him any more reason to hurt me.

"Hello, yeah, I'm leaving in a minute. I'll see you in a bit. K, bye."

I'm watching him and my body is still shaking uncontrollably. Tucking his phone into his scrub bottoms, he glances down at me as he shakes his head. I don't know why, but I'm not surprised when his foot connects with my ribs causing me to cry out before wrapping myself up in a ball. In a way I was asking for it. I should have just agreed, let him think he is controlling this while I try to find a way out. It seems as if I'm wasting my time though. He has made it blatantly clear that I have no out and every time his fist, feet, or anything else connects with my body, I feel like getting away from him is more and more out of my reach. I should have stayed with my mom; I was stupid to come back. But, then again, that doesn't feel right either. I need to do this on my own. I can't run. I have to be able to stand on my own two feet and fight back. I have to or I'll hate myself forever.

Holding myself as the tears continue to fall down my face, pain shoots through my side and chest. I don't think I can move, but when he crouches down again, getting in my face, I find myself balling up tighter before backing up against the counter.

"Do I look like I care what you can take?"

When I don't answer, he shakes his head.

"That's what I thought," he says. He then he takes my face roughly in his hands before saying, "Tell everyone that is so concerned with your home life to back the fuck up and if you tell anyone, I swear, Violet. Things will not be good for you."

I didn't realize they were good for me now but I don't say that. Instead I lay on the floor, holding myself as tears drip down my face onto the hardwood floors.

Something has to change. It has to before I give up.

The next day, I'm sitting on a bench in one of the examining rooms as Tucker softly probes my ribs. Through the night, the pain got worse and taking aspirin wasn't working. I didn't want to go to the ER because it's at the hospital where Rob works and word would get to him that I went in. That would get me in more trouble so instead I asked Tucker to take a look for me. Something tells me that Tucker doesn't believe my lie about falling down the stairs at the airport. He seems to always see through my lies and I am just waiting for him to say something. It's coming, I can feel it. I just don't know what I'm going to do when it does.

"I think you broke a rib and if you did, then you have every right to sue the airline, you know," he says as his fingers dance over my ribs. I know this is not the time to get turned on but this man has some kind of power over me and my stomach has turned itself into a swarm of butterflies.

Looking up at him, I nod as I say, "Yeah, but I tripped. I doubt I can sue for that."

"You can say the stairs were icy?" he says with a grin.

I smile. "You want me to lie, Dr. McCloud?"

"Nah, I was just joking but yeah, I'm going to send you to get an X-ray and then I'll confirm it but there really isn't anything I can do but prescribe you some pain meds."

"That's fine, thanks."

"No problem," he says before sitting down at the counter and writing a script. I sit up, pulling my shirt down as he hands me the script. As I try to get off the bench, Tucker's hand comes toward me to help. I take his warm hands in mine and smile when my feet hit the ground.

"Thanks so much, I guess I'll go over and get that done, and then get back to work," I say as I reach for the door.

"Hey, Violet."

"Yeah?" I ask turning to look at him.

"I ran into Rob yesterday at the hospital."

My smile falls and I can only blink. "Okay?"

"Well, I really didn't want to tell you, but the more I think about it the more it bothers me. Especially with us going to the conference this weekend. I don't want him thinking things that aren't true."

"I'm confused. What did he say?" I ask even though I'm pretty sure I know exactly what was said.

"Rob threatened to rearrange my face if he finds out anything is going on between us. Even though the thought of him rearranging anything on me is comical, I assured him that nothing has happened between us, but he didn't seem to believe me. He told me not to touch you and to stay away from you. Instead of entertaining his assumptions, I walked away. I really didn't want to beat up your husband. I doubt you'd appreciate that."

Actually, I would appreciate that very much. "I'm sorry; I don't know why he does this. He's very jealous."

"I get that because if I was married to someone as beautiful as you, I'd be jealous too."

It's the second time he has said that and, just like the first, my heart flutters and the butterflies in my stomach form a tornado. I don't know what to say and before I can even utter anything, he says, "But that's beside the point. The main reason I bring this up is because I suspect that he is more than just jealous."

The butterflies still and my heart is beating so loud, I can hear it in my ears.

"I'm sorry?"

He looks away, moving his hands together before taking in a deep breath. Turning to look at me I can tell he is struggling with what he wants to say. "I may be completely out of line and might be wrong, but I have to ask because I care about you, Violet. A lot and well…" He pauses again as he holds my gaze. I'm frozen in place because I know what is about to come out his mouth and I have no clue what I'm going to say. I whip through every excuse I know, every reason for why his assumptions are so off that it isn't even funny, but I can't bring myself to find them. He's right and a part of me wants to admit that. But if Rob has already threatened him, the next step is hurting him and I can't let him hurt Tucker. I just can't.

Meeting his gaze, he asks, "Violet, is Rob hitting you?"

I start to say something but nothing comes out. I know I'm moving my lips but no words are leaving them. Tucker is watching me, waiting for my response, and I have no clue why I'm unable to answer him. Maybe it's because I don't want to lie anymore. I don't want to hide. I need help and, as much as I don't want to involve him, maybe I should. But like any other time I've started to talk, we're interrupted when the door opens and Elizabeth, the receptionist, pops in her head.

"Dr. T, your dad is calling, says it's important."

Tucker eyes leave mine to look at Elizabeth before saying, "Okay, I'll take it in here."

"Great," she says before shutting the door, but I stop it from closing. This is the perfect time for me to leave.

But as I'm about to leave, Tucker says, "Violet, I get that you don't want to answer me, but know that you don't deserve to be treated like this. And when you're ready to talk, I'll be here for you. I always will be here."

Tears pool my eyes and I want to scream that yes, he hits me, that I don't know what to do to get out and please God, help me, but before I can, he reaches for the phone, turning his back on me as he answers.

Chapter
TWELVE

I haven't see Rob in three days.

It shouldn't be a bad thing but it makes me nervous. I'm about to get in the car with Tucker and Dr. McCloud to leave for Atlanta and I can't get a hold of Rob to let him know. I don't want there to be any reason for him to freak out on me when I get home on Sunday, but he isn't answering any of my calls and I don't know why. I feel like I'm being set up to fail and it's making me inwardly panic.

I know I shouldn't care. Fuck it, you know? Who cares if the house is a mess, if there's no food? He doesn't deserve any of it, but for as long as it takes me to get my shit straight to leave, I need things to go smoothly between us. I can't go to work with any more marks. I need to stay under the radar with Rob. I just need time to get things together, make some money, and then I'm blowing this Popsicle stand. I've already set up my direct deposit and I feel good about it. I like my plan and I hope to God it works.

No, it *will* work.

I have to stay positive. I have to stay glass half full. I can't doubt myself because I can do this.

I can.

Looking around the kitchen, I make sure everything is clean, that nothing is left out. The house is spotless. Opening the fridge, I read each note that says what each dish is. I have cooked a meal for him every night but I'm not sure if it is enough. I'm nervous and skittish and I feel like I should call Tucker to tell him I'm not going, but I need to go. This is for my career. This is to better me and to also build a good relationship with Dr. McCloud so that he'll give me a raise and a great reference when I leave.

That's the other part of my plan. I plan to move back to Colorado and I'll need a job, so I need to make sure Dr. McCloud and I are on great terms. I know Tucker will speak highly of me but if I could get both of them to do it, I would have a sure in when I get to Colorado. I might even meet a doctor from Colorado at the conference. Wouldn't that be fantastic? If I start networking now, it will be easier when I move because they'll remember me.

Okay, to be honest, even though having all these references and stuff will be great, I mainly want to go because of Tucker. We're driving up there. That means four hours in the car with him, and it's going to be a blast. I'm excited to talk and just enjoy him. We have a great relationship at the office but I want to know him outside of the office. Why? I don't know, but I just do. Is it stupid that I've included him in my plan? I know I couldn't convince him to move but maybe we could keep in touch and when my divorce is final and everything, I could visit. I don't know — but I feel like I need him in my life.

I need him to be a part of it, even when I'm gone.

Okay, enough about that, I need to make sure this house is clean one more time but before I can reach the hallway, my phone goes off.

It's Tucker.

"Hey," I say breathlessly as I run through the house, checking each room.

"Hey, I wasn't sure if it was a good idea for me to come in and get you but I'm here."

"Oh, Rob isn't here, but I'm coming, give me two seconds," I say before hanging up the phone and doing one last run through. Satisfied and knowing that I should be okay coming home Sunday, I put on my big coat and I grab my weekend bag before locking the door behind me and heading down the steps. When I look up, Tucker is getting out of the car and he smiles as he reaches for my bag.

"Thank you."

"No problem. Hurry, get in the car; it's colder than Antarctica out here!"

I laugh as I walk around the car. "Are we picking up your dad? Should I get in the back?"

"He isn't coming," he says as he reaches for the passenger door and opens it.

"He isn't?" I ask as I get in. I wait for him to run around the car before he gets in and looks over at me.

"Nope, my mom wanted to go to some knitting thing and asked him to go. He's trying to do whatever she wants now."

I reach for my seat belt as I say, "Well, that's nice, but has he not always done that?"

He shakes his head as he pulls out of my driveway. "Nope, it was always about work. My whole life it's been like that. My mom says that's why me and Blaine traveled and did what we wanted first because he was such a workaholic."

"Did retiring change him?"

"No, my mom has cancer. That's what changed him."

Oh no. I love Mrs. McCloud. We had become so close in the weeks she trained me. She is such a sweet, loving lady, one who would do anything for anyone. My heart sinks as I watch Tucker's profile. His mouth is in a straight line and I can tell that this is hurting him. "Will she be okay?"

"Thankfully, yes. It's breast cancer, and they caught it really early. We're very lucky. I don't think any of us are ready to lose my mom."

"Yeah, it's hard," I say softly as I look out the windshield. The pain of my loss of my grandma is still very raw and honestly I don't know how long it will be until it dulls even a little. I miss her and I would give anything to have one more time to tell her how much I love her. I would hate for Tucker to go through this kind of pain and I'm glad that Mrs. McCloud will be okay. That's a blessing.

"Well, that's no way to start a road trip, sorry," he says with a laugh. He glances over at me with a huge grin and I return it, putting my pain on the back burner. I can be sad later, right now I need to enjoy what is in front of me.

"Ready for Atlanta?"

More than he'll ever know. With each mile we drive, I'm that much farther from Rob and man, what a feeling that is.

"You're crazy! Wolverine is not better than Spiderman."

I roll my eyes. "Hugh Jackman."

"That means nothing. That's only the actor! Spiderman is quick and agile; he spits webs from his hands, Violet! He can fly!"

"He swings," I say, bored because obviously Wolverine is ten times the superhero. "Wolverine is played by the gorgeous Hugh Jackman."

"You are delusional. That does not make him the best superhero!"

"Yes it is, because he has adamantium claws that come out and can cut Spiderman's web thingies. He wins. Hands down. Did I mention that Hugh Jackman was naked in the movie, too?"

When Tucker's head falls back in frustration, a smile pulls at my lips.

This ride is going to be fun.

Another hour later…

"You're kidding me? *National Treasure* is by far the greatest movie ever."

"No way, it's boring. Oh wait, do you think Nicolas Cage is hot? Is that why you like it?"

I give him a look as I say, "No, it's about the history. I love history stuff like that. It's exciting. I want to be a treasure hunter!"

"You're a dork. That stuff isn't real."

"Sure it is! Don't rain on my parade! You're just jealous because I won't take you on my treasure hunt," I tease.

"Of course I am," he says flashing me a grin. "I am completely hurt by it. But no, really, the movie sucks. You're crazy."

I laugh as I roll my eyes. "Blasphemy! Fine, then, what is the greatest movie ever?"

"That's easy."

"Okay? What then?"

He glances over at me before saying, "*Say Anything*, classic 80's movie."

"Seriously?" I ask.

"Seriously. It's a masterpiece."

"Shut up," I say with a shake of my head.

"No really, and if you haven't seen it, I'll pray for you. Everyone needs a little *Say Anything* in their lives."

"I know! It's my favorite, too!" I yell out, smacking his arm. "After *National Treasure*, of course."

"Of course," he laughs.

"My mom used to watch that movie all the time."

"Mine too. It's a great flick. Blaine makes fun of me for loving it, but I don't care."

"Me too!" I gush. "The part with the radio, pure magic! What girl wouldn't want that?"

"This is true. I actually did that to a girl in high school."

My mouth drops. "No way!"

"Sure did," he says with a grin. "She loved it and all, but she didn't get the whole *Say Anything* reference. It was depressing."

"Ugh! What the hell! You wasted it on someone who didn't appreciate it, that's so sad!"

"Ugh, I don't know about wasting it. I did get laid that night."

I try to hold in my laughter but I can't and soon he is laughing with me but then he stops, suddenly, sparing me a glance before he belts out the chorus to "In Your Eyes" by Peter Gabriel. I giggle before joining in with him. We both can't sing worth crap but I don't think either one of us cares. I feel so alive. So free. It's been so long since I've done this.

It's refreshing.

It's perfect.

It's everything I've been missing.

Three hours in….

"You have no tattoos?" he asks and I can tell he is completely stunned by this.

"No! Why? Did you think I did or something?"

He nods. "Yes, I was sure of it. I thought you had a tramp stamp!"

"What the hell!? I'm no tramp!" I say offended.

He laughs, shaking his head before saying, "No, I mean the lower back thing. I thought maybe you had a butterfly or something."

"No way. Needles scare me."

"Chicken."

"Damn right, I am. The truth is, though, I'd really love one. But I'm too scared to do it. It's sad really."

"It is. It doesn't hurt that bad."

I look over at him and ask, "You have tattoos?"

Surely not. He's such a clean-cut guy. I mean his hair falls perfectly in place. He always wears suits or nice clothes. I may be stereotyping, but he does not look like a guy who has tattoos.

"Yup, I have a plane on my forearm and on my other forearm, I have *McCloud.*"

I am stunned. "Seriously?"

He smiles. "Yeah, see."

He then lifts the sleeve of his Henley up, showing off the bright colors of the intricate plane flying through the clouds. I am surprise that I recognize the plane. It's a North American P-51 Mustang, my grandmother used to love them since my great grandfather flew one back in the war. The colors are fascinating, and I have to have a closer look. Taking his arm in my hands, I bring my face forward to look closely at the detail of the plane. It seems so real, like it's about to fly off his arm. Each part of the plane so defined and perfect, it's mesmerizing.

"Does it mean something?" I ask.

"Yeah, it's for me and Blaine. He has the same one. Then Dad, Blaine and I all have McCloud on our forearm; Mom has it on her ankle."

I smile. "Did you guys all go together?"

He nods. "Yup. Mom cried like a baby."

That has me laughing and soon his laughter is filling the car, too. Once we settle down, Tucker asks, "What would you get if you weren't scared of needles?"

A smile plays on my lips as I admit, "A butterfly."

Tucker laughs out loud before saying, "Told you! I had you pegged from the start!"

I push into his arm as he continues to laugh. "Oh, shut up."

"No really, though, you should go get it. It doesn't hurt."

"I don't know," I say with a shrug. Rob hates tattoos. He doesn't have them and wouldn't let me get one when I wanted to.

"I'll go with you, hold your hand and all that."

I'm pretty sure I'd like that more than he would. "I'll think about it."

"We could do it while we're in Atlanta," he suggests. "A cute little butterfly on your wrist or something."

I shake my head. "Not now, but soon. Let me save for it," I say but really, I need to get away from Rob first. Just thinking of him makes my skin crawl and I glance down at my phone to see if I've somehow missed his call. I haven't and I don't understand one bit. He should have been home almost an hour ago and I know that he knows I'm gone so why hasn't he called me? Even with being so far and without talking to him, he still has a hold on me and I hate that. I wish I could just ignore the fact that I haven't talked to him or told him where I'm going but the fear is weighing on me. I feel like he is doing this on purpose, to justify why he beats the crap out of me later.

A part of me wants this weekend to end, while the other part doesn't because every time Tucker looks at me, or smiles at me, I forget about everything. The fear is there, but I feel safe. As if nothing can touch me and because of that, I never want to leave. But the hours are counting down until it's time for me to go home, until it's time for me to face him. And when that time comes, I won't have Tucker there to protect me. But I can't think of that. No, I need to enjoy my weekend. I need to learn. I need to better myself because yeah, the time is counting down until I see him, but it's also counting down until the moment I leave.

And that thought alone brings a smile to my face.

The only thing separating Tucker's room from mine is a door.

I've been staring at the damn thing and my phone for the last hour. It has been taunting me since we arrived at the hotel the night before. After going to a seminar, we had dinner and then both went to our rooms. While it seemed easy for Tucker to shut the door and disappear in his room, it wasn't for me. I wanted to follow him in there and continue talking the way we had the whole day. I had never talked so much in my life and it felt amazing. I feel like the old me is back—the one who was fun and had a good time no matter where I was. I was never scared, never worried about what I said or how it would affect me later. I was fearless. I was young and I had fun but Rob took all that.

Now the old Violet is coming back. I feel her inside me, begging to come out and I'm slowly but surely allowing myself to let her. I have to, but it's easy when I'm not around Rob. Being around Tucker, I feel like I can be anything I want to be. When I talk, he listens. I feel like he cares, like I matter, and that feeling is unbelievable. I haven't felt like I've mattered in a really long time and I've missed that feeling.

I feel so alone in this room. I want nothing more than to open the door that separates us and go into his. I don't know what I'll do once I get in there, but I don't want to be alone. I want to feel like I matter and all I'm doing by sitting in here alone, is staring at my phone. I still haven't been able to reach Rob. I've sent texts and even left voicemails but he is completely ignoring me. It scares me to the core and I feel like I'm coming out of my skin. I don't know what to do and a part of me wants to not worry about it but I can't. I'm supposed to be getting ready to go to dinner with Tucker but instead all I can do is stare at my phone.

This is stupid. Throwing my phone down on my purse, I go to the bathroom to get ready. If he doesn't want to talk to me, fine, fuck it. I'm going to go enjoy dinner and talk about all the neat stuff we learned today because it was a great day. I met so many doctors, unfortunately none from Colorado, but a lot nonetheless. Tucker introduced me to a lot of great people. I talked with other office managers and I swear the guy who was running the seminar was tired of me after I asked over a thousand questions. Tucker liked it, though, he liked that I wanted to know so much and he loved that I had taken notes to give to Dr. McCloud. After hearing all the benefits of being completely digital, I don't understand why we aren't yet. I have a feeling that will change once we get home though.

After curling my hair and pulling up one side with a bobby pin, I try to ignore my need to rush to my phone and call Rob again. Instead, I pick up my foundation and do my makeup. When I'm satisfied with my smokey eyes, I smear gloss along my lips before admiring myself. My blond hair looks perfect, cascading down my shoulders in different lengths. My makeup looks flawless and I wish I would do this more often. I look great so made up. And that smile — that's a real smile, a pleased one.

I actually look happy.

Something I plan on always being after leaving Rob.

Walking out of the bathroom, I head to where my dress is hanging on the door. It's a simple little black dress that I bought at Target the day before I left for Atlanta. Putting it on, I try not to mess up my hair as I pull it down my body. It comes to mid-thigh and the lace overlay goes to my knees. It's low cut, showing off my breasts beautifully, and I hope that distracts people from looking too closely at my shoes. Since I spent so much on the dress, I had to go for not so great shoes. I mean they are still cute, black heels that are covered in lace, but they don't live up to the dress.

As I look myself over, a satisfied grin sits on my face. I look beautiful. Gorgeous, maybe, and I wonder if Tucker will like the way I look. I can't help it. I want him to think I'm pretty. I want to feel wanted, I want to feel important, and every time I'm around him, I do. Walking toward my purse, I pick up my phone and check it one more time. Still nothing. Dialing his number I wait until his voicemails comes on.

"Hey Rob, it's Violet. Calling to let you know I'll be home tomorrow. Call me back, okay?"

Hanging up the phone, I sit on the bed and fight the urge the cry. He's never done this. He's always answered my calls. It doesn't make sense, and I have no clue what it means. I try to still my shaking hands but it doesn't work. I feel like I'm about to have a panic attack but before that can happen, a knock comes at my door. Looking at the door, my stomach does a flip as my heart starts to race. I wasn't nervous about going out with Tucker before but I am now. How does that make sense? I have nothing to be nervous about. I'm going to dinner with my boss. It's not as if this is a date. No, just two co-workers going to dinner to discuss everything we learned today. Even through dinner last night, I was fine, so why am I just standing here staring at the door, forgetting how to talk or move.

Pulling myself together, I go to the door, opening it for Tucker.

He looks unbelievably exquisite and all my worries from before instantly vanish. In a crisp black suit with a green shirt underneath that brings out the honey in his eyes, I find myself breathless. He is wearing no tie, the first three buttons opened in a casual way. His hair is brushed to the side, his chin dusted with a light brown hair, and damn, he's sexy as hell. I don't know what it is. It isn't like this is a new look for him; he always dresses like this but something is different. Something I can't figure out. Maybe it's his eyes. They're running over my body like water, taking in every single inch of me, almost like he is memorizing me.

When his eyes meet mine again, I can only blink as he says,

"Wow. Violet, you look amazing."

I feel my face flush before looking down at the floor. "Thanks."

"You're welcome. Ready?"

"Yes."

I grab my purse off my bed and then follow him out of the room. Walking together, we make our way to the elevator and I feel his eyes on me. I can't bear to look over at him. I might giggle or do something else equally crazy. Don't laugh at me. This is serious. I don't know how to act and I hate that. This is my friend. My boss. He's the same guy he's been for the last couple months. I need to get it together before I embarrass myself completely, but for some reason, I can't. Things feel different and that makes me more nervous than I was before. Shaking my head, the doors of the elevator open and we step out.

As we walk, I can feel his hand resting on the small of my back and I'm inwardly giggling. We're having dinner in the hotel restaurant and from what Tucker says, it's fantastic. I'm excited and hope my nerves calm down so I can actually eat. After talking to the concierge, we're led to our table. The restaurant is beautiful. Big white columns fill the hall, giving off a plantation home time feel. Each table is set with roses as a centerpiece and candles. It feels very high class, very expensive. I've never been somewhere so beautiful to eat and my excitement is growing with each step we take to our table.

Tucker pulls my chair out for me and I smile in thanks as I sit down. When he sits down across from me, I watch as he pulls out the menu and begins to read it. I do the same thing but when I see the prices I cringe. Seventy-five bucks for chicken!? Jeez!!

"Do you like wine?"

I look up, meeting his gaze before shrugging my shoulders. "I've only had cheap stuff."

Nothing like this. Two thousand dollars for a bottle of

wine? Good God.

"Okay, do you like Pinot Noir?"

I have no idea but I feel stupid not knowing if I do or not, so I say, "Sure."

He chuckles as he says, "That doesn't sound very confident."

I smile as I blush. "Yeah. I'm not."

When the waiter comes up, Tucker smiles as he says, "Welcome, sir and madam, my name is Raoul and I'll be your waiter tonight. Would you and your beautiful wife like to start with one of our premium wines?"

Before I can correct him that Tucker is not my husband, Tucker says, "Yes, can we please have a bottle of 1999 Domaine de la Romanee Conti La Tache?"

He says it like he has lived in Italy, drinking that wine his whole life. It's incredibly sexy and I sorta wish he would talk Italian to me all night. I'm pretty sure I'd end up being a puddle of goo. With a nod, the waiter scurries away as Tucker looks across the table at me, a grin playing on his lips.

Jeez, have you ever seen anything sexier?

"Since we're celebrating a successful weekend, I think we need the best wine, don't you?"

I nod quickly, excited not only for the wine but for the night ahead of us. With his whiskey gaze on mine, I'm breathless. I feel this pull between us and I'm trying to ignore it, but it's so damn hard. When his mouth curves up in a grin, I can hardly breathe as I say, "I sure do."

Chapter
THIRTEEN

I cannot believe it, but I think I might be drunk.

Or tipsy, I'm not sure, but really, I don't care. This wine is fantastic.

The food has been amazing, too. I've only picked at my main course but that's because there were three courses before it. Even with all the food I ate, this is the best chicken marsala I've ever eaten. It is exquisite. It's been a long time since I've eaten somewhere that blows my mind and it isn't only the food; it's Tucker too. He's kept the conversation going effortlessly. We've talked about everything, it seems, and I swear I feel like we've known each other our whole lives. I feel comfortable with him and it's such a refreshing feeling. I don't know when I'll get the next chance to sit in a fancy restaurant with a sexy guy sitting across from me, his eyes glued to mine, so I need to enjoy this.

And I am. Looking across the table, I take in everything about him. His eyes are light, playful even, and I feel so beautiful in his gaze. I don't know why, but I feel different right now looking at him. Something is happening between us, and I'm scared to put a label on it. I know that I'm developing more than a crush on him and that's stupid on my part. I can't fall for him when I have a husband I have to get away from first, but how can I not when he is smiling at me like this? Holding me in his gaze like I'm the only woman in the room? I feel so important, so wanted and it's hard not to fall for someone that gives me everything I crave. Every moment I spend with him, the more I know I can't leave him behind—he'll always be a part of me. Maybe after I get away and get some help, get myself established, I can admit the way I feel and maybe he'll feel the same. I know it's crazy to assume that he will but when I look at him, I feel he does and that alone gives me hope.

One day, my life will be what I want it to be. It's in my grasp; I just have to grab it and hold on and fight. Right now, though, I'm going to drink my wine and enjoy the view in front of me. Tonight, nothing matters but me enjoying myself.

Sipping my wine, I look at up at Tucker. "I feel that going digital is the best option for us."

Tucker nods. "I agree. I think when my father sees your notes, he'll agree. I have no doubt about that."

"I think the girls will love it, too. It will be easier."

"Yeah, but after we merge completely into it, we'll have to let go of Amy and Rita," he says sadly, and I bite into my lip. Amy and Rita are our filing girls, and he's right, unless we can find another job for them.

"Maybe they can be floaters? They always help when needed, so maybe we can float them or better yet, send them to school for Medical Assisting so we can have floaters for the patients," I suggest.

"That's a fantastic idea, Violet. God, you amaze me," he says and his eyes look into mine with such intensity that it's hard to deny he means what he says.

I smile shyly as I look down at my uneaten chicken. "Stop,

you're making me blush."

"Good, I love the color on you."

I glance up to see his eyes have darkened and when they fall to where I'm working my bottom lip with my teeth, I swear my heart stops. He is looking at me like a man about to pounce and I think there is a chance I'd let him. Ack! No! No, that's a bad idea. Not yet. Not now. One day but not now.

"Are you finished eating?"

"I'm full," I admit shyly. "I'm not used to all the food we got."

"Yeah, it's a lot but that's why I like this restaurant. I love to eat."

"I know you do," I say with a laugh. "You ate your weight in snacks on the way here."

He laughs along with me before saying, "I know, I'm horrible."

"But hey, at least you look hot. Lots of people can't do that, but you can," I point out before taking a sip of my wine. When he doesn't say anything I look across the table to see him staring at me. "What?"

"You think I'm hot?" he asks playfully.

My cheeks burn with embarrassment. I did say that, didn't I? Shit. Working my lip, I look away as I try to figure out what I'm going to say.

"Well, yes, I do, but I shouldn't have said that," I say, still not looking at him.

"Maybe not, but it's only fair."

I look up there, confused as I ask, "Why is it fair?"

"Because you know I'm attracted to you, so it's nice to know you're attracted to me."

"I can think you're hot, Tucker, but it doesn't mean I'm attracted to you," I inform him with a smile and to my surprise, I'm flirting. Holy crap, I don't even remember the last time I did that. I didn't even think I remembered how. When his grin grows, I have to look away as a giggle escapes my lips.

"Oh, you're attracted, it's just wrong to say you are and I understand that."

"You're right," I agree looking back at up at him. "So let's just accept that we're attracted to each other but we can't act on it."

"We could if you left him."

He did not just say that.

"Tucker," I say softly.

He sits up, leaning against the table, his eyes glued to mine as he says, "No, hear me out, he doesn't deserve you—"

"Not here," I say, cutting him off. "Please."

He eyes me for a moment and then softly, he whispers, "I would be good to you."

I look away as I slowly nod. "I know."

I can't do this. If he keeps it up, I'm going to tell him I want him to be good to me. That I want to be with him more than I want to breathe. This can't happen. Not now. I don't have the will to deny him of what we both want. Before he can say anything else, I feel someone beside me just as they say, "Hey!"

When I look up, an older version of Tucker is standing beside our table. Holy crap! I suspect that this fine man is Tucker's brother and when Tucker stands up, hugging him tightly, my suspicions are correct.

Tucker pulls from Blaine and smiles at him as he says, "How'd you know where I was? Why are you here?"

Blaine laughs. "I was driving back from Savannah. I'm going to go see my little guy. When I texted you and you said you were at dinner with the most gorgeous woman in this universe, I had to come and see if you were right," he says before looking down at me. Reaching out, he takes my hand in his and looks right into my eyes before placing a kiss on the back of my hand. Guys still do that? "And you weren't lying, Tuck, she *is* gorgeous."

I know I'm blushing, but really, who wouldn't be? He's as devilishly handsome as his brother and his voice is thick with an accent. I know damn well these two had the ladies chasing them when they were younger.

"Hey, let her go," Tucker says pushing into him. "This is my knucklehead older brother, Blaine McCloud; Blaine, this is Violet Moore."

I smile, feeling a little insecure under his gaze as I say, "Nice to meet you."

"You too," he says before sitting in the empty chair beside me. "I've heard a lot about you."

I watch as he downs Tucker's wine, wagging his eyebrows at Tucker's protest before turning his gaze back to me.

"I hope good things?" I ask.

He nods. "Of course, you're the golden child at the McCloud office. Not only does my younger brother here talk constantly about you, but so does my mom and dad. Everyone seems to worship the ground you walk on."

I laugh nervously, meeting Tucker's gaze. His cheeks are red and he looks a tad bit nervous. With a smile I say, "I think very highly of them, too."

"You'll think that of me, too," he adds with a wink.

"Is that true?" I ask Tucker.

"Maybe, he is the wonder of the family but he is a stand-up guy," he says punching Blaine in the shoulder.

"Jeez, jerk," he says, rubbing his arm. "That hurt."

"Pansy."

"Ass."

"Oh wow, the joy of brothers," I joke and I mean it. These two are probably going to make this the best night of my life.

"So then, stop laughing. You're making me laugh," Blaine says between his own laughter and mine. I can't even breathe, I'm laughing so hard my stomach hurts. Tucker is sitting across from me, glaring at his brother as he goes on. "He's standing there, a radio above his head, crying as he sings that God awful song to her."

"I wasn't crying," Tucker supplies. Blaine waves him off as I continue to sputter with laughter before he goes on.

"Yes, he was, but anyway, she's sitting in the window, watching him, with this look on her face that told us that she was in no way impressed by his declaration of love, and I swear, the only reason she slept with him was because she felt sorry for him."

"She loved me!" Tucker exclaimed.

"Maybe, but that's not the point. The point is declaring your love that way doesn't work in the long run," he says with his hands out in front of him. "Not only is that an example of my case but here is another one. I wrote my ex-wife a beautiful love note telling her that she was my everything and I wanted to spend the rest of my life with her – and I did – but tell me why, after only a year, she divorces me because I don't give her what she needs? I hadn't changed. I loved her, did everything in my power to love and provide for her, but she still kicked me to the curb, taking my son in the process. Why declare love if it gets you nowhere? Love equals heartbreak, I tell you. Pure bullshit."

My laughter stops as silence fills our table. I look over at Tucker as he says, "Wow, Blaine, you're drunk."

And he was. I hadn't realized how much he drank until I looked down and saw all the empty beer mugs and shot glasses. I was feeling pretty drunk myself but I wouldn't change the last couple hours for anything. Blaine and Tucker have to be the funniest guys I've ever met. They play off each other and you can tell how much they love each other. Sometimes it's hard to tell who is the oldest. Blaine is a free soul, I can tell that. His stories of women, booze, and the greatest food imaginable are proof of that. He doesn't care about anything but his family and his son. He has made that clear many times, and I admire that about him. He also doesn't want to be tied down. He is so different from Tucker, but at the same time, so much alike. All the things I love Tucker for, the loyalty, the stand-up guy quality, the caring, and the charm are all there in Blaine. I've lived most of my life thinking there are no good, stand-up men in the world but after tonight, I know that isn't true. Mrs. McCloud raised two amazing men and the girl to settle Blaine down will be one special and lucky lady.

Blaine laughs as he shrugs his shoulders. "Maybe. I guess driving to see little man tonight isn't going to happen. Might have to wait till the morning."

"Yeah, I think so. I'll go get you a room." Tucker's about to get up but Blaine stops him.

"Nah, I'll go sleep in the car."

Tucker shakes his head. "No way. I'll get you a room because I'm not sleeping with you." Looking over at me, Tucker says, "He kicks the crap out of you when he's asleep. I'll be right back."

"Alright," I say as Blaine starts to laugh.

"I do kick a lot."

I laugh as he looks over at me. I stop laughing when his gaze meets mine, though. Like Tucker, his eyes are the same whiskey color I've come to love. His face mirrors Tucker's, just more scruff, and more wear and tear. Blaine has been everywhere, done the most amazing things in the world and you can tell by looking at him.

"I miss my kid."

My smile falls as I slowly nod. "I couldn't imagine."

"I hate my ex-wife. She's an evil bitch who doesn't understand that my son needs me and I need him."

"I'm sorry," I say because I don't know what else to say.

"I'm lucky though. Tucker goes and gets Nicky for me, so I can see him. Elaine, the ex, loves Tucker and for good reason; he's a great guy."

"He is," I agree, still trapped in his gaze.

"The best I know and the thing, Violet, is he's not used to

not getting what he wants."

My face scrunches up in confusion. "I don't follow."

"Tucker. He always fights for what he wants. Our whole life he's been that way and always succeeded. But you, he can't succeed with you. You're the one thing he can't have and it's wearing him down. I don't know you well enough, but I can tell that you care for him. It's apparent with the way y'all look at each other but please, don't mess with his heart. It's pure gold and I have a feeling you could ruin him."

"I wouldn't dare," I proclaim, my heart speeding up. "I care for Tucker. He's a good man but right now, I can't give my heart to him. Not that he has asked for it."

"But he will. One day the flirting and the almost kisses will turn into something more and he will ask for everything, and if you can't give it to him, then walk away. Don't bring him down. Get your shit straight and then come back, but don't ruin my brother."

I look down at my hands and take in a deep breath. When I look up, his eyes are still on me. "I can't walk away from him, but I promise you, I won't hurt him."

Blaine nods before draining the last of his mug. Looking over at me, he says, "I hope I can trust you."

"You can," I say automatically.

We share a long look and I hope my eyes are conveying that I mean what I say. When Tucker's hand comes down on Blaine's shoulder, he looks up and smiles. "Your room key."

"You rock, bro, thank you," Blaine says, standing up. When he wobbles a bit, Tucker's hands come out to steady him.

"Can you make it?"

"Sure, piece of cake."

It's obvious he can't though. Standing up, I take a hold of his arm while Tucker flanks his other side.

"Come on big guy, let's get you to bed," I say with a smile. Blaine smiles back at me, leaning against me as we walk toward the exit. As we walk, Tucker and Blaine make plans to get together the following weekend to spend some time with Nicky; all I can think about is what Blaine said. I never want to hurt Tucker and the thought of walking away is inconceivable. He has given me light when all I saw was black before. He's here when I need someone and he's also giving me a great opportunity by allowing me to work for him. After Blaine's comment, I'm scared that I'm using him for my own selfish needs. That I'm latching on to the only person who treats me well, but that doesn't feel right. I'm not that person. I really do care for him. I would do just about anything for him and I plan to once I'm away from Rob. I will give him all of me and then some as soon as I'm away from Rob and I heal. I've done my research and I can't jump out of an abusive relationship and think that Tucker and I will survive. I want a fighting chance with him and I want to be the woman he deserves. I just have to get there and I will.

I'm just scared he won't wait for me.

When we reach Blaine's room, Tucker opens the door and lets him in, laying him on the bed.

"Do you want me to undress you?" Tucker asks, running his hand through his hair. I can tell he is nervous, maybe even embarrassed.

"Nope, I'm good. Y'all go on, have a good night."

"Alright. Goodnight, Blaine," Tucker says walking back toward the door.

"Night, bro. See ya later, Violet."

I smile over at him, receiving a goofy grin from him as I say, "It was great meeting you, Blaine."

"Likewise. And I mean what I say, you're the most gorgeous girl he has ever been into."

I smile as Tucker groans. "Thanks man."

"No prob, now leave me be," he says before he promptly drops his head into the pillow.

I hold back my laughter as I walk out with Tucker behind me. Shutting the door, he shakes his head before looking over at me. "Sorry about that."

"What?"

"He likes to drink a little too much sometimes," he says as we head for the elevators.

"That's fine, no big deal."

Tucker shoots me a grin as we get on the elevator and go up to our floor. "Did you have fun?"

I nod as I beam up at him. "Yes, it was a beautiful night."

"Good, I'm pleased," he says.

"Did you have fun?"

Fire swirls in his eyes until they're smoldering and I've turned into a veritable pile of human mush. "I did. Anytime I'm with you, I have a great time."

I look away, breathless, as the doors open and we step out. As we walk toward our room, something seems different. My body is humming and my heart is racing as our doors come into view. Stealing a peek up at Tucker, a content smile rests on his upturned lips as he looks ahead of us. He is gorgeous, and I wish that I could just go up on my tippy toes and taste his beautiful mouth. Feel his scruff under my fingers before running my tongue along the hollow of his neck. I know for a fact that if our lips touch, I won't be able to stop.

I want him.

Bad.

It's the alcohol, damn wine and shots! It's heightening my hunger for him and making me want to act on my need for him when, in my sober state, I'm able to hide it just fine. What I need to do is go straight to bed and put all these feelings of want and desire back where they belong. No stupid mistakes, Violet. I have to push through the hazy thoughts and remember what's at stake here.

But when we reach our doors, I turn to look at him and I'm stunned by what I see. His eyes are dark and glued to mine. Reaching out, he takes my face in his hand and with a low voice he says, "You deserve the world, Violet, the whole damn thing and I know I can give it to you."

I close my eyes as my heart sings for this man. "Things are a mess right now."

Leaning towards me, I can feel his breath on my face and then he says, "Then let me fix them."

Before I can answer, tell him that he can't help me, that this is all on me, his lips are on mine, kissing me. And instead of pulling away, I wrap my arms around his neck and kiss him back.

Chapter
FOURTEEN

Somehow we find our way inside before he pushes me up against the wall, holding me up with his own body. My hands are in his hair, his hands holding my ass while we both get lost in sloppy kisses. I've never felt like this. So out of control. I want to feel every inch of him all at once. My hands are shaking for their chance. His mouth is hot and his hands quick, touching me everywhere. Finding the control I need, I move my hands down his body, feeling each of his muscles through his shirt and jacket before pulling his jacket down. Taking a hold of his shirt, I rip it open, causing buttons to fly. As I move my hands down his exquisite body, I look up to see that his eyes are shut, basking in the sensation of my hands on him. I'm basking in it, too. He's solid muscle and I want every piece of him in my mouth. It's as if his body is a song, singing only to me, begging me to do what I please.

"I've been waiting for a long time for this," he whispers. He reaches for the hem of my dress, whipping it up and over my head and leaving me in nothing but my black panties and bra. I know I should stop—I need to stop—but I can't. I just can't. I'm drowning in him, and I can't see through the desire clouding my head.

I want him.

I need him.

Now.

Pulling away, I kiss down his neck. His head falls back as his hands squeeze my ass gently. Meeting my mouth with his again, he moves away from the wall, carrying me until we fall onto my bed, his body covering mine before I capture his mouth with a hungry urgency again. I could get lost in his kisses. I could do nothing else in my life but kiss this man and I would be okay with that. They're intense and I find myself completely addicted to them. Why did I wait so long to do this? What the hell was I thinking?

His hands are soft against my skin, tender as they move up my rib cage to my breasts. Softly he squeezes and molds my breasts, causing me to arch against him, begging for more and boy does he give it to me. Pulling the cup of my bra down, his mouth replaces his hand and I cry out when his tongue circles my hard peaks. Warmth floods between my legs and I find myself thrashing under his hungry mouth. Moving his mouth back to mine, I groan against his lip when he presses his hardness into me.

Oh my God, I want this man so bad.

When his hands move up my thighs, I want to scream out to keep going, take me, but then that all changes when fingers dance along the crotch of my panties. I quickly tense up as his lips dust along my throat. My heart constricts and I can't breathe. What did I think was going to happen when we fell into this bed? Tucker must have felt me tense up, because he sits up on his elbows, moving his hands along my face, moving my hair out of it while looking at me like I'm the most gorgeous girl in the universe.

"Too fast?" he whispers, dusting his lips along mine.

I feel my whole body flush with embarrassment as I look up into his face. How am I going to tell him this? I can feel the length of him between my legs. He wants me as much as I want him and I'm pretty sure that it isn't going to work. It never does. I'm broken. That asshole I married broke me for any other man out there and that has tears stinging my eyes before I look away from him.

"Whoa. Whoa, Violet, sweetheart, what's wrong?" he asks, catching my tears with his thumb before bringing my face back up to look at him but I can't. I can't look into his beautiful face and admit that I'm broken. That I can never have the connection that men and women have been practicing since the beginning of time. I'm sure that as soon as I admit it he'll think I'm worthless, just like Rob does.

Why did I let this happen?

"Violet, look at me." But I won't. When he moves so that our eyes meet, I close my eyes as the tears leak out and down the side of my face. God, I feel so stupid.

"Tell me what's wrong? You can tell me. I care so much about you, Violet, I won't hurt you. We can stop. I won't be mad, just please, tell me what's wrong. Let me fix whatever it is."

Can I believe him? Can I trust him?

Yes.

Yes, I can. I know what he says is true because it's Tucker. He'll understand. He's nothing like Rob. Tucker is good, he is sweet and he would never hurt me.

I open my eyes slowly and take in a deep breath as my lip wobbles. I'm scared and so embarrassed but somehow, I whisper, "I have Vaginismus. I haven't had sex in eight months since being diagnosed with it."

I can see the confusion on his face as what I have just said sets in. When it finally does, concern fills his eyes before he cups my face, his lips only a whisper away as he says, "I don't know how it is with Rob and I don't care. This is about us, this is about the connection we have. I don't need to have sex with you to feel the connection. I just have to be with you."

"But I'm broken," I whisper.

"You've been hurt, Violet, not broken, and I'm going to do everything I can to help fix you."

"You can't fix me, Tucker, I'm—" I start but his lips stop me. His mouth moves against mine, moving his tongue along my bottom lip before dancing with mine. When he pulls back, a smile rests on his lips as he looks down at me.

"I want to please you, Violet. Let me."

Tears are clouding my vision but thankfully, I can still see the amazing man that hoovers above me. Slowly nodding, his smile grows before he kisses me again, his fingers lazily moving my panties down. When his midsection touches my bare center, I fight for oxygen, while his tongue runs down my neck to the spot between my breasts. My breathing is labored, my heart is about to come out of my chest but most of all, I am so fucking scared that it is messing with my head. I want to tell him to stop, but then I don't, instead I want to scream for more.

I'm confused and freaked out and feeling borderline bi-polar. It's ridiculous, but then my bi-polarness is the last thing on my mind when his tongue dips into my belly button, before he leaves leisurely kisses along my belly. I feel like my whole body is on fire and I want more. I need more. Running my fingers through his hair, I close my eyes and try to relax but it isn't working.

Moving his fingers up my body, his hands rest right under my breasts before he softly says, "Relax, Violet. I swear you'll like this."

I nod with my eyes still closed tightly as I will myself to relax. It still isn't working, but then his lips lightly kiss my moist flesh and everything stops. My heart, my mind, my world. Taking in a shuddering breath, I open my eyes and find him watching me. He bends his head down and places a whisper kiss to my flesh again before slowly running his tongue down the slit of my vagina. When his fingers slowly open me, I cry out as all my wanting becomes a reality. Moving his tongue inside me, he blows my world to pieces as he sucks and licks me in the most pleasurable way. I'm lost beneath his mouth. I don't know if I should scream, thrash, or what, but I find myself doing all of those things.

When I feel his fingers tease me, I tense up but I can tell he isn't giving up. Cautiously, he works my opening while giving me the most unbelievably pleasure in the world. When I feel his fingers completely inside me, penetrating me, I cry out but not from pain. No, it's pure, agonizing pleasure, and I want more.

"Please don't stop," I cry out.

"Never," I hear him say and then he is skillfully fucking me with his fingers. I can't breathe and I know my body is about to spontaneously combust. I'm lost in the passion and soon the pleasure is so intolerable that I'm screaming as my body squeezes his fingers while ripples of ecstasy flood through me. I heave for breath as he slows his fingers to a stop, his mouth pulling away from my throbbing clit before I feel his eyes on me but I can't move. I haven't come like that in ages and I feel unbelievable. So free. So beautiful. So loved.

Tucker's lips make their way up my body, kissing, licking, and sucking before he's lying on me, moving my hair out of my face from when I was thrashing. Kissing my lips, I can taste myself on them and I don't care one bit. This man has me.

All of me.

"See, I took care of you didn't I?" he asks with a satisfied grin on his face.

"More than you know," I whisper as I move his hair out his eyes. It's the first time I've seen it all crazy and out of whack. It makes this moment ten times better for some reason. When he moves his nose along mine, I feel so cherished. He then pulls back and looks into my eyes and I want to cry. I'm surrendering myself to this man in more ways than one and I'm not the least bit scared. I feel completely and utterly protected in his arms, and I want this. I do. It will work. It has too.

"I want you inside me. I'm not sure it will work, but I want to try."

Holding my gaze, he slowly nods before kissing my nose. "Are you sure?"

"Yes."

His mouth curves into a beautiful smile before he rolls off me and stands up. Reaching into his pocket, he pulls out his wallet and takes out a condom. Holding it with his teeth, he throws his wallet on the floor before unbuttoning his slacks and pushing them down along with his boxers. My eyes go wide when the size of him springs up for me to see. He is big, extremely big, and I'm scared he won't fit but then I mentally shake myself. I want this. He will fit. He'll be careful.

He watches me as he slowly slides the condom down his long shaft. "I'll go slowly. I'll be careful."

Swallowing loudly, I say, "I know."

Crawling back on the bed, he hovers over my body as places himself between my legs. Lying softly against me, he kisses me as his fingers tangle in my hair. I feel his hand at the back of my knee and then he is moving it up, bending it so I am completely open to him. Going up on his knees, I watch as his eyes roam along my body before he reaches out and runs his finger down my dripping wet center.

Looking up into my eyes, he smiles before he asks, "You're sure?"

I nod quickly and, to my surprise, I'm not freaking out. I'm not even scared. I know this is going to work. Taking his shaft in his hand, he positions it and carefully enters me. I close my eyes, my fingers digging into the blanket as I take him, inch by beautiful inch, inside me. When he's fully inside me, I open my eyes and his gaze is boring into mine.

"You're beautiful, Violet, so fucking beautiful."

This moment is so intense and I want to cry, I do, but somehow I push that to the back of my mind and I enjoy this exquisite man. I enjoy the pleasure he provides and soon, I'm actually moving with him. Heightening the splendor that our bodies create and I can feel myself about to come again. Arching my hips, he hisses, his fingers digging into my hips as he starts to go faster. The speed and angle is just right and instantly I'm coming, crying out as my body squeezes his. My fingernails bite into the backs of his ticeps, but he doesn't seem to care; he's delving deeper into me with each rhythmic push. Moving in perfect unison, he groans out in blissful agony, stilling inside me as he explodes. I watch as his face contorts in different ways until his head falls back and I can't see him again. Sweat drips down his body and his erratic breathing matches mine. Letting go of my hips, he moves his hands up on both sides of my head before letting his body crash into mine, sweaty and warm, as we both try to catch our breaths.

"I didn't hurt you did I?" he asks and a smile instantly appears on my face.

"Not at all."

"Good, sorry. I kinda lost it at the end."

I reach up and hold his face, running my thumb along his bottom lip. He playfully chases my thumb and bites it before smiling down at me. I smile back, my heart so full of happiness before I whisper, "It was perfect."

With the biggest grin ever on his face, he nods. "Yeah, it was, and I want more."

Me too.

My body feels amazing.

Perfect, even. The spot between my legs aches and so does most of my body. I haven't been worked that hard or experienced that much pleasure in a long time. The room is destroyed from us and a room service cart is parked beside the door from when we got hungry last night. It was one of the best nights of my life but even with the afterglow of it all, my fear has found a way to ruin it all.

I've been lying in this bed, by this man, for the last six hours. Three of those hours were spent making sweet, beautiful love while the other three consisted of me freaking the hell out.

What did I do?

How could I have done this?

I had a plan. One that would help me get to where I needed to be — not only to be the woman Tucker deserves, but also one I would love. I want to be able to stand on my own two feet. I want to make sure I never feel this fear again, ever. I want to be able to give myself completely to this man and never have to worry about watching our backs for Rob. I want to have money in the bank to have at my disposal, so I never have to depend on a man again. I want to be able to fight when I need to fight and most of all I want to love myself the way I used to. I'm getting there, but now everything is blown to shit.

I know Tucker. I know his personality and even though I wanted everything that happened last night, and in no way do I regret it, it was wrong. I not only cheated on Rob, but I also gave him free range to go on a killing spree if he wanted. I also broke my promise to Blaine. I said that I wouldn't hurt Tucker and I know there's no way I'm going to be able to walk out that door without hurting this man. But I have to — for his sake and mine. I have to protect him and I have to do this on my own or I'll never be able to live with myself. I know something will happen to him if I allow this to go on and I can't let that happen. I'd rather hurt him than ever let Rob get his hands on him.

Pushing the blankets off me, I start to get out but Tucker's arm comes around my waist, pulling me back into the bed and up against his chest. Kissing my neck to my jaw and then to my lips, I kiss back, even though I know I shouldn't. It isn't going to make it easier but I can't help it. I love to kiss him and I'm not really sure when my lips will meet his next.

It will probably be never.

"Where are you going?" he asks, a smile on his lips as he runs his nose up and down mine.

"I need to get dressed."

He shakes his head. "No, let's stay in bed."

"I have to get home, Tucker."

Pulling back, his brows are together as he asks, "What? Why?"

"Because Rob knows I'm coming home today; I have to get there," I say, holding back my tears as I wiggle out of his arms and out of the bed. I can feel his eyes on me but I ignore them as I put on my bra. I have to get dressed. I have to get out of here.

"Seriously?"

I glance up at him and shrug my shoulders. "I'm sorry, Tucker, but I have to get back. I understand if you don't want to drive me. I'll rent a car, but I have to go back home."

Looking away, I reach for my panties and then my dress and when I turn, he's pulling up his own boxers, a perplexed look on his face. I hate that I've put it there but I have to believe I'm doing the right thing.

"Can you just stop for a minute, please?"

Sliding my dress over my head, I turn to look at him. I take in the body I loved the night before and then looked up into the face of the person that will always have a special place in my heart. Even if he decides to hate me after this, I'll always cherish him and maybe one day I can explain why I had to do this. And maybe, he'll forgive me. God, I hope he will.

"Yeah?" I ask.

"Does what happened in that bed not matter?"

I look away as I say, "The booze was flowing last night and I felt special, important. You wined me, dined me, and I let the night get to me and fell into bed with you. Yes, it's what I wanted, more than anything, and Tucker, you have to believe me when I say I'll never forget what happened, but I'm not a cheater. I shouldn't have done this. Not only does this hurt you and me, but if Rob finds out, I'm scared to even think what will happen, so please."

"Violet, please. I can protect you. I will always be there for you and I won't ever let anything happen to you."

"You can't protect me from him; he's my husband."

"But he doesn't deserve you," he said a little louder, stepping in front of me, looking deep in my eyes. I'm holding back the tears but I'm not sure how much longer I can. I can see the hurt in eyes and I hate it. I don't want to hurt him, not after all the good he has done for me and to me. "Violet, I don't think you understand."

"No, I do, and I'm sorry. This should have never happened. I'm sorry I disrespected you. You deserve better than that," I say and I mean every word.

"No, I know you're not a cheater, but the reason why you did it is because we belong together. When I said you don't understand, what I meant is that you don't understand how much my heart belongs to you. I've been completely yours since the moment our eyes met. I've never felt this intense about someone and I don't think I ever will again. Last night was everything I dreamed of. If you walk out that door, it will crush me." Taking my face in his hands, I gasp before he whispers, "I promise I'll never let you down. I'll never hurt you, I'll only love you. You deserve better than what he gives you. I can do better. I can give you the world because *you* are my world. I'm laying it all out, Violet. I love you and I need you to take a chance on me. Leave him. Be with me."

I knew fighting my tears wasn't going to last long and soon they're rushing down my face, over his hands and onto my dress. I didn't realize until this moment that I have fallen for Tucker and this is going to be the hardest thing in the world, but I have to do it.

Because I love him.

Slowly shaking my head, I pull out of his reach and whisper, "I can't Tucker. I'm sorry."

"Why? Why can't you? I would treat you right, I would love you the way you deserve."

Looking away, I take in a deep breath. I hate what is about to come out of my mouth but I know it will be the thing to get me out this room. It will be the only thing that saves us both because it will hurt him and he will let me go. With that urging me on, I look back at him and say, "I love Rob."

"No," he says, dropping his hands from my face and stepping back. His face is twisted in pain, his hand on his chest as if I've shot him square in the chest. My tears come faster down my face and my heart feels dead. How could I do this to him?

"I don't believe you."

Mustering up all the strength he gave me, I look over at him and say, "I do. I'm so sorry. I never meant for this to happen and I'm truly sorry, Tucker."

I turn to grab my shoes because I can't stand the way he's looking at me. I have to get out of here before I tell him I'm lying, that I don't love Rob, I love him. That I never want to see Rob's face again, only his for the rest of my life, but I know I can't. As I gather the rest of my things, he stands there, watching me with a gut-wrenching look on his face. Walking toward the door, I spare him one last glance and I wish I hadn't.

His face tells me the one thing I feared—there is no fixing what I've just done.

Chapter FIFTEEN

The drive home was a haze to me. I don't remember anything except that I cried the whole way. I did what I thought would help me in the long run, but in reality, I just made everything worse. So many times I wanted to turn around and go back to Tucker. Beg him to forgive me and to understand why I acted the way I did, but I knew it wouldn't help. I'm pretty sure I've ruined the possibility of anything happening between us in the future and I have to live with that. Thankfully I'll always have our night together, but in a way, I wish I didn't.

I broke him, and it's killing me.

I'm not sure if what I did was right, and I hate that I'm not as confident as I was when I was in that room with him. I knew what needed to be done, what had to happen, but now I feel like I've just fucked up everything and I'll never have the chance to hold that man in my arms or feeling his lips on mine. I'm scared he'll hate me for the rest of his life and I don't know if I can live with that. I can't help but think maybe I should just admit everything but I know I can't.

Like I've said before, Tucker, God, he is perfect. But he's a fixer and he'll want to fix it all. I mean, you heard him. He wants to put me back together but I can't let him. I have to do it myself. You understand why I had to do it? Yeah, I know I should have skipped the sleeping with him part but the passion took over. I have been denying myself of this man for months and I couldn't resist anymore. I need him and I can't bring myself to regret any of it. I will always hold our night deep in my heart and I'll never forget how amazing I felt being held by him, but I'm not sure how the hell I'm supposed to face him every day with the constant reminder of what I did.

God, I've really messed up. I've not only lost the one person who was in my corner completely, my best friend, but I've lost my strength. Everything inside me is gone and I don't want to go back home. I want to run and hope no one finds me but I know that won't work. If I don't come home, Rob will be after me in a New York second. I know his games and I know that he's ignoring me because he's mad I went, and when I walk inside my house the pain I'm inwardly feeling won't match the pain he'll cause me. I've prepared myself for this, I know it's going to happen, but I hate it. I am so tired of living like this but I can't change it yet.

I have to believe in myself. I hurt Tucker to protect him. I will walk into my house and take whatever Rob dishes out in the hopes that all this will be worth it in the end. It has to be. I have to have faith in that or I'll give up. And I can't give up, not after what I did to Tucker. I have to stay strong and I have to work toward my goal. Another month should do it and then, I'll be gone and never have to live with the fear and pain Rob causes. Now the pain from Tucker will always be with me, but maybe one day he'll understand and forgive me. It's a long shot but I can hope.

Hope.

I wonder when all my hoping will actually do me some good. It hasn't helped at all yet but maybe my time is coming. Maybe things will completely change for the good once I'm gone. I guess all I can do is hope since giving up isn't an option.

When I take a right onto my street, my heart starts to speed up. I don't want to go home. Not in the least. I want to go to Tucker's and wrap myself up in his arms and stay there. Instead, though, I pull into my driveway and park the rental behind my SUV. Grabbing my things, I get out, locking the door before heading to the front door. I have to drop off the rental tomorrow which I'm not looking forward to because I'll have to ask Rob to pick me up from work.

Ugh, work. I have no desire to go there tomorrow and I can't stand that I feel that way. I love my job and I'm excited about making the announcement about us going digital once Dr. McCloud approves it, but seeing Tucker, knowing that I crushed him, will make tomorrow and the rest of my time there extremely hard. I should have thought about that before I slept with him. I made my bed, now I have to lay in it.

Opening the door, I step inside to find the house not the way I left it. It's disgusting. The living room is littered with beer cans, takeout, and clothes; the sink is overflowing with dishes. I'm completely stunned by what I'm seeing. I was gone two days. How did he mess up the house this much in two days? Turning toward the kitchen, I find Rob with a beer in his hand, glaring at me.

"Why are you in that car?" he asks, nodding his head toward the window where there is a perfect view of the rental.

"Dr. McCloud had to stay in Atlanta for another night and I had to get back to open the office tomorrow, so I couldn't stay. He rented me a car and I drove home," I say as if it was all the truth.

I had been practicing that lie the whole way and I must say, it's a damn good lie. Turning from me, he makes a noncommittal noise and throws his can in the trash before reaching in the fridge for another one. That was easier than I thought. Happy with the outcome of that, I turn and head down the hall to my room. Laying my stuff on the bed, I sit on the edge and take in a deep breath as I look around the room. I hate this house. I hate everything about it. I just want to leave, but I know I have to be patient. My day is coming and happiness is within reach.

Looking down at my hands, I blink back the tears as I take in deep breaths. Because the truth is, I left my happiness back in that hotel and I might never get him back. Not that I deserve him anyway. Blah. I hate feeling like this. I hate feeling sorry for myself. I put myself in this position, and, in a way, I deserve everything that has happened to me. But no more. I'm going to change my destiny. It's mine for the taking and I'm going to do what I need to do to be happy. If that doesn't include Tucker, then so be it. At least I had him when I did and I will always feel something for him. Reaching into my purse, I pull out my phone and go to his contact. I know I shouldn't do this, I should just leave him alone but I have to tell him this. When my text opens, I quickly type until I am happy with what I've said.

> Me: *Thank you for a beautiful weekend, Tucker. I apologize for any pain I have caused you and I hope that one day we can still be friends. I would miss your friendship dearly if we can't work this out. I just want to say I'm sorry and that I do care for you very much but the timing isn't right for us. I know that right now you probably hate me but I just wanted to tell you I was sorry.*

When I hit send, I instantly regret it. I should have just left him alone but it's hard. I just want to fix what I've done. I want to fix us when really all I need to do is worry about is myself. I need to leave him be. Our time will come.

Wiping away a tear, I take in a deep breath. Throwing my phone down, I get up and start unpacking my things. When I get to the dress that Tucker had peeled off my body, I pause, holding it my hands as my tears cloud my vision. I will never be able to wear this dress ever again and that's such a shame. Reaching for the hanger, I put it on before putting it in my closet. I stare at it for a long time until the dinging of my phone brings me away from it. Picking up my phone, I see a text message from Tucker. My heart stops as I open it to ten little words.

> *Tucker McCloud: That's the problem, I don't hate you. I miss you.*

He doesn't hate me? I cover my mouth with my hand and take in a shuddered breath. My tears start to roll down my cheeks just as another text comes in.

> *Tucker McCloud: I need time Violet. You've crushed me and as much as I want to forgive you and let it all go, I can't. I need time to get over what I thought we could have. What I had been hoping and dreaming of for the last couple months. I hope you can understand that.*

I wipe away my tears and I'm about to type back when my door opens, knocking into the wall, making me jump. I delete the texts real quick before turning to look back at my husband. He is shirtless, his scrubs hanging low on his hips as he looks me over. I can tell that he is drunk and that fact has my heart race. I don't like when he is drunk.

"Aren't you wondering why I ignored your calls all weekend?" he asked.

I shrug my shoulders. "I figured you were busy. I left messages, notes and texts on where I was."

"Yeah, with that fucking asshole."

"Tucker isn't an asshole," I say, turning from him to put away my shoes. "And you knew I was going."

"I told you not to!"

I try to not jump or seem affected by his yelling but I'm not sure I'm coming off that way. Turning to look at him, I say as calmly as I can, "I told you I had to go. It was for my career. I worked and slept and called you. You have no reason not to trust me."

"I don't trust whores," he slurs, taking a step toward me.

"I'm not a whore, so there is another reason why you have no reason not to trust me," I say, taking a step back.

"Yes, you are, you're a nasty little whore."

He takes another step toward me, and I know I'm in trouble. I thought I was good, he didn't say anything when I first walked in which is when he usually does. Why is he coming at me now and why does he have that look on his face? I can feel my hands going clammy and my face turning white. I'm thoroughly scared out of my mind. My pulse is erratic and my shoulders tight, waiting for whatever he's about to give me. He keeps coming at me, until I'm glued to the wall, looking up into his dark, hateful eyes. Reaching out, I jump as he grabs me by my face and smashes his mouth to mine.

I balk, pushing away, but he pushes into me harder, forcing his tongue into my mouth and I cry out, trying to push him away. Finally he pulls back as I scream, "What the hell, Rob!"

His eyes narrow before his hand comes up, backhanding me, causing me to see black. Shit, that hurt. I move away but he grabs me, pulling at my shirt and then it's gone.

"What the fuck are you doing? Stop!" I cry out as he starts to remove my bra, sloppily sucking and licking my breast. "Rob, quit," I say in a shrill voice, pushing him away, but he isn't stopping. My nails are digging into his skin but it's like it doesn't even bother him. He isn't stopping.

Oh fuck, he isn't stopping.

I push and start to kick but he has me pressed against the wall and I can't move as his mouth moves along my breast and chest. When he bites me hard on my breast, I scream out and pull my hand out of his, smacking him alongside his head.

"Fucking stop!" I cry out. When he looks up at me, his eyes are dark and his nostrils are flaring.

"You are mine," he proclaims, his nails cutting my skin and I can't move, I'm frozen in fear. When his mouth comes down on mine again, I can taste the beer, and it makes me gag. I need him away from me, so I bite his lip but then I instantly wish I hadn't. Pulling back, he brings his hand up to his bleeding lip before glaring down at me. "You want it rough, huh? I forgot you liked it like that, you dirty whore."

I am speechless, my eyes are wide and I am gasping for air but I know I have to get away. I try to move away again, I try to kick, I try everything, but he isn't letting go and I'm panicking. I cry out but he covers my mouth, squeezing it hard as he pushes up the bottom of my skirt and I can't believe it.

He is going to rape me.

No, no this can't happen. I smack his hand away, stomping my feet on his, trying to get him to stop but he rips off my panties, throwing them to the side before he takes hold of my vagina, squeezing it hard in his hand. I scream against his hand, trying to bite his fingers while beating him in the side of the shoulders with my fist. My throat is hoarse, and I can't get away. He dips his fingers inside me and I know he can't get in. I'm too tense, too scared out of my mind, but he doesn't care.

"You're going to give me what I want. Now. I'm done waiting."

"No," I cry against his hand but it's muffled; not that I think he would have listened anyway. When he reaches to pull his scrubs down, his shaft springing up toward me, I start to thrash and fight harder against him, screaming, but he doesn't care and soon he is jamming into me with his cock. The pain in unbearable as he continues to try to enter me but it's as if he's hitting a wall and he's screaming his frustration at me.

"You're going to open for me, or I'll tear you open, bitch. Open your legs, stop fucking fighting me! You're my wife, you cunt! Now!"

Tears are falling in heaps down my face, my chest is heaving with sobs and I don't know what to do. I close my eyes and turn my face to the side, wishing I would just die. This pain is unbearable and when he puts his fingers in me, trying to spread me open, I scream out, slamming my fist against the back of his head. He take a hold of my hands, squishing them against the wall as he looks in my eyes before he proceeds to thrust inside me. With each thrust, it's like fire is ripping through my vagina and soon I'm bleeding. I feel it running down my leg.

"Please stop," I cry and then I look up at the ceiling and whisper, "Please God, make him stop."

Taking a hold of my chin, Rob squeezes it before whispering, "God can't help you. You're mine."

With one last thrust, he is finally completely inside me. Tearing me and causing so much pain that I swear I'm about to black out.

"That's right, yeah," he breathes against my face and I'm going to puke. To my surprise, though, I don't. Instead I close my eyes shut and try to imagine myself somewhere else but I can't. The pain is overwhelming. Finally he stills with his climax and I hate him. I hate him so much, I want to cut off his cock and stuff it in a blender. I want to make him feel what I feel. When he lets me go, I fall to the ground, wrapping myself up to protect myself from him and also to try to comfort myself.

"Ugh, you got blood all over me. Gross," I hear him say as he walks toward the bathroom while I shake with terror. My heart is pounding in my chest and my vagina feels as if it's been chopped up into a billion pieces. When the door opens, I watch as he walks, naked, through the room, putting on a new pair of scrubs before looking back at me.

"You okay?" he asks and I quickly shake my head. "Yeah, might want to go to the doctor. You're super tight, and with the bleeding you might have ripped something."

My lip wobbles as I say, "I might have ripped something? You fucking raped me."

He laughs, shaking his head. Crouching down, he looks at me with a condescending smile on his face. "Is that what you think? Is that what you think you're gonna tell people? You're my wife, Vi, I tried to have sex with you and your shit was tight so I pushed through to pleasure both of us. It isn't my fault your shit is broken and you're worthless. That's your fault, so don't blame me."

"I didn't do anything wrong," I cry and when he laughs, I want to scream.

"Vi, sweetheart, everything you do is wrong and if you go and tell anyone I raped you, they won't believe you. We're married; a husband can't rape his wife. Now go clean up," he says, standing up and heading for the door. He stops though, turning to me and says, "Oh, by the way, your check didn't deposit into my bank. Fix that, I'm running low on money."

When the door closes, I break down, shaking so hard while the sobs rip through me. I'm in so much pain that it hurts to even breathe. Falling to the ground, I lay my face on the hardwood floor and let my tears fall down onto the floor. I can feel the filth of him in my bones and I need it off but I can't seem to find the strength to go to the bathroom. As I lay here, I want to give up. I want to accept that this is my life. That nothing good will ever come my way. I feel defeated and I feel as if I'll never find the fight, or the will to leave. I mean what for? If I tell the police or anyone, no one will believe me. I've been hiding it for too long and Rob's right, who will believe that a husband has raped his wife? I feel completely broken. Every piece of me shattered and I just want to die.

No. I can't. I can't give up.

I know the fight is inside me. It has to be. I have to believe in myself. I have to believe that the light is at the end of the tunnel. I know I am strong—I can get away—and laying here isn't going to do anything but make it all worse. I have to figure out a way to make sure this never happens again and I will. I have to show him I'm strong. I'm done being the victim of Rob Moore. I'm ready to be the woman who Tucker McCloud deserves and one that I will love.

My legs wobble as I pick myself up off the floor, cringing with each step, but I know that it's going to take one step at a time to get me to where I need to be.

I'm going to fight.

I'm going to get my life back because it's mine for the taking.

Chapter
SIXTEEN

"**V**iolet, sorry to bother you but Tucker sent me to get the expense reports for y'all's trip to Atlanta."

I look up to Ms. Yolanda from my desk and let out a breath. It's been five days since certifiably the worst day of my life and I feel like a zombie. Dead. Everywhere. Trapped in a body I hate. A body that has no meaning, and the worst part—Tucker hasn't said one word to me. He hasn't even looked at me and it's been pure torture. As if dealing with what Rob did to me hasn't been enough, I have to look at a man who I know can comfort me and keep my distance to give him the time he needs.

I just want to run to him and ask him to hold me. I feel so empty without his friendship, his companionship, and I just want what we had back. But he's made it clear that it'll never happen. I have ruined him like Blaine said I would if I didn't let him go. How could I have been so stupid, so selfish? I needed his friendship, and because of my selfish need, I have no one. I'm alone.

This needs to stop. I don't expect him to open his arms and forgive me, even though that would be nice, but this no communication stuff has to stop. I know our employees are starting to wonder. I've seen them whispering and who can blame them? Tucker walks around this office looking the way I feel, like a zombie. He won't even look at me when before all he did was talk and joke with me on a daily basis.

"Is he in his office?" I ask.

"Yes."

"I'll take them over."

I wait for her to leave and when she doesn't I look up. She is looking at me with a worried look on her face, so I ask, "Yeah?"

"I'm stepping out of line here, I know that, but is everything okay between you two? It seems as if there is some tension between y'all and I'm just wondering if there's anything I can do to help."

No, she is just being nosy, but that's fine. With a bright smile, I shake my head and say, "Everything is fine, no worries. I'll take care of this."

With a curt nod, she starts for the door. "Okay, thank you."

"No, thank you."

When my door shuts, I stand up and cringe. My vagina hasn't been the same since Sunday and because of that, I'm going to the OB-GYN today. I don't know what's going on down there, but it hurts. It's a constant reminder of what happened and I need that to stop. I hope that nothing serious is wrong, but I have a feeling it is more than a bruise. Since the incident, I haven't had to deal with Rob. Thankfully, he has been working, and I haven't had to see or talk to him. It's been great and for the past few nights, I've decided that all I need is a month and I should have enough to live on in Colorado to get me by until I get a job. It will also be enough to start my divorce proceedings, which is great. It all scares me because I'm not really sure how I am going to get away. But I am ready for the change.

Reaching for the files Tucker wants, I head across the hall, knocking on his door.

"Come in," he calls out and I push open the door.

When his eyes meet mine, he quickly looks away and I want to cry.

"Violet, what can I do for you?"

"The files you needed," I say before laying them on his desk. I wait for him to look at me, but he doesn't. He ignores me, writing away in the patient's file. I want to yell at him to look at me, to allow me to apologize, but I don't think it will help.

"Thank you, anything else?"

I hate how short he is and I want my Tucker back. "Can you please look at me?"

"I'd rather not," he softly says as the pen he is writing with stills. "I have work to do."

"Tucker, people are starting to notice that something is going on."

"I don't give two shits what people notice. As long as they do their jobs, I don't care about anything else."

I'm stunned. "You don't mean that."

He looks up at me. His eyes dark, his mouth in a straight line as he says, "You're right. I love my office and they deserve the best possible boss but the problem is I don't want to be here. I care so much about you and looking across that hall at your door is killing me because I know behind it you're sitting there not caring one bit about me or how I feel."

"That's not true, Tucker."

"Sure it is, because if you did, you would admit that he's hurting you but you keep lying to me and hurting me in the process. All I want to do is help you and you won't let me, so unless you're going to share something more than a lie, I have nothing to say to you."

I can see that looking at me is hurting him and I know I just need to walk away. That's something I should have done a long time ago but instead I've hurt us both by allowing our feelings to develop. I should have stopped this from the beginning but I couldn't. No matter how hard I tried and I did try. I knew it was wrong to get involved with him. I just couldn't help it and now I am paying for it.

I nod before taking in a shuttering breath. "I'm so sorry I've hurt you Tucker."

When he shakes his head and looks down at his desk, my heart breaks into a billion pieces and I fell like my world is caving in. I've ruined the one good thing in my life besides my mom and I didn't realize it was going to hurt this bad. I want to tell him everything, apologize for lying and tell him that I will never utter another word but the truth but that would defeat everything I'm trying to do, which is protect him from that monster I married.

As a single tear trails down my face, I turn and open the door, shutting it behind me and rushing across the hall to the protection of my office. Falling into my chair, I allow a sob to break from me as I wrap myself up in my own arms, silently crying so that no one hears me. When my computer dings, I look up to see it's a message from Tucker.

Dr. T: Don't cry.

I close my eyes, squeezing the tears out of my eyes before leaning forward to type back to him.

VioletM: I hate that I've hurt you.

Dr. T: Me too.

VioletM: Is there a way to fix us?

I work my lip as I wait for his answer.

Dr. T: Stop lying to me.

Stop lying to him. That's all he wants but I'm not sure I can give that to him. My whole life has been based on a lie and I'm not sure how to change that. I don't know how to admit that I have a monster for a husband and that I'm a victim of abuse but it is becoming clear that I need to figure out how.

Because I need him in my life.

My day went from bad to worse.

Slamming the door, I find that son of a bitch standing at the counter with a sandwich in front of him. I can tell he is about to go to work and this is probably the worse time to do this but I don't give a shit. I going to give this man a piece of my mind and I don't care about the repercussions. It needs to be said and I'm going to say it. I'm not going to allow this to happen to me ever again.

I'm done being the damn victim.

Stomping to the counter, I put my hands on it and glare up at him.

"What the hell are you looking at?" he asks before taking a bite of his sandwich.

"I went to my OB-GYN today."

"I don't care," he says, "leave me alone, I'm eating."

"Well, I'm sorry but you need to stop because I think you'd like to know that after dodging question after question about if I was raped, I found out that not only did you cause lacerations in my vagina but to my surprise, you gave me fucking chlamydia."

He pauses but soon covers it up with a scuff. "No, I didn't."

"Yes, you did."

He shakes his head, taking a drink before looking over at me. "No, you're delusional. I never touched you."

What? Is he fucking serious?

"Excuse me? Yes, you did. You raped me."

He looked up at me from his sandwich and with the most sinister look on his face, he asks, "Where is the proof?"

Oh my God. This asshole. Taking a step back, I place my hands on my stomach, taking in deep breaths as I watch him eat his sandwich. He acts as if he did nothing wrong. As if the rape never happened. Like he didn't cause me the most unbelievable pain in my life. How can he stand there and think that what he did wasn't wrong. How can he be so callous, so uncaring about the pain he caused me? But what makes me the maddest is that he's right. I have no proof but a sick vagina, and since I lied to the doctor, I have nothing. No one.

"Why do you do this to me?"

He looks up and smiles. "Because I can and since you don't know how to leave me alone and you're obviously in the mood to fight with me, let's discuss the fact that you have an STD? Who're you fucking, Violet? 'Cause it isn't me."

He says it so calmly but his eyes tell me that he isn't calm at all. I'm not sure why, but I can tell that he knew I would have chlamydia because he has it too. He is turning this on me.

"I'm not fucking anyone but that's not the point. You did rape me and you made me sick."

"I did not, I'm clean. You're the nasty one."

"You asshole! I have always been clean, you're the one probably fucking some whore at the hospital and bringing home her disease, but let me tell you something, if you ever touch me again without my consent I am calling the cops and reporting it."

His laughter fills the room as he shakes his head. Licking his fingers, he looks across the room at me as he comes around the counter. I take a step back and then turn to go down the hall, but as I'm about to walk away, Rob has me by my hair, slamming me into the wall face first. Pain shoots to the back of my head and all I see are white spots as I try to focus. I scream out, trying to get away but he has me by my hair, pressing his body into mine, holding me in place.

"Calling the cops, huh?"

I struggle against him and yell out, "Let me go! Now!"

Ignoring my demands, he says, "Call the cops, Violet, and you wanna know what they will do? Nothing. I know most of the force here. I went to school with them; I see them daily at the ER. They love me. Do you think they'd believe any claim you make? You are nothing. You are worthless. No one would believe anything you say. So shut your fucking mouth and do what you were put on this earth to do."

Pushing off me, I turn around and put my hands up to hopefully soften the blow but he pushes my hands away, taking my face in his hands before getting so close to my face I can smell the mustard on his breath from the sandwich he was eating. There is even residue on his lips and I want to gag from the smell and sight of him. Squeezing my jaw, he says, "And that's to do whatever the fuck I say."

Smacking his hand away, I move quickly away from him causing his eyes to widen and his mouth to curve into a surprised grin.

"Keep your fucking hands off me."

I thought I would see it coming but I don't. He quickly takes me in his hands, slamming me up against the wall causing my head to bounce off the wall. It hurts and I know I'll have a mark but I have to get away so I push away from him but his grip is tight and my attempts are futile.

"Sorry, baby girl, you're mine."

I shake my head as I continue to try to get away. "Why do you do this to me when obviously you have someone else on the side. Go to her, leave me alone. Let me go."

He shakes his head, holding me as if I weigh nothing and that my fighting is doing nothing to him. I can see where I have scratched him, but he doesn't seem to care. He is proving his strength to me and it scares the shit out of me.

"Never. It's till death do we part Violet and don't forget that."

No. It's not.

Glaring up at him, I say, "Let me go."

"No."

I feel that he isn't holding my legs so I kick my knee up and get him right between the legs, causing him to fall over, grabbing himself. He groans and I know I should run but I can't move, he's blocking the door and I know if I run that way he will grab me.

"You stupid bitch. I'm going to beat the fuck out of you."

"No, you're going to keep your hands off me or I'm going to call the cops," I say, reaching for the home phone, just in case, but he surprises me, grabbing it before throwing it up against the wall, shattering it. He reaches for me but I move out of the way and run down the hall from him. Entering my bathroom, I slam the door shut and fall to the ground as tears started to fall down my face. I saw this going differently. I'd threaten him and he'd leave me be but, like always, he does the opposite of what I want.

"You think this door is going to keep me out?" I hear him scream before he starts pounding on the door. "I'm going to teach you to keep your hands to yourself, you bitch."

"Leave me alone!" I scream just as his fist comes through the door. I scream out, balling up cause it's only a matter of time before he gets in. I should have run out the door instead of the bathroom, but if I did get by him and I got to my car, where would I go? I could go to a hotel but knowing him, he'd show up at my work and that would involve Tucker and there is no way I'm going to involve him. I should just run, I should just go to my mom but I can't risk him going out there. Anywhere I go, he'd find me, and that would put anyone I go to for help in trouble.

I thought by now I would have this figured out. I thought I would have a foolproof plan. One that would keep me safe but it seems that I'm in the same position as when I married him. I know what I want. I know what I need to do to get there but I just don't know to get away from him scot free. I should have just kept everything I learned today locked up but I needed him to know that this can't happen to me. I need him to know that I'm not some rag doll for him to beat. That he has to treat me with respect but it seems like he doesn't care. He doesn't have any respect for me. He doesn't care about me, and he sure doesn't love me. It's insane. It seems that everything I do is wrong and nothing good ever comes out of it.

But maybe I'm wrong. Maybe what I did was right because I think that he knows he can't do what he did, ever again, because now I know I can get help. That's why he's so mad, that's why he's trying to get to me, because I have shown him I'm done taking all his shit. And now he wants to show me he doesn't care. I honestly believe that he'll kill me before he lets me go and I have no clue what to do.

When the door finally cracks and swings into me, I scramble, trying to get away but there is nowhere for me to go. In seconds he has me. Pinning me to the ground with his hands and weight. I try to get away but there's no use. He has me. Looking down at me, he shakes his head as he presses his knee into my vagina, causing me to cry out.

"Are you going to call the cops?"

When I don't answer, he presses into me again and I cry out, "No, please, that hurts." Tears are streaming down my face and I can't breathe as I look up into his face. He's a monster. He doesn't care that he is hurting me. He doesn't care about anything.

"That's right, now stop this mess. You understand me? The next time you kick me, I'll make you regret it."

I nod, choking on my tears as he presses his knee into me again. "Okay. I'm sorry. Please, stop."

He lets up and I take in a lungful of breath as my tears run into my ears. He then bends down and puts his face beside mine. I cringe away, but he follows and then whispers, "Stop fighting me, Violet."

Then he slams his knee down onto my stomach, knocking the air out of me. I gasp for breath as he lets me go, standing up over me. I ball up into the fetal position, trying to ease the pain but all I feel is fire. Closing my eyes, I squeeze out my tears, begging God to make the pain stop, to help me as Rob says, "You won't win. You'll never win."

I listen as his footsteps retreat and when I hear the front door slam, I cover my mouth, letting the tears fall as I sob. Slowly I sit up, cringing from the pain but I know if I stay down, I'll never get up. And I have to get up. Just like before. I hate him, with everything inside me, but I won't let him win. I can't give up. I won't give up.

Taking in a deep breath, I wail, "Yes, I will!"

A sob escapes from me and I gasp for breath as my heart pounds in my chest. Looking around the room, I blink away my tears as I whisper, "I will."

Even though no one hears me, I continue to say it as I slowly get up.

I may have not won right now but I will.

I will…

Chapter SEVENTEEN

Another week passes and with each day, I slowly begin to hate my life.

I live with a man that I hate. For the last couple days, I have sat and thought of ways to kill him, but I won't do it because I'm scared of what would happen to me if I did. I have completely shut down when he is around. I don't talk to him, I don't look at him, and I walk on eggshells around him. I'm biding my time until the moment I can leave, but each time I make a plan and think it's going to work, I always remember that there is a good chance I won't get away. I can't help but think that all this will be a failed attempt. But I refuse to give up, despite working every angle to get away and discovering that each time he finds me. It's driving me crazy but I have to get out of here, I have to keep trying.

Rob isn't the only thing that is making me hate my life and myself. It's my job too. I used to love this place. I used to get so excited about coming here but now I dread it. Now it's the place I go to make money to leave this state. Tucker is still not talking to me. He didn't even come to work for the first three days of the week. Dr. McCloud did, claiming that Tucker had to go out of town for something. Tucker hadn't even told me he was leaving town when usually he tells me everything. He won't answer my calls or texts and it's killing me.

I know what you're thinking. Just tell him. He could help and you would feel better and honestly, I'm starting to feel the same way but each time I look across the hall at his door, I freeze. I can't do it and I don't know if I ever will. I'm not sure I can handle what he will say and I'm not sure he'll understand. He'll want to fix it but, like I've said before, I don't know if this is something he can fix—I need to do it myself. I'm stuck between a rock and a hard place and I can't get out.

Going through my emails, I glance at the clock and even though I'm glad it's almost time to go home, I have no desire to go there. Rob is on a vacation of some sort and has been home for the last four days. I hate it. Everything I do, he's there, watching me and yelling that there is something better for me to do than work on the computer. I miss my time to myself and I wish he would go away.

When a knock comes at my door, my pulse speeds up at the possibility of Tucker walking through it but when I look up, it's Ms. Yolanda. Trying to mask my dismay, I smile and ask, "What can I do for you?"

"Dr. T has called a meeting."

My brows come together. "He has?"

"Yup, everyone is gathering in the break room. He asked me to come get you."

Fantastic.

Still with a bright smile, I say, "Wonderful, I'm on my way."

She sends me a grin before walking out and I crumble onto my desk. I have no clue what this meeting is about and I really don't want to go. Sitting up, I grab my notebook and pen for notes and slide my feet back in my heels before leaving my office. When I reach the break room, everyone is there, laughing and carrying on with Tucker but when he notices me, he stops laughing and turns to grab his things.

Well then.

"Since everyone is finally here, we can get started," he deadpans, making it clear that he is talking about me.

Sitting down, I send him a look as I get my notepad ready to be written on. "I didn't know about the meeting, so sorry I was late."

I may have said that a little rude, but he was rude first. Yes, that was a tad bit childish. I don't care though. He's acting like a jerk.

"I sent you a message," he says back and I shrug my shoulders.

"Didn't get a message, must have gotten lost in cyberspace, huh?"

Turning from where he is grabbing things, his eyes narrow as our gazes meet. It's only for a second but it feels like a lifetime and that's all it takes for my breath to hitch and my heart to slow. I want to run to him, beg him to forgive me but before I can, he looks away, picking up the files he had on the counter. Everyone is watching us, I can feel their eyes on us and I want to scream from frustration.

"Okay, so, I have exciting news. After my trip to Atlanta, my father and I have decided, after very careful research, that we want the office to become completely digital!"

His trip? His research? Hmm. Okay...

I sit back and watch the faces of my co-workers. Some are excited while others, like Amy and Rita, look nervous. Tucker seems oblivious to it though; he's talking about how great it will be for the office. How checking in patients will be a breeze and how everyone will benefit from it. While he goes on and on, I get madder and madder. Where is my credit for looking up all these facts? It could still come, so I sit back and watch, giving Tucker the benefit of the doubt, but I don't think it's coming.

When Rita's hand goes up, Tucker points to her before asking, "Yeah Rita?"

"Um, is this going to affect my and Amy's job?"

Tucker smiles as he shakes his head. "No, I was going to offer you and Amy the opportunity to go to a trade school for Medical Assisting on the company's account. I would need help getting the office in order too, so no, your job is sound. Everyone's job is."

Amy and Rita are glowing with happiness, so is everyone else. Except me. I'm fuming. Really, I'm not sure I have the right to be mad but at the same time, I think I do. I feel like I'm not even a part of this office anymore. No one is talking to me when usually I run these meetings. Tucker hasn't even looked to me for help; he's doing it all himself. Does he even need me anymore? Am I going to get fired?

Oh shit.

"Everyone good?"

Everyone nods and Tucker grins as everybody gets up to leave, saying bye to him first but not even sparing me a glance. Maybe I'm imagining this all. I am so hurt and upset with everything that I'm thinking things are happening when they really aren't, because surely my office wouldn't do this to me. I'm a great office manager, loving and attentive to everything they need. Everything Tucker needs.

Tucker.

Pinning him with a look, I watch as he laughs with Amy and Rita. I want to go over to him, smack him upside the head and ask why he's being such a jerk. Why he didn't credit me for anything or even act like I was in the room except to scold me? Folding my arms, I sit back in my seat and wait for them to get done talking. When they do, Rita and Amy head for the door, not saying anything to me, while Tucker heads down the hall, without even acknowledging that I'm still there.

Frustrated, I throw down my pen and paper and follow

behind him. When I reach his door, it's shutting and I catch it before it close, swinging it back hard so that it slams into the wall. I didn't mean to but I'm a little upset.

Whipping around Tucker sets me with disgruntled look. "Excuse me?"

"Excuse *you*? No, excuse me! How long are you going to treat me like this, Tucker?"

He rolls his eyes, sitting down in his chair before laying his papers down and looking at his computer. "I'm not treating you any way, Violet."

"Yes, you are. You're treating me like a villain!"

"That's a little dramatic, don't you think?" he asks, still not looking at me.

"It very may well be, but answer me. How long am I going to have to take this?"

"You don't have to take anything," he mutters, hitting the off switch on his monitor and looking up at me with a dismissing look.

"So you want me to quit? You want me gone?" I ask and saying the words is like taking a knife in the throat. My lip wobbles and I know he sees it because he looks away, shaking his head.

"No, Violet, I don't want you to quit."

"Then what, Tucker? What do you want from me?"

Slamming his fist down on the desk, he stands up, sending his chair back, hitting the wall and startling the shit out of me. "I want you! All of you and it's killing me with each passing second that I can't have you."

I can't hold them in, and soon tears are dipping down my face as I stay locked in his gaze. "I can't give you that. Not now, not yet."

"I know that," he says, looking away as he runs his hands through his hair. "That's why I'm just trying to survive you."

"Survive me?"

"Yes, because it is so hard to pretend that I don't love you, that I don't want you every minute of every day. That I don't think of you all the time. And yearn to hold your body in my arms. Every time I see you, it's like ripping the bandage off the wounds I've spent all night trying to mend. I'm hurting Violet, and I don't know how to handle it because I can't pretend that nothing happened. I just can't."

I cover my eyes with my hands, crying into them as I take in a deep breath. My insides are ripping apart with each word. I know how much I need him, but I didn't know this. I knew he was hurting, but jeez, all that? How can I fix that? How can I make anything better when I can't give him what he wants? When I feel his arms come around me, I come undone, sobbing in this man's arms.

"Please don't cry, I hate when you cry," he whispers against my hair.

"I don't want to hurt you anymore," I cry, hiccupping a sob before looking up at him. His eyes are soft and locked on mine. He reaches up and cups my face as he takes in a deep breath.

"Then be with me."

"I can't, Tucker. I'm sorry."

Shaking his head, he lets me go and turns from me. I want to reach out, hold him but I doubt that would help the situation. I don't want to make this any worse than it already is.

Before I could make any hasty decisions, he turns, his eyes on me. "Don't you know we belong together? I would love you until my dying day, Violet. We could be the forever kind of couple. I believe that, because my love is soul deep for you."

"Tucker—"

He shakes his head, stopping anything else from coming out of my mouth before taking my hands in his. "Let it be me, Violet. Let me be the one to love you forever. To kiss your sweet mouth every day and to make love to your beautiful body. I would treat you like a woman deserves and I would never make you cry, except tears of happiness. Don't waste your life on him. Spend it with me."

I'm shattered. My face is flooding with tears as he leans his head against mine, moving his nose along mine. "Just please, let it be me. Pick me. Love me." I want to say yes and wrap my arms around him and never let go. To feel his heart beat next to mine. To secure my place at his side and fall asleep beside him like two spoons. I want this. I want all of him. Every bit, but I'm not the woman he deserves at this moment. As much as I want to give in, I can't. Not yet.

Cupping my face in his hands, he places his lips on mine but I can't do it. I can't allow this to happen. Pulling away, I shake my head as I walk across the room and when I turn to look at him, he looks as if I've beaten him with a bat. He looks so broken, so hurt and as much as I want to comfort him, I can't. I'm scared out of my mind but I have to tell him. I have to tell him the truth because I love him too and I need him in my life.

I'm not sure how it will go and I'm scared to find out what he will think of me, but I've been doing this by myself and it isn't working. I need someone to give me advice and since I don't want to worry or scare my mother, who better than the man I've fallen for?

But before I could even get a word out, Tucker asks, "Why, Violet? And don't tell me you fucking love him because I know you don't."

"You're right, I don't."

His brows squish together as he cups the back of his neck, looking at me in the most flustered way. He spreads his arms out in front of him in confusion. "Then why? Don't you feel the same about me?"

I look up at him and wipe my face with the back of my hands before slowly nodding my head. "That's the thing, Tucker, I do. So much. But, I can't leave him for you. I can't seem to leave him period. I'm trying, I'm trying so hard, but—"

I pause to take in a deep breath and I can't believe I'm going to tell him this but I am. I'm going to do it. I'm going to let him fully in.

"But why?" he asks, taking my hands in his.

Looking up at him, I take in a shaky breath as the tears rush down my face, down my lips onto my shirt.

"Because he'll kill me."

I did it.

And oh my God, I feel like the world has been lifted off my shoulders. I told him everything and it was so easy. So freaking easy that I am mad at myself for waiting. Like the good man he is, Tucker listened, not saying a word as I told him about the last three years. About how we met and how we were so in love. I told him about the abuse, the rape, and how I've hid it for years. I told him about how Rob stole all my money, how he noticed that my check isn't going into his bank, and that I'm worried he'll retaliate. I told him about Rob attacking the doctor in Colorado and how that's the reason I haven't told him or let him in. All he did was support me and encourage me to go on when I wanted to break down.

He is amazing.

"Okay, so beating the ever loving fuck out of this dude is off the table, right?"

I nod. "I know you're doing this whole alpha male thing and believe me I completely believe in your strength and know you'd give it to him, but Tucker, I couldn't risk it. I couldn't live with myself if he hurt you."

"Wouldn't happen, but okay, I understand."

"I have to do this myself. I have to get out. I just need to figure out how. I feel so alone and I don't know what to do."

He nods, reaching for my hands and running his thumb along the back of them. The whole time I talk, he held me in some way, whether his thumb was rubbing easy circles into my palm or he was touching my shoulder, but gave me space at the same time. "Okay, we'll disappear."

I shake my head, my shoulders falling. "You have this practice, Tucker. I can't ask you to leave it for me. Plus, he'll find us. I promise you, he would."

"Hit man?"

I laugh as I shake my head. "No, it has to be legal."

We sit for a minute, and I can tell he is racking his brain for anything that might help, but I've been doing it for weeks and I can't seem to think of anything.

Looking over at me, he says, "I have the best lawyer ever and if you don't like mine, Blaine's is spectacular. I'll get him to draw up a restraining order to hold you over until the divorce."

"He'll go right through it or fight it, plus I don't have the money for your kind of lawyer."

"But I do and I'll say it's a business expense."

"Tucker, I told you, I have to do this. You can't have anything to do with it. He'll find out, he'll come after you, and I won't let that happen."

"Okay, I won't point out that I work out almost every day. Instead I'll say we can do strictly cash, so no one will know anything about my involvement."

I look down at my hands, tears welling up in my eyes. "It won't work."

"I don't accept that and I'll be damned if I'm going to allow this to happen any more than it already has. We will figure out something. I'll contact my lawyer, see what he says."

"But I have no evidence. I have nothing proving what he's been doing to me. It would be my word against his."

He shrugs his shoulders as he gets up, walking toward his desk. "So? People divorce every day without even putting anything down. We'll figure it out. Give me a day or two. I promise, you'll get away from him."

He looks back at the computer and I watch as he types and clicks his mouse, not knowing what to say. I want to tell him again that he can't do this for me, but I knew this would happen when I told him. The damn fixer in him is shining right now and I don't know how to dim it. I know he wants to take over, and fix it all, but dammit, it's so frustrating. I wish Rob would just go away and leave me alone, but that won't happen so I'm left figuring out a way to get out while Tucker puts his cape on to save me. I can't let him, though, and I have to reiterate that.

"Tucker, you can't do this for me."

His fingers stop typing and he looks over at me. "I know, but I can help. I can be there and I can be the person in your corner since you won't let me hire to have him killed or beat the living shit out of him."

"But you have to let me do this. You can't send your lawyers off on him, you can't confront him or even act like you know. It has to stay between us. Ugh, dammit. You can't do it for me. Thank you and I wish I could give it all to you and let you do it, but I wouldn't be able to live with myself. I want to be the woman you deserve—one who is strong and worth being with—so I need you to promise me that. Promise you won't do it, for me. You'll let me, because if I don't get away, successfully, it's my own damn fault."

Looking back at his screen, he shakes his head. "First, I will never deserve you, you're too good for me but we'll get to that later. Second, this is not your fault. It's that piece of shit's fault and don't ever let me hear you say that again."

"But—"

"No buts, listen to me. I promise I'll let you do this yourself and we'll do it your way but you have to trust me, you have to believe that I'm going to do everything in my power to help you. You're going to get away from him and you're going to live a long and beautiful life, I can promise you that."

I glance down at my hands and take in a deep breath. "Thank you."

"Anything for you."

I look up to see him typing away. Standing up, I walk over

to the desk and reach over, taking his hands off the keys and pulling him up. He looks surprised but he goes with it, until he is fully up, looking down at me with concern in his eyes.

"Tucker I don't know how to thank you. I want to kiss you, but—" I say but he stops me, placing his finger over my lips before smiling down at me.

"As much as I would love that very much, I know that it can't happen and I'm okay with that because we'll have our time. You need to get away, you need to heal, and then we can be together. We can be happy."

His hand comes up and slowly he rubs his thumb along my bottom lip.

"Until then though, I'll be behind you one hundred percent. I will be here when you need me. I'll give you the strength and support you need, every step of the way. You will never feel alone ever again."

My tongue is thick but somehow I'm able to whisper, "How did I get so lucky to find you?"

He smiles before enveloping me in a tight hug. Kissing the top of my head, he whispers, "I wonder the same thing and I thank God every night that I found you."

Closing my eyes, I hug him close to me, holding him as if I never want to let go. Things are changing and it's all because of him.

Chapter
EIGHTEEN

Tucker McCloud: Everything okay?

Me: Yes, I'm about to leave.

Tucker McCloud: Okay, see you soon.

Me: Thanks.

Tucker McCloud: Anytime.

I smile as I lay my phone down before running a brush through my hair. It's been three days since I told Tucker about everything and he has been simply amazing. He's always texting to make sure I'm okay; he even offered to let me stay with him or in his family's condo. Of course, I declined – for obvious reasons – but it was nice to have the option. If I could get away with staying with Tucker or even in a condo, I would, but I know Rob would find me in no time. He knows too many people in this town and I know for a fact he'd come to my work.

Laying my brush down, I head to the kitchen to grab my things so I can leave. When I reach the living room, the door is opening and Rob glances at me as he lays his keys down on the table near the door.

"Where are you going?"

"To work," I answer, reaching for my purse. I walk around the counter and slide my feet into my heels before turning, and when I do, I run right into Rob. He gives me a look as I scramble back, running into the counter. He rolls his eyes before looking over at me.

"Did you get that shit fixed with your check?"

I shake my head. "Tucker isn't sure why it isn't going in because it is pulling from his account. He's looking into it."

"Doesn't he know you need money?"

I shrug. "He said it's the bank. He offered to write me a personal check but I figured we're fine."

His eyes narrow as he takes a step toward me. "Don't you think that is something you should have asked me? You should have taken the check, we need money."

"How, when you work?" I ask, confused. "You are always working so I don't know why you depend so much on my money."

When I notice that his eye is beginning to twitch, I take another step back, rounding the counter to put some space between us. "I didn't ask for your opinion, I said to ask me next time. Ask for the check. I need money."

I shake my head. "No, Rob, I don't feel right asking for it."

"I don't care what you feel right doing, do what I say."

I don't want this to turn into a fight. I want to get to work and then I won't see him for the next couple days because he is going back to work. I just need to get out of here, hopefully by the next time I see him I can figure out what to say to him. Just with the two paychecks I've gotten in my bank, I'm already sitting with over three thousand. All I need is another thousand and I'm pretty sure I'll be able to get a lawyer and have money to live in Colorado until I find a job. That's my goal at least and I am hoping it will work but he is pressing me really hard about this money and I have no clue what I'm going to do.

"Alright, I'll ask," I say, picking up my purse and then my keys before heading to the door.

As I'm about to close it though, Rob says, "If you don't ask, I'll ask him. I see him every week at the hospital and you better hope you aren't lying."

I shut the door and let out a breath. Dammit. What am I going to do? As I drive to work, all I can do is think about what I am going to tell Rob, or how I'm going to hide that I'm keeping the money for myself. I'm having the hardest time thinking of anything else to say. When I pull into the parking lot of the office, I lean back in the seat and let out a long breath. For the nine hundredth time, I scold myself for getting in this situation but I have to remember that I'm almost out.

Almost.

Opening the door, I grab my workbag and head into the office through the back. Everyone is moving around, getting ready for the day, and as I pass everyone wishes me a good morning. It's nice and I know I'll miss these people once I'm gone. I'll come back though. Or at least I hope I will.

I lay my things on my desk once I enter my office and then grab my mug before heading to the break room for some coffee. When I get there though, it's full when usually it's empty. Looking around, I know I look confused as I ask no one in particular, "What's up?"

"Dr. T called a meeting," Mrs. Yolanda says before handing me a pamphlet. My brow rises as I read the first line.

Learn to defend yourself!

What the hell? Opening the pamphlet, I discover that it is for a self-defense teacher, Gary St. Claire, who goes anywhere to teach a class on how to defend yourself. Just as I'm about to ask why the hell we're having a meeting about this, Tucker strolls in looking dashing as ever. He wasn't wearing his white coat, just a black button up shirt with a red tie. His black dress pants fit him perfectly but that wasn't what had my attention. Like always, it his eyes. They're dark but light at the same time, giving off the perfect combination to brighten my day. He captivates me completely, and I wish that we could explore our feelings. I wish I could look at him and tell him the three words he has said to me, but it's not the time. Like he said, we'll have our time. We just have to wait. I just hope that I'm worth waiting for because I know he is.

"Alright ladies, hope everyone is well this morning. Did everyone get a pamphlet?"

Everyone nods before he goes on. "Good. Okay, here's the deal. There has been an outbreak of attacks in Tennessee this year and I have decided that I couldn't bear having anything happening to any of you, so I'm bringing in Mr. St. Claire to train you in the art of defending yourself."

There is silence until Amy raises her hand. "Is it mandatory? Because as much as I appreciate you worrying about us and all, I dare someone to attack me. I'd kick their butt."

Everyone laughs, even I do, but Tucker doesn't. His mouth is in a straight line before he says, "Yes, Amy, it is mandatory. Unless you have health problems that would keep you from training, I want everyone to do it. It's paid training and it's something I feel you all need."

No one says anything as he looks down at the piece of paper in his hands. He then looks up at us, and says, "It isn't even about being attacked for your purse or something; it could be rape. Over eighty-nine thousand cases were reported last year in Tennessee for rape and did you know that one in four women have experienced domestic violence in her lifetime? That's scary stuff."

He pauses to let that soak in and all I can do is look at my lap.

It's scary to know that there are other woman who go through the same thing I do. Everyone always thinks they're strong and that this kind of thing will never happen to them and, at one time, I thought that too. I thought I was untouchable, that Rob loved me, and look at where I am now. It's a vicious thing that I'm going through and I'm glad that Tucker is doing this. I'm proud of him and thankful.

"I know you may think I'm crazy for this, but I work in an office with ten ladies, the only other male being my father whenever he shows up. I care about each and every one of you as if you were my family. I know a lot of offices that offer this to their employees, and I think we need this. It will not only protect you, but it will unite us as an office. The class will be on Friday afternoons at three, here in the back. We'll need to reschedule our patients for Friday since we'll be closing early. I don't want it to run into your everyday schedules so I've decided to close early."

The two front office girls nod their head as Rachel says, "I'll get that done today. You want the last appointment to be what? Two?"

"Yes, thank you, Rachel. Any other questions?"

When everyone shakes their head, Tucker claps his hands before saying, "Okay, that's all I got. Everyone have a nice day."

I smile brightly at Tucker as I stand, and he grins back before turning to look at Ms. Yolanda who is asking a question. I want to tell him how proud I am of him, how amazing this all is but it can wait. Everyone disburses in their own direction while I go the coffee pot to get the cup I had initially came for. As I pour my cup, I feel someone behind me and when I turn, Tucker is looking down at me.

"Good morning, Violet."

A grin pulls at my lips as I say, "Morning, Tucker."

He smiles as he looks away. "Everything okay?"

I nod. "Everything is fine, well," I pause and let out a breath.

I hate to trouble him with this but no sooner do I say the words before he asks, "What?"

"He's been asking where my money is. I'm trying to figure out what I'm going to say. He says he will ask you if I don't tell someone or at least have the money in the account."

He scoffs as he looks off the side. "Please let him come to me."

I reach out, wrapping my fingers around his forearm. He looks down at my hand and then back at me as I say, "Please, you promised you wouldn't say or do anything to him."

"And I won't," he answers, putting his hand over mine. "But only because you've asked me too."

"Thank you."

He shakes his head, moving his hand off mine before saying, "As much as I'd rather you let me kill him, this excuse will get you by until you have enough money to leave. I still think you should go to the cops but since you won't, here is what you do. Say that you got demoted because you've missed so much for being sick, your grandmother's passing and all. Take your raise money and deposit that in your account."

I'm confused. Raise? "Huh? What raise?"

"The one my dad approved after seeing the notes and the ideas you had for the digital office. I told you it was coming."

"I know but I didn't think it would be this soon."

He smiles before chucking my chin softly. "When you're as amazing as you are, things come quickly. My dad loves you and decided you didn't have to wait the normal ninety days before a raise."

I smile, feeling as if some of the weight has been lifted off my shoulders. It's the perfect excuse and it will work but I really don't know how I will ever repay Tucker and his family. "Thank you," I whisper, "I know that's not enough, but tell your father, thank you."

"Your performance is what got you the raise. You do a great job around here. I don't know how many times I have to tell you that, but I will keep saying it until you believe me."

"It may take a while."

"I got all the time in the world for you," he says before turning and walking away. I watch as he heads out the break room toward his office and I wish I could tell him how wonderful he is but I can feel eyes looking my way. Turning back to my coffee, I finish pouring it and then head down the hall. When I enter my office, I find him standing against my bookshelf with his arms crossed over his chest.

"Hey, I thought you went to work."

He shakes his head as I close the door. "No, Amy was watching us, that's why I walked away, but I wasn't done talking to you."

"Oh okay," I say going back to my desk and setting down my coffee. "What's up?"

He walks around a bit before turning to look down at me. "Are you okay with the self-defense class?"

I nod, a small smile resting on my lips. "Yes, of course. Thank you."

He lets out a breath before letting his shoulders fall in relief. "Oh good, I was nervous you would think I was overstepping."

"No, not at all."

"But calling my lawyers, getting the biggest suit imaginable against him or hiring a hit man is overstepping?"

I laugh as I roll my eyes. "Yes, Tucker. Very much so."

He makes a face as he falls into the chair in front of my desk. "Okay, how about this?"

He lays down a piece of paper on my desk and I pick it up, reading. It's a support group for battered women in the next town over. They meet every Tuesday and Thursday at eight p.m. and offer all the support a woman needs to get out of their current situation or stay away. I look up at Tucker and I can tell he is worried.

"No, it's not, but I don't know," I say, dropping the piece of paper. "It took me forever just to talk to you."

He scoots to the edge of his seat, nodding as he folds his hands in front of him. "I get that, but the percentage of women who get out and stay away from their abuser is higher when they go to support groups or therapists. Since you won't take any of my money to go to a therapist and I know you can't spend your money since you're saving it, I figured this is the best thing for you. To help keep you away from Rob. It's in Williamsburg, so no one will know you, or Rob; it will be safe."

I love that he is so caring. This man is a gift from God, I swear he is. With a smile, I say, "When I get away, Tucker, you won't have to worry, I'll never go back."

"I hope so, but this will help you get away too. These women have either been through it or are going through it. They're just like you. They can help more than I can, more than anyone can. I'm only asking. I'll take you so that no one really knows you're there. I'll sit in the car or I'll sit with you. It's whatever you want. I just want to help."

I look back down at the paper, re-reading what it says. I can feel him watching me and in my head this isn't happening. In my head, we're happy, together, and completely in love. Instead of talking about support groups and self-defense courses, we're talking about when we will move in together. When we will get married and have babies but that isn't my life. I chose a life that has done nothing but make me think I was ruined but that was until Tucker came along. He believes in me when I don't.

Looking back up at the gorgeous man that has been here even when I didn't want him to be, I smile. "I will think about it."

"That's all I can ask," he says before standing up and heading toward my door. "Have a great day, Violet."

"You too," I say before he leaves my office. I look back down at the paper and push it to the side. I don't know if I'm ready for something like that. It took years for me to open up to Tucker and I'm not sure I can go sit with a group of women and tell them all about my deep dark secrets. It just doesn't seem like something I could do. But the thing is, Tucker is right. I need to start healing, I need to know I can get out and live a successful and meaningful life. Hearing it from Tucker is one thing, but hearing it from a group of women who have left their abusers is what I need. Looking back over at the paper, I read the headline again:

Are you being abused?

Never once have I admitted that I was a victim of abuse. I believed for so long that he really did love me and then it was fear that kept me there, but now reading those words, I know the answer.

"Yes. I am."

"My name is Leann, I was in an abusive relationship for two years before I got out. I have been away from my ex-husband for seven months now."

"I have been in an abusive relationship for ten years. I don't know how to leave, we have children and he has all my money. I'm scared but with each of these meetings, I'm starting to see a way out. I finally told my mom about it all. She knew. It's crazy, but she did, and well, yeah, I'm gonna get out. I have to. Oh, and my name is Tabitha."

"My name is Ellen, hi, I was being raped and abused by my boyfriend for six months before I left. After leaving him, I jumped into another relationship with another abuser, but that only lasted a couple months. And when I left him, I ended up getting with another abuser. I finally left him and I have been single for almost a year now. I am learning to love myself. That I am worth the love of a good man who won't raise his fist to me."

"Hi, I'm Rena, I left my husband three weeks ago after four years of abuse. It's been hard. He has begged me to come home but I won't. He has come to the place I'm staying and physically tried to drag me out, but my brother stopped him. I'm thinking of moving to New York where my mother and father live. Not sure though. I have a great job in Nashville that I don't want to leave."

"I'm Ann Marie, I went from my father abusing me, and my uncle sexually abusing me, to my husband who sexually and physically abuses me. I'm planning on leaving this Friday. I'm going to go to a shelter first and then once I can save up some more money, I'll fly out to Germany where my mom is. I'm just scared. He loves his daughter but he is so mean and hateful to me that I can't risk something happening to my sweet angel."

"My name is Tammy and my boyfriend continues to beat the crap out of me on a daily basis, but I continue to stay. I don't know why, but it's nice to meet you."

"I'm Rachel. My husband beats my children and me daily. I dealt with it for a long time until he raped me in front of my three-year-old. I left two years ago, and I'm finally dating and I'm happy. It's hard and I was scared for a long time, but no more. I won't be anything but happy."

"This is our group, and I'm Marci, the group counselor. I have been doing this line of counseling for over three years after spending years in a physically, emotionally, and sexually abusive relationship with my husband. I decided to help people who were in the same position I was in since my husband told me I'd never get out. I welcome you and I'm glad you came. So please, introduce yourself to us."

You know, it was simple to admit that I was abused in the privacy of my office but now, sitting in a circle of eight women, I don't feel as brave. I look at each of the women that sit in the circle with me. We're all of different races, different sizes, and different ages. I thought I'd be the youngest but the girl across from me, Ellen I think was her name, looks like she's only eighteen. Rena looks like she's a businesswoman, her clothes are all designer, the purse that sits in her lap is a Coach. Ann Marie has her newborn baby on her lap. Tammy is covered in tattoos and has a shiny black eye that she had tried to cover but I can tell it is there. The others look just like me, just normal women, trying to get by.

I think I've made a mistake. Standing up, I look around and say, "I'm sorry, I can't do this."

Marci, the leader of the group, smiles before she slowly nods. "We'll be here when you can. Every Tuesday and Thursday."

"I'm sorry," I mutter again as I start for the door.

"It's okay. Hope to see you back," she calls toward my back as I slam the door shut.

Closing my eyes, I take in a deep breath before letting it out in a whoosh. I should have never come here. This was a waste of my time and theirs. I'm not ready for this, and I'm not sure I'll ever be. Opening my eyes, I start to walk to where Tucker is sitting in his car, reading patient files.

God, what am I going to tell him?

I open the door and hop in just as he looks over at me. "That was fast?"

I nod as I look down at my hands. "I couldn't do it."

He doesn't say anything and I wait for what seems like forever for him to say something. Instead, I hear the car start and then it is moving. When I sneak a glance at him, he is looking forward, his face calm.

"I'm sorry," I whisper.

"What for?"

"For wasting your time."

He reaches over and squeezes my hand. "Helping you is never a waste of my time, Violet. So you walked out? We can try again next week. It's okay."

I look back down. "What if I don't want to go back?"

He lets out a breath before he squeezes my hand again. "As much as I want you to, I won't make you. This is your battle and as much as I want to fight it for you, I know I can't, but what I can do is be the guy who encourages you and gives you the tools you need to win. I think with the help of these women, you can win, but if you don't want to go back, then we'll find another way to win."

I don't say anything else as we ride back to the office where my car is. He is so sweet, so helpful, and I honestly don't know how I'll ever repay him for what he has done for me. I glace over at him and admire his profile. He could be with anyone right now. Someone amazing and beautiful, who has her shit together—but instead, he is with me, helping me find the strength I thought was lost.

When Tucker enters the parking lot to the office, I look away, watching as my car comes into view. When he pulls into the spot beside my car, I don't want to move. I don't want to go home. I know Rob is there and he is the last person I want to see right now but I know I have to go. I gather my things, reluctantly, and then slowly reach for the door handle before turning to look at him.

"Thank you for taking me."

He smiles. "Anytime, Violet. Can you text me when you get home?"

I nod. "Sure."

"Okay, see you tomorrow. Remember we have self-defense class tomorrow."

"Yeah, I know," I say, sending him a smile as I climb out of his car. When I go to shut the door, I stop; Tucker is giving me the tools to help me and all I have to do is use them. That's all. Bending down, I look over at him.

He is still smiling at me and I find myself smiling back as I say, "Can you take me next Tuesday?"

He doesn't even pause, or think it seems. With a wide smile, he nods. "Of course."

Chapter NINETEEN

Three weeks have passed and I feel like nothing has changed. I've been to six meetings and I feel like I'm wasting everyone's time. I still haven't admitted my name, or even said what I'm going through. Nothing. I just sit there, listening to everyone's stories and as soon as Marci asks me if I'd like to tell my story, I blanch. Each time, Tucker is supportive, telling me it's going to take time, but surely he's getting tired of it all. He sits in the car, working, playing on his phone and each time all I can do is tell him 'I'm sorry, but I didn't say anything'. It's starting to stress me out because it makes me think I'm not ready to leave. That I'm not ready to start my life because I can't even tell anyone else that I am abused.

It's scary.

Along with the six meetings, I've been to three defensive courses and I've discovered that I love them. They are fun and I feel so powerful, smacking the shit out of the guy when he wears the padded suit. It's fun but I'm not so sure that I will remember any of this stuff if Rob ever comes at me again. I haven't had that problem because every time I'm home, he is gone or asleep. It's been quiet, and he's been calm, but that makes me nervous.

You know the saying, the calm before the storm. That's Rob. Usually when he is quiet for a long length of time, I have to be extra careful because he can blow up at any moment. He's a ticking time bomb and I have been staying out of his way, watching what I'm doing at all times, but I know it's coming. And even with my training, I'm still nervous.

Will I remember it all?

Will I defend myself?

Or will I do exactly what I've always done and just try to get away.

I hope I don't have to do anything. I hope he stays away from me. I only need a couple more weeks. I know, I know, I said that three weeks ago but the thing is, my mom isn't doing well. I spoke with her last week and found out that she is hurting for money. Because of this, I figured I needed a little more money so that I wouldn't have to burden her at all. I could support myself completely and maybe even her. Only two more weeks, that's all, and then I'm gone.

Gone.

Away from Rob, but also away from Tucker.

I wish Tucker will come with me, or maybe we can figure out a way for me to stay here but those are fantasies. As much as I don't want to go, I have to. I wish I could put Tucker in my pocket and take him everywhere. In a way I guess I can with the way technology is now but still, I can't imagine not physically seeing him every day.

In these three weeks my feelings for him have become stronger, more deeply rooted inside me. It's crazy because I have honestly never felt this way about anyone. Not even Rob and I thought Rob was my all-time love at one point. I don't know what it is, but something about Tucker has me completely entrapped in him. He is so supportive, so nice and kind. He calls to check on me, to make sure I'm okay. He's constantly asking if I need anything and it's so refreshing.

I was convinced that he was going to ride in and take control but he hasn't. He is letting me do it and I think I have fallen for him even more because of it. He is everything I always wanted but I can't have him and as much as I want to ask if he'll wait for me, I can't because I feel like it's a selfish thing to ask. He deserves the world, and I don't know when I'll be able to do everything to give it to him. It could be months, maybe even years before I can be the woman he deserves and I can't bring myself to ask him to wait for me.

Like right now, I'm watching him on the phone. He is smiling, his dimples prominent, as he laughs on the phone with whoever he is speaking with. I have a smile on my face because his grin and laughter are infectious. God, he is so beautiful. When he looks across the hall at me, he winks and the butterflies go crazy inside me. I smile and wave at him before going back to work since I don't want to seem like a creeper but soon I'm back at staring at him when my phone rings. I look down to see that it is Rob and my stomach quickly drops.

"Hello?"

"When is this demotion shit going to be over? This check isn't even worth you going to work every day."

"I'm on it for another month, I think."

"Bullshit, tell your asshole boss that you're quitting," he demands.

"No, I love my job."

"It's a waste of time."

"No, it's not. I'm happy."

"I don't care if you're happy. I said quit, damn it," he yells.

I roll my eyes and try to speak calming as I say, "How does that make sense? You're complaining because my check is not enough but if I quit then there will be no money. So why am I quitting? Shouldn't I stay and make some kind of money and then in a month it will go back to normal?"

He doesn't say anything for a moment. My heart is jackhammering against my chest. I shouldn't have said anything, I should have waited for him to get done bitching and then hung up but I know I'm right. Plus, I have to keep this job. I need the money.

"You think you know everything, huh?"

"What? I didn't say that," I explain, "all I am saying is—"

"I don't give a fuck what you're saying. You're walking on a thin rope, Violet. You better watch what the hell you're doing," he says before the line goes dead.

I lay down my phone and let out a long breath. Closing my eyes, I let my head fall on the desk and I just lie there. I wish I could have a do over. Like instead of falling into this clusterfuck with Rob, I wish that there were something that would have told me what kind of man he was but no one knew in Colorado. Everyone saw only what he wanted them to and that was a charming guy until he beat the crap out of that doctor. As I much as I want to say I wish I never met him or married him, I truly believe that it happened for a reason. This time in my life is supposed to make me stronger and I also believe that it had to happen so that Tucker would come into my life. As much as it has hurt and caused me to hit rock bottom, I know I have to start somewhere.

It's all up from here and I have to believe that. I have to believe I'm doing everything I can to change my life and it will be worth it. I hope so.

"Sleeping on the job?"

I pop my head up to see Tucker and Blaine looking at me from my doorway. Between them is a mini version of them both and I can't help but think *damn this family has strong genes.* They're all so damn good looking. The mini version of them has hair that is shaggy and falling into the same eyes as the rest of the McCloud men. He comes up to his father's waist and is as cute as ever. A smile spreads over my face as I stand up and come out from behind my desk.

"Not at all. Just trying to breathe," I say in a cheerful voice as I make my way toward them. Tucker is smiling and so is the little guy who I assume is Nicky. Blaine on the other hand, he isn't smiling. He's just looking at me like I betrayed him and I know I have. I promised this guy I wouldn't hurt his brother and I did. Even if had my reasons and Tucker knows them, I still hurt him and by the looks of it, Blaine doesn't know my reasons nor does he care. So why is he in here?

"I hope we aren't bothering you, I just wanted you to meet Nicky McCloud, my nephew."

I bend down, holding out my hand for Nicky. "Nice to meet you."

He smiles shyly before looking up at Tucker. "She's pretty."

I blush as Tucker laughs, his eyes meeting mine as he agrees. "She sure is."

"Well thank you, you're very handsome yourself, Nicky."

He's blushing this time as he turns into his father's leg, peeking out at me with the same eyes I love on Tucker. I stand up and smile over at Tucker before glancing up at a glaring Blaine.

"He's darling," I say to Blaine, but he doesn't say anything.

"Well then," Tucker laughs before reaching for Nicky and throwing him over his shoulder. "Come on man, say bye to Ms. Violet and let's go see if Ms. Yolanda has some candy."

"Bye, Ms. Violet!"

I grin as I wave. "Bye Nicky, it was great meeting you."

He sends me a toothless grin before being whisked away by Tucker. I wait for Blaine to leave but he is still standing there, looking at me.

"Is there something I can do for you, Blaine?" I ask and his eyes quickly narrow.

"I trusted you," he says causing me to look away before taking in a deep breath.

"I know."

"Why don't you just leave him alone?"

Yeah, he doesn't know anything.

"How? I'm not doing anything. I mean what do you want me to do Blaine? Quit?"

He nods. "Yes, and leave him alone; it hurts him having you around."

I'm surprised by this. Surely Tucker hasn't said that. "Has he told you that?"

"Yes, not lately, but before he had." he says, shaking his head as he looks at me in disgust. "I thought you were better than this. I thought you were a good person."

Tears well in my eyes as I slowly nod. "I'll be gone in a matter of weeks, Blaine."

"Good."

I look up and meet his eyes. "But just to let you know, I am a good person and I'm sorry for what happened, for hurting him, but it was out of my control. We both weren't thinking and one thing led to another, but I promise you, I care about him so much and I want nothing but good things for him."

"Yeah, well you can care all you want but leave and never come back. He deserves someone so much better."

With that he walks out of my office and I know I can't take everything he has said to heart. He doesn't know the whole story and I know he is super protective over his brother but even with knowing all that, it still hurts. I really like Blaine but it is obvious that he despises me and it's my fault entirely. I made a promise and not even twenty-four hours later, I broke it. He has every right to hate me, I just hope that one day I have a chance to explain myself, to tell him my story and to make a new promise.

And that is to never, ever hurt his brother again.

"Blaine hates me."

Tucker looks over at me with a confused look, as he says, "No, he doesn't."

I nod my head as I watch the town pass by through the window. We're driving back from another failed meeting. All I did was sit there and this time, no one said anything to me. It's as if they are getting used to me just being a mute. It's depressing and I wish I could just say what I'm thinking, but I freeze up every time. Tonight was a good night for Tabitha though, the one who has been with her husband for ten years. She finally left him. It's only been a week but she looks so much happier and it gives me hope. Tucker says that means the group is working but if it was working why am I not talking? Why am I not telling my story?

Looking back over at Tucker, I remember that we're discussing Blaine. "He told me to stay away from you and that I was a horrible person."

He shakes his head before reaching over for my hand. "I'm sorry. He is so overprotective of me, especially after his ex-wife. I haven't told him anything because that's your business, so he only has this negative view of you. I promise I'll fix it."

"No, don't," I say, shaking my head. "He has every right not to like me and hopefully one day I can explain myself and fix it myself."

Tucker smiles as he tangles his fingers with mine. "One day."

I smile back as he pulls into the parking lot of the office beside my car. I go to gather my things, but he doesn't let go of my hand. I look up at him and his eyes are full of concern as he looks at me.

"How's everything at home?"

"It's okay, he's working a lot and then sleeping any other

time. He called today but I handled it."

He nods as he looks down at his lap. "So you're thinking what? Two more weeks?"

"Yeah. Then I'll be gone."

I watch his profile as he takes in a deep breath. "Are you ready?"

I scoff. "Hell no."

He laughs as he leans back against the seat. Looking over at me, he smiles and I instantly smile back. "You're going to be fine. I believe in you."

"It's going to be hard."

"Of course it is, but you're strong, Violet. You got this."

"I'm scared," I admit before looking away.

"I know but I promise, you're going to succeed, I can see the fight in you."

"I hope so." I look over at him and then say, "You've been amazing, Tucker, I don't know how to repay you for all your kindness."

"It's easy," he says with a smile.

"Really? How?"

"Be happy. That's all I want for you."

I want to kiss him so bad that I have to look away before I do it. Looking out the window, I beg my heart to still from the pounding. This man is unbelievable and I want nothing more than to lose myself with him but as I look out in the parking lot, I forget all about my desire as my eyes land on a very familiar car.

I instantly freeze.

"Violet? What's wrong?"

I don't move and watch as Rob slowly shakes his head before speeding out of the parking lot and onto the main road. Oh god. How long had he been sitting there? Why was he here? Oh, my God.

Quickly I grab my things and reach for the door handle but Tucker stops me. "Was that Rob?"

"Yes," I say, scrambling out the car and rushing to my SUV but Tucker stops me again.

"Whoa, whoa, no way. You can't go home," he says.

I pull my arm out of his hand as I say, "I have to, or he will know something is going on. I have to act as if it isn't a big deal. That we went out to dinner with the office or something. Fuck."

I'm shaking and my heart is thrashing wildly in my chest while I feel like I'm going to puke. What am I going to do? Why was he here? Maybe I shouldn't go home but then I know he'll come after Tucker because I was with him last. When Tucker's arms go around me, I close my eyes tight and lean into him as the tears start to slowly fall down my face.

"Come home with me. I'll put you on the first plane out, please don't go there."

"I have to, he saw me with you. He'll know you're a part of this."

"I don't care, Violet, because I *am* a part of this and I'm going to do everything I can to help you."

I slowly pull away and move my hands along my face, wiping away my tears. I have to act as if everything is fine or he's never going to let me leave. I have to protect him. He has done so much for me. I have to do everything I can to make sure he's safe.

"Everything is going to be fine. We didn't do anything wrong and I will tell him that. It's nothing. I'm overreacting," I say, shaking my head. "It's no big deal. I promise. I'll go home and tell him that we all went out to dinner and that I didn't call him because I thought he would be at work."

Tucker eyes me and I know he doesn't want to let me go but slowly his shoulders fall and he looks away. "You'll call me if something happens?"

"Yes, but you can't do anything if it does."

He shakes his head. "Now, Violet—"

"Tucker, you promised."

Letting me go, he threads his fingers through his hair before kicking the side of his tire. Looking back at me with concern and frustration all over his face, he says, "I don't know if I can stand here and let this happen. I can't let him hurt you!"

Slowly taking in a breath, I look away as I say, "I'm sorry, Tucker. You have to let me do this. This is my fight. I don't want you to have to save me. I want to be able to come into your arms free and clear once this is all over. I want to be the woman you will be proud to have on your arm. The one you will love because I love you with all of me, but I can't give you all of me yet."

"I will love you always," he proclaims.

My heart stops and my breath hitch as I look up into this man's face. "You have to let me do this," I stress.

"So what? I'm supposed to watch you get in that car and leave? And just pray you'll come to work tomorrow?"

We stand, staring into each other's eyes for a long time before I whisper, "Yes."

"This is fucking insane," he says turning from me and walking to his car. I watch as he yanks his car door open before looking over at me. "I know you don't want me to save you, Violet, but I don't know if I can just stand by and hope this all works out. You have my heart and I can't let something happen to you. It would break me."

I pause before asking, "You believe in me right?"

"Of course."

"Then believe that I can handle this."

He looks up at the sky and I can tell he is about to lose it. Looking back over at me, pleading with his eyes, he says, "Text me so I know you are okay."

"I will."

"Alright, talk to you soon," he says before he reluctantly gets in the car. I get into my SUV and I know he's watching me leave just like he has for the last three weeks. Once on the road, the calmness I exhibited in front of Tucker is gone and I'm shaking with fear. I tried to be confident and reassure Tucker that I would be fine, but I know Rob and I know he is pissed. I still don't know what he was doing there though. It doesn't make sense because it is nowhere near the hospital or anything else that would bring him to this side of town. It's almost as if he was checking up on me...but I don't understand why? He hasn't spoken to me at all. It's like he has been ignoring my existence for the last three weeks, so why was he checking in on me? Was he looking for Tucker? Was he going to say something to him about my job? He saw us together and I know it was innocent but Rob won't see it that way.

It doesn't take long for me to get home and soon I'm parking the car behind Rob's. I get out and make my way up to the porch before entering the house. The first thing I see is Rob at the counter, a beer in his hand and his face twisted in anger. I lay down my purse, hoping like hell that he can't tell I'm scared shitless. Because I am. So scared that it takes everything out of me to take steps toward the counter and act as if everything is fine in the world.

"Why aren't you at work tonight? I thought you had to work that's why I didn't call to invite you to dinner with the office. It was Ms. Yolanda's birthday."

His eyes are dark. His voice menacing as he says, "I got sent home tonight and I came by the office to pick you up because we needed a new washer but you weren't there and so I waited and waited until finally you pull up with that asshole," he says before coming out from behind the counter. His steps are feral as he stalks toward me. "I thought what the hell is she doing with him? I watched as you laughed and giggled and flirted with him until finally I had enough and had to drive away but then you saw me, and I saw your face. And I knew that you knew. You were caught. You're fucking around on me."

He reaches for me, but I move quickly out of the way, batting his hands away, but I can tell that only makes him madder. His eyes narrow before he goes for me again but this time, I go for the door, reaching for my keys as I pull the door open but he is quicker, slamming me face first into the door. I scream out as he turns me around, and I swing the keys, hard into his face. He yells out, smacking the keys out of my hand before holding me by my throat up against the wall. I try to remember the class. Eyes, throat, groin, anything, but all I am doing is thrashing, trying to get away, which only causes him to squeeze my throat harder, until I stop struggling.

My eyes are clouding with tears as I look up into his threatening eyes. Where I hit him with the keys is a spot and it's bleeding, maybe even bruising. I want to be proud of myself but then I can't be because he still has me in his grips. He is still controlling me, and I can't get away.

"I'm gonna ask you once. Are you fucking him?"

I quickly shake my head. "No, I promise, I'm not."

"I don't believe you," he instantly says, squeezing my neck, making me dizzy.

"I'm not," I cry as I try to gasp for breath.

"Maybe I'll pay him a visit. He's a fucking pretty boy, I'll scare him straight and teach him to stay away from what's mine."

"No," I cry. "Please, nothing is going on. We went to dinner for Ms. Yolanda's birthday."

"SHUT UP!" he screams. I start to swing my fists, hoping to connect with his face. When I do, he growls at me and then his fist comes slamming into my nose. Lights go off, and I feel dizzy as I reach up to cover my face. I can taste the salty, metallic taste of blood as it runs down the back of my throat and over my mouth. He lets go of my throat and I fall to the floor, where he promptly kicks me in the chest, knocking the wind out of me. He then punches me in the back of the head, screaming that I'm nothing but a whore. I try to kick him away but his kicks are harder and when one connects with the middle of my chest, I gasp before completely stopping and balling up.

I give up. I'm fucking giving up.

"Stop fucking fighting me and just take what is coming! You deserve this! You're cheating on me!"

"I am not," I whisper but I doubt he can hear me because he screams, "You are such a whore! How dare you do this to me?"

I only shake my head as my tears and blood mingle on my face. "I'm not doing anything, Rob," I say as I sit up and look up into his face. "Nothing."

"How many times do I have to tell you that you are mine?"

I can't see through my tears so I close my eyes, resting my head on my knees.

"You will listen to me. You will do as I say or I will continue to do what I need to do to make you listen."

I don't say anything; I only wait, until finally, he stomps away. I jump when the door slams and when I look up the room is empty. My face is swelling. I can feel it and I fear that my nose is broken. Tears rush down my face as I just sit there, my face throbbing. Why does this keep happening? I tried to de-escalate the situation but it didn't work. It never works. I tried to fight back but it was no use, I wasn't strong enough. Nothing ever works with this fucking man and I really don't think I can wait two more weeks to get the hell away. I know I have to though. I have to, because if I don't get everything I need and make sure I can keep him away, I'll end up right back here.

And I can't let that happen.

Chapter
TWENTY

"**A**re you okay?"

"No," I answer as I catch the blood from my nose with a cloth. It's hard to hold the phone and keep blood from getting everywhere but somehow I manage as I take in deep breaths.

"What happened?" Tucker asks, and I can hear it in his voice, he's freaking out. But he's also trying to hide his anger from me. It isn't working, though. I take in a shuddering breath as tears sting my eyes. Looking at my reflection, I hate the girl I see. My eyes are swollen, my nose running with blood and there is a cut along my cheek.

"I think he broke my nose," I say before choking on a sob.

"Violet, please," he pleads, "I can't take this anymore. Let me call the cops, let me kicks his ass. No, better yet, let me fucking kill him!"

I close my eyes. "You can't."

"Yes, I can, it's very easy. I take him by his shirt and slam my fists into his face. I hate this guy, I hate what he has done to you. Please let me help. Let me get rid of him, let me help you get away. Please."

"You promised, Tucker," I reminded him.

He pauses for a moment. "Okay, fine. Then please, tell me what I can do, because I'm going crazy here. I'm trying to respect your wishes but, Violet, this is getting out of hand. Either leave him or let me kill him."

"I need only two more weeks," I whisper, "I promise. I'll leave."

"No, leave now or I'm taking matters in my own hands."

I open my eyes and a tear slowly rolls down my face. "You said you believed in me."

"I do."

"Do you really think I want this? Do you think I want to stay? I just need time."

"I understand that but hell, I'll give you the money you need, just leave."

"No, I want to do this myself. I got myself in this mess, I have to get myself out. I just need two more weeks."

"I don't know if I can give you that long. I feel like less of a man for letting this happen to you. It's hurting me. I can't do it much longer."

"I understand that and I'm not asking you to do anything," I say softly. "You don't have to stand beside me."

"Yes, I do. I love you."

Silence comes over the line as my tears continue to roll down my face. "Please leave him," he begs. "Let me pay for it all, let me help you leave."

It would be so easy. Just take his money and run, but I can't. I can't allow him to win. I want to be able to do this on my own. I want to show Rob that I don't fucking need him. I want to come back here in the near future and show him that I can do it all myself. That I'm a strong, smart, beautiful woman who deserves the world. I can do this. I can.

"Give me two more weeks."

"Violet. I don't think I can."

"Please. Just two more weeks. After that, I promise I'll leave."

"It's not that I don't believe you, it's that I am scared for you," he says, his voice full of emotion. "What if he hurts you again? What if he kills you? I think it's best that you just leave without him knowing."

"I plan to, in two weeks."

"Dammit," he whispers, almost so quietly I can't hear him. "I'll give it to you as long as he keeps his hands off you. The first time he touches you, you have to tell me and I need you to leave. Please, do that for me."

I nod even though he can't see me. I plan to completely stay out of his way. "Yes, I can do that."

"Good. Do you want to go into the office? Let me look at your nose?"

I look at my reflection and know that if I go anywhere near Tucker, he'll freak. With good reason of course but still, I need to just stay away. At least until the swelling goes down.

"No, I'm fine."

"It would make me feel better."

"Or it would piss you off," I speculate.

"I'm already pissed so just please come in, I'll meet you there."

I'm about to agree when I remember that Rob isn't working. I look down at the blood soaked rag as my fear grows. I don't know what will happen when he gets back. That is, if he even comes back. I don't know, but fuck, I'm scared. "I can't. Rob might come back."

"Bastard," he says, his voice dripping with acid. "Fine. I'll check on it tomorrow."

"Do you think it's a good idea that I come to work?"

"Yes," he says almost automatically. "I don't want you there unless you have to be. Show him that you aren't scared anymore, that he can't knock you down."

I smile at the mere thought of that. I wish I could exhibit that kind of confidence but I'm not sure I can. "I wish."

"No wishing needed, you can do it. I know you can. I'll see you tomorrow."

I look back up at myself and even with my bloodied nose and swollen face, my smile remains because he is right.

I can do this.

"Yeah, I'll see you tomorrow."

I spent the night in the bathroom.

I know you think that is ridiculous, and I couldn't agree more. When Rob came home, he was drunk and he spent the night drunkenly beating on the door and swearing at me. I don't know how he didn't get in but he didn't, so I spent the night curled up, holding the door closed. When I woke up this morning, he was passed out on the bed so I quickly changed, grabbed my things, and left. I'm at the office an hour before I'm supposed to be but I couldn't risk being around him.

I had to get away.

Cleaning up my mess from yesterday, I do little things until finally my door opens and Tucker comes barreling in. He looks tired as if he hadn't gotten any sleep the night before. His eyes are wide when they set on me and I stand up, my hands out as I say, "It's not as bad as it looks."

It is, but I'm trying to downplay it. I can see the rage building in his eyes. I can see his hands start to shake, and he looks like he's about to track Rob down and beat him to within an inch of his life. Now, as much as I wouldn't mind this and would gladly pay to see it happen, it can't.

"The hell it isn't, Jesus, Violet," he says, coming around my desk before reaching out to softly touch my face. His hands are gentle and slow, tender as he probes my face, feeling along my cheekbones and nose, the light touch of his fingertips giving me gooseflesh. Biting on his lip, he looks up my nose and before saying, "I don't think it's broken, I think he got you more on your cheekbone than your nose. I'm not sure though, there is so much swelling. I want to do an x-ray and then I'll know more."

"Okay," I agree looking up into his beautiful face.

He softly cups my face, running his thumbs along my bruises, his eyes clouded with worry and concern. Leaning forward, he rests his forehead to mine before whispering, "I worried about you all night."

I close my eyes, our breath mingling as I say, "I'm sorry."

Wrapping his arms around me, he holds me close and I let him. I wrap my own arms around his middle, resting my face in the middle of his chest. His lips touch the top of my head and my arms tighten around his waist. When I feel his hands on my face again, I look up, tears gathering in my eyes as he holds my gaze. Leaning down he presses his lips to the spot between my eyes, ever so lightly before pulling back only an inch to look into my tear filled eyes.

"I never want to let go," he whispers. "I never want anything else to ever happen to you."

Again I want to kiss him. Who am I kidding; I always want to kiss him. His lips were made to be devoured by mine and no matter how fucked-up the situation is, I want to get lost in them. But before I can, a door slams and slowly we part because that means that our staff is arriving. Looking down at me with his mouth set in a worried line, he says, "Get the x-ray done as soon as possible, please."

"I will. Hopefully that's Andrea."

"Yeah, hopefully. I'll come check on you in a few."

"Thanks."

"Anytime," he says before reaching out and running his thumb along my bottom lip.

A smile curves my lips causing his to do the same before

he moves away from me and out of my office. Sitting down at my desk, I call up to the front to find that Andrea, our x-ray tech, isn't here yet. Laying my phone back down, I sit back in my chair and let out a long breath. My face hurts and I'm just waiting for Rob to call me. I know it will happen and I dread hearing his voice. Reaching for a file that I need to submit, I start to do just that when my cell phone rings. I glance at the time before reaching for it out of my purse. It is too early to be Rob and when I read the display, I find that it is my mom.

"Hey, Mom."

"Hey, are you okay?"

I look around the office, confused. Why would she ask that? "Yeah, why?"

"Just worried, something feels off this morning. I wasn't sure if it was you or Pilar; I'm going to go check on her after I get off the phone with you."

"Oh, okay," I say, taking in a deep breath. I don't know what I thought she meant by that but it worried me. "How are you?"

"Alright, getting everything figured out with Mom's estate. It's a pain in my ass."

"Yeah," I agree and maybe I should wait a little longer before going home. She sounds stressed out and I hate to add to her stress but if I don't go home where will I go? I can't go to Tucker's, but maybe a shelter? Or maybe I can stay in a hotel? Shit, I don't know. I won't have the money for a hotel and a lawyer but I don't know if I can put my mom through that.

"What's wrong? You're quiet."

"Nothing, just thinking."

"About? Is everything okay?"

"Yeah, Mom, I'm fine."

"No, I can tell something is wrong. Tell me before I fly down there and make you tell me," she said with the authority of a mother.

"Mom, it's nothing. Everything is going to be fine."

I shouldn't have said it like that. My mom catches everything and now is no different. "So it's not now? What's wrong? What do you need?"

I know I have to tell her. I can't just show up and be like 'Hi, I'm moving in!' I need to give her some warning but I know that I can't say I'm coming to stay with her without an explanation. She's going to want to know everything and I can't tell her all that right now. I'm not ready. Or maybe I am but I am scared. Hell, I don't know. I just know I need to tell her something. I need somewhere to go and if she can't take me in, then I need to know that.

"Is the offer for me to come live with you still on the table?"

She pauses. "With or without Rob?"

I swallow loudly before saying, "Without."

"Absolutely," she says quickly. "When are you coming? Are you flying? Or driving? Do you need money?"

"Mom, whoa," I say, completely overwhelmed.

"What? Are you leaving today?"

"No, I don't know, things are a little crazy right now," I say and I can't believe she didn't ask why. "Are you sure? I don't want to add to the stress that you're going through with Grandma's estate and everything."

"Yes, I'm sure, you being with him adds to the stress, Violet. Leaving him will make a lot of my stress go away."

I hate myself for that. I knew she worried about me but it hurts to hear that a situation I hide from her stresses her out. I don't want to do that to my mom. Closing my eyes, I can't believe she hasn't asked yet. I could have sworn that would be the first thing she would ask about. "You don't want to know why I'm leaving him?"

"I don't care why as long as you leave. It's about time, is all I have to say. Do you need money?" she asks again.

I wouldn't tell her yes even if I did. I can't take anything from her. "No, Mom, I don't. I'm still figuring things out."

"There is nothing to figure out, leave everything behind

and come home."

"I can't, not yet."

She doesn't say anything as I slowly work my lip. I'm still waiting for all the questions, for her to want to know what Rob has done to me, but they never come. Instead, she says, "I am here when you need me. I always will be. I want to remind you, though, to trust your heart and no matter how much you think you need to stay there for a certain amount of time, know that your heart knows best. When it's time to go, go. Don't worry about anything else. We'll worry about all that when you get here. I love you, Violet. So much."

Tears sting my eyes as I swallow past the lump in my throat. "I love you more, Mom."

"Call me as soon as you know when you'll be here."

"I will."

"Okay, I'll let you go, I'm still gonna go check on Pilar, but Violet?"

"Yeah, Mom?"

"I'm so proud of you for leaving him, for getting past your fears."

I choke on a sob and all I can do is nod, knowing that no words are able to leave my lips.

"Alright baby, talk to you soon, bye."

"Bye," I manage to say before I end the call, set the phone down, and allow my sob to escape. Everyone wants to help me and instead of reaching out and getting the help, I've hid it all. I don't understand why I've let this happen but I can't dwell on that. I have to look forward because I'm about to take back my life. I don't have time to cry the way I want before the phone dings and Ms. Yolanda's voice is filling my office.

"Violet, Andrea is here and ready for you."

I clear my throat before answering, "Okay, thank you."

"No problem."

When the line goes dead, I sit back in my seat, wiping my face while being careful around my nose and cheeks. Taking a mirror out my desk, I check my face, hoping it's clear of tears but when I see myself all I want is to cry again. It's going to be hell walking through this office and into the x-ray room. I have to pass everyone to get there and I'm scared to go out there and let them see me. I know that they don't know anything about my struggles but I don't want the questions. I plan on lying but what if they all suspect that and think that I'm weak? I know it doesn't matter what they think but it scares me. I've spent the last three years of my life trying to put on a show and I'm tired. I want out. I need out.

I wait another minute, looking at myself, and I wish like hell I could see the girl I used to love and know. I know she is in there somewhere. Behind the bruises, behind the broken face and watery eyes, but all I see is a woman who is scared. A woman who has allowed a man to use her as a punching bag and allowed him to completely control everything and I hate her. I don't want to be that woman and I know I can't let him win. I can't keep being so scared. I don't want to do this anymore. I want to be strong. I want to be the woman my mom is proud of and also the woman who is worthy of a man like Tucker. Sitting here, crying and feeling sorry for myself, is not going to do that. I have to get up and I have to truck on.

Taking in a deep breath, I stand up, running my hands down my skirt and shirt to make it straight. I slowly walk to my door, my heart pounding, my stomach churning but I ignore it all. I can do this. When I reach for the handle, I let out a breath as I repeat those words again:

I can do this.

My nose is broken.

After getting a couple shots in my face and having it reset, I go home early and sleep most of the day away and well into the night. I'm not sure where Rob is, but I don't care. My face is aching and I need to sleep. I wake up around four a.m. because my face was hurting so damn bad. Tears cloud my eyes as I sit up and look at the clock beside my bed. I groan because I'm not supposed to be up for another two hours. Stumbling out of the bed and to the kitchen, I grab some aspirin before popping two with some water. When I turn to go back to my room, I let out an ear-deafening scream.

Rob is standing in the middle of the living room watching me, the whole room is black except for the light on the counter. With a bored look, he says, "What the hell?"

"You scared me. I thought you were at work."

"I got sent home early again. The damn charge nurse has it out for me, she's changed my whole damn schedule. I don't even work four twelves anymore. I work every night because we need someone to work overtime. It's fucking stupid," he says walking past me to get something out of the fridge. He acts like it's just another morning. As if he didn't break my nose two nights ago. I don't say anything else and start walking toward my room but then he says, "You went to work yesterday?"

I look back at him and nod. "Yeah."

He eyes me curiously, carefully. "With your face like that?"

"Yeah."

I try to sound confident and unaffected by him but I'm not sure if it works. He is annoyed, though, and that makes me nervous. I'm supposed to be staying out of his way, not pissing him off.

"Did that asshole doctor say something? 'Cause when I see him at the hospital, he is a jackass to me. I'm pretty sure he's the reason the charge nurse hates me. They're all buddy buddy."

I would roll my eyes but I'm pretty sure that would hurt plus not help this situation. With a shrug of my shoulders, I say, "That's because he doesn't like you, but I don't care about any of that. I had to go to work so I did. You keep bitching about money, so I don't know what you want."

"I want your boss to leave me the fuck alone."

I shake my head. "I gotta go to work in a couple hours, I need to sleep this headache away."

His eyes narrow but I ignore them and turn to go back down the hall to my room. To my surprise he doesn't say anything else and once there, I shut the door and lock it before getting back in my bed. Reaching for my phone, I send a text to Tucker.

Me: Are you sleeping? Or working out?

I know he wakes up early to work out and like I thought, it only takes a second before a text comes back.

Tucker: Just woke up, you okay?

Me: Yeah. He came home early.

Tucker: Is he bothering you?

Me: No. I'm in my room, I just wanted to talk I guess. Sorry if I'm bothering you.

Tucker: Not at all. I was thinking about you.

I can't help the grin that spreads across my stiff face or the butterflies that take flight all at once in my stomach.

Me: He is surprised I went to work.

Tucker: Good. He should be worried.

Me: Yeah. He also says that you are the reason his schedule is all messed up. Any reason why he would say that?

When his response takes a while to get there, I know he is lying.

> *Tucker: Nope, not at all.*

> *Me: Liar.*

> *Tucker: I have no clue what you mean.*

> *Me: You are trying to keep him away from me.*

I'm not mad. How can I be? He found a loophole around my request.

> *Tucker: Yup and I'm not apologizing for it.*

I shake my head as I type back.

> *Me: You don't have to.*

> *Tucker: Good…enough about him. Are we going to the meeting tonight?*

I pause, reading his words over and over again. If I show up with my face like this, there is no way I could just sit there. I'd have to talk and you know what, maybe it's time I did. I have to try, I have to believe in myself like my mom and Tucker do. I have to be strong.

> *Me: Yeah, but I'm pretty sure I'll have to say something. I can't just sit there. They'll know something is up.*
> Tucker: Yeah, I'll go in with you if you want.

He is amazing, isn't he?

> *Me: I'm gonna try to do it myself.*

Tucker: You can do it.

Tears cloud my vision as I type back.

Me: I hope so.

Tucker: I know you can. You got this.

Do I?

Nope. No, I don't. Not even in the least. Oh, I am fucked. Everyone is staring at me. My palms are clammy and my heart is beating out of control. I want to run. I want to hide. I don't want to be here but I'm not moving. Instead, I'm scanning the circle, watching as everyone watches me.

When I look at Marci, I swallow loudly as she says, "I'm glad you have been coming back, but maybe today you'd like to tell us what happened to your face. Or maybe even your name. We're here for you. You understand that, right? Nothing ever leaves this room. I can promise you that."

I look down, picking at my nails. I start to say my name, just my name, but it doesn't come out. I don't understand that because I know my own flipping name, but it isn't coming out. When I look up, everyone is watching me and I feel like I can't breathe. Tears cloud my eyes and I can't help but think what the hell am I doing? If I can't even speak to them, how am I ever going to leave this part of my life behind me? How am I ever going to get my life back if I can't get the help I need? I don't know, but I can't do this. I feel like I'm about to have a panic attack and I know I have to get out of here. I shake my head and I'm about to run but as I go to get up, a hand comes down on my shoulder.

I look up to see Tucker smiling down at me. "You can do

this," he whispers.

My breathing hitches and a tear slowly roll down my cheek as I shake my head. "I can't."

He reaches down, slowly catching my tear before nodding and saying, "You can. I believe in you."

"We're here to help you," Marci says but I can't stop looking into Tucker's eyes. His eyes are full of love and concern for me while urging me on and I want to believe his words. I want to be strong.

I want my life back.

Looking back at Marci, I clear my throat as Tucker softly squeezes my shoulders. Closing my eyes, I slowly repeat the words that surprisingly help me.

I can do this.

"My name is Violet and-" I pause as a large smile appears on Marci's face, urging me on. When I look around, everyone is smiling at me, waiting for me to go on, but I'm scared. I close my eyes and take in a deep breath before opening them again. I don't know what I was expecting but everyone is still watching me, smiles on their faces. And when I look up, Tucker is still there, smiling and giving me the strength I need. He believes in me. He loves me. He knows I can do this and I can, because I believe in myself too. I want to love myself the way he loves me and the only way that can happen is if I heal.

Looking back at Marci, I clear my throat again and wipe my face. She is waiting for me to finish and after taking in one more long breath, I say, "I have been in an abusive relationship with my husband for three years and I am ready to leave. I am ready to get my life back—"

I pause and look up at Tucker. "I'm ready to be happy."

Chapter
TWENTY-ONE

I couldn't get through my whole story without crying.

I mean, really who could go through what I have been through without crying? I thought telling Tucker about everything was amazing and perfect but opening myself up to these women was really what I needed. Each one of them listened and cried and I know that each of them is here for me.

With Tucker still close to my side, tears drip down my face as I look up at Marci and take in a deep breath. "I only need another week and then I'm gone. As much as I would love to leave now, I need one more paycheck. I need to be able to support myself."

Marci nods as Tammy asks, "But can't you borrow the money from your family or maybe even him?"

I look at over at Tucker and shake my head. "I got myself into this mess; I need to get myself out of it."

"I understand that completely, but sometimes you need to lean on someone and it's obvious that this man wants to help you. With everything you have told us, I truly believe the only reason you are here is because of him," Marci says.

I wipe away my tears and nod and offer a smile. "You're right but I can't ask him for anything else. He has done so much for me plus I wouldn't feel right taking a hand out."

When Tucker squeezes my hand, and I look over at him, leaning into him, into his strength. "It wouldn't be a hand out though because I want to help you. I want you to get away and I want you to one day be ready to love me back, Violet. I'd do anything for you, don't you understand that?"

I blink, my chest rising and falling while our gazes are locked. Marci breaks our silent reverie. "The thing is, you're making excuses for why you can't leave. It is always going to be give me one more week, oh, I only need one more, because in your head you're too scared to leave. Your fear of your husband and the fear of the unknown is what is keeping you in that house."

Ann Marie raises her hand and everyone looks over at her. She is holding her sweet baby in her arms and I know it hasn't been that long since she left her husband but she looks better. Her eyes aren't so dark and she isn't working her lip nervously. Instead, she is smiling, holding her baby close as she looks at me.

"I left with two hundred and fifty dollars. It has only been thirteen days and I am still scared out of my mind. I wasn't sure how I was going to get back home and when I shared that last week, after the meeting Rena offered to pay my way to Germany."

Everyone's eyes cut to Rena and she just smiles as she looks down at her hands while Ann Marie goes on. "I refused to take it but then he found me and I realized I can't do this on my own and I can't bring my parents into it, so I took the money and I'm leaving Saturday."

"That's wonderful. We'll miss you, but that's great. That was very generous of you, Rena," Marci says with a bright grin on her face.

"I am hoping that helping her will make me save myself. We can't keep doing this. We all need our lives back. I hope that you realize that," Rena stresses, her eyes on me. "This man wants to help you. Take the help."

"We all want the same thing here, Violet. We want you to get away and be happy like you want, but I'm telling you, you're never going to leave if you keep waiting until you're ready. Because, honestly, you'll never be ready. You have to just go. You have to do this. You're ready in my eyes. If you weren't you wouldn't be here. You wouldn't have been strong enough to share your story. No, you'd be sitting there, staring at us all. This is the time. Go. And don't look back."

Tears roll down my cheeks as I look down at my lap where little dark spots are all over my jeans from my tears. I'm torn between what's right and my own fears. Do I believe these people? Do I take the chance and Tucker's help and run like hell? Or do I plan? And I can't help but wonder if Marci is right? Have I been using the excuse of saving money as my crutch? I have all the people who want to help me, my mom and Tucker, and I think my fear has been pushing them away. If I don't have the money, I can't leave and that means he has won.

What am I doing?

I mean, what do I want? That is the real question.

It doesn't take long for the answer to come. I want my life back.

Closing my eyes, I whisper to myself, "I can do this."

When I feel a pair of arms that I know belong to Tucker come around me, I open my eyes and look into his. "Yes, you can."

"I don't know if I can do this."

Tucker looks over at me from the driver's seat. We're sitting in the parking lot of the office and we have been for the last hour. Nothing has been said; we have only been holding hands like teenagers, still thinking about all that went on at the meeting. After a tearful goodbye to the women who I will always be indebted to, I promised that I wouldn't see them again because I was leaving. But now that I am away from them, I am scared that I can't do it.

I am just so scared.

Turning in his seat, he looks as me as he holds my small hands in his large one, rubbing his thumb along the back of my hands. "Tell me something."

"Okay?"

"You said you want to be happy."

I nod. "Yes, I do."

"Are you happy with him?"

"No," I say quickly, with a disgusted look on my face. What kind of question is this?

"Okay, what would make you happy?"

I still don't understand his questioning, but I decide to play along. "To leave and one day be with you."

He nods, his eyes boring into mine as he says, "Then do it and let me be there with you every step of the way."

"But Tucker-"

"No, no 'but Tucker' anything. You want something, then you do it, Violet. You are strong. You can do this. Don't let him hold you back; don't let him control your life anymore. Take it all back and leave."

I shake my head but before I can say anything, he says, "I believe in you. Your mom believes in you and so does that group of women from the meeting."

Shouldn't I believe in myself if everyone else does? It should be easy but every time I play it all out in my head, all I see is me failing. I'll get to Colorado and not have the money for a divorce or he'll come after me. He'll find me and kill me.

Or worse, he'll hurt my mom. I can't help but think that maybe this is what I'm supposed to do. Just be with Rob but when I look at Tucker, I instantly know that whole thought is stupid because Tucker is the man who I am meant to be with one day. Rob is the hurdle I have to get over to get to what I really want.

I have to believe in myself. I have to believe I can do this.

And I can.

Can't I?

"What if I fail?" I ask as my tears spill over and run down my face. "What if I get to Colorado and he comes after me?"

"Won't happen because we are going to make sure you're safe. I am going to get the best lawyer and I swear to you, no harm will ever come your way."

"He can't know you are helping me," I stress and his hand comes up to cup my face as his eyes soften.

"He won't. No one will know. Just let me help you. Say the word and I swear to you, I will help you find happiness."

I reach up and put my hand on his. "My happiness is right in front of me."

His eyes soften as he leans his head against mine. "Then fight. Take back your life, and when you're ready, I'll be here. Just fight."

I blink back my tears and slowly nod my head. "Okay."

He lets out a breath, his face relaxing in relief before he presses his lips to mine. I close my eyes tight as my arms come around his neck, pulling him closer. When he pulls back, I want to whimper, but he pulls completely away and takes in a deep breath.

"We can't do this. Not yet. I need you away from him, Violet. The next time I kiss you, I want you to be mine, and I want you to love yourself and your life."

My lip quivers as I slowly nod, pulling away more. Looking into his eyes I know what I have to do. If I want this man, if I want my happiness, I have to fight. I have to take back my life.

I can do it.

Reaching for the door, I push it open but then Tucker stops me by grabbing my arm. "What are you doing?"

"Going to go get my stuff. I'll call you in a few, it shouldn't take me long. Rob should be a work, I should be able to get away just fine."

"I'm coming with you," he says, sitting back in his seat.

"No, I told you, Rob can't know."

"He's at work," he points out.

"But what if he comes home? Since someone has been messing with his schedule, I never know when he will be gone."

Tucker ignores my comment and says, "What if he does come home?"

I look away because I don't know the answer. I mean what am I going to do? Do I just run? Do I tell him the truth? That I am leaving his sorry ass? I don't know but I know I have to do this. I am ready. I need this. Pushing the door open, I jump out before he can stop me.

Bending down so I can see him, I say, "He won't be. I'll call you in a few."

"Hurry," is all he says before I shut the door and jog to my SUV. Once there, I jump in, throw my purse into the other seat, and start the engine. My heart is erratic in my chest. My palms are dripping with sweat and I am shaking. My breathing is labored but not from me jogging—from my fear. I am scared out of my mind but I have to do this.

I can do this.

I'm not folding anything. I am frantically stuffing all my clothes and belongings into my two bags. I dump my jewelry box of all my grandmother's jewelry on top of my clothes and reach for the next thing, stuffing as fast as I can. When I drop my brush, I scream. I am freaking out and I swear, I feel like he is going to walk through that door at any moment. It has me on edge. Rushing through the house, I take my pictures off the walls. I take my grandma's cookbooks and even her cast iron skillet but I leave mine behind because they are replaceable. Running back to my room, I stuff everything in the bags and then do one final walkthrough. I'm pretty sure I have everything.

Looking around the room, I wonder if I'll miss it all. I wonder if I'll think of this place that I tried to make into a home. Will I miss my life here? Will I ever want to come back? The answer is plain and simple. No fucking way. I won't miss a damn thing about this place and I sure as hell won't miss the man that has kept me here. I swear, I think the stupidest stuff sometimes. Grabbing my bags, I head down the hall and into the living room. I lay down my bags and reach for my purse, placing it on my forearm, before picking them back up to go but before I can even take one step, he is there, his eyes wide as he looks me up and down.

"Going somewhere?"

The hairs on my arms stand to attention as my hands to shake. I drop my bags and lick my lips because my mouth has gone dry. My whole body feels like it's frozen and I don't know what to do. I don't know what to say. Slowly my hand goes into my pocket for my phone, but it's not there. It's in my purse. The same purse I dropped down with my bags. Fuck. I glance down to see how far it is but before I can even grab it, Rob kicks it away before putting his body in front of me, looking down at me with a look that could kill.

As I look up in his cold dark eyes, I can't believe I ever loved this man. I mean yes, he is a very good-looking man but how did I let that distract me? Why did I allow him to completely take over and control me entirely? I let him own me. I let this happen. He was such a good guy to me back then. And now? I am so fucking scared I feel like I'm about to have a panic attack. My heart is going nuts in my chest. My hands are shaking so bad that it almost hurts. I am terrified. Completely terrified of this man.

But I can get away. He is not my enemy right now. No, it's my fear and I can overcome all that. I can do this. Nothing else is holding me back from obtaining my happiness. Raising my chin, I look up at him and with all the strength I have, I say, "I'm leaving."

His head cocks to the side. "You are?"

"Yes. I want a divorce. I'm tired of the way you treat me and the things you have done to me."

He scoffs shaking his head. "Where are you going to go?"

"It doesn't matter to you. My lawyer will be in contact."

"Lawyer, huh? Where did you get the money for that?"

"Nothing you need to worry about," I say but I fear my confidence is wavering. He is getting closer, his fist balling up, and I swear I see nothing but hatred in his eyes. "Now, if you will please move, I'd like to leave."

He laughs and before I can even move or get out of the way, he takes a hold of my shoulders, his fingers biting into my skin.

"Stop!" I yell, trying to get out of his grip but he has me. He doesn't have my legs though.

"Let me tell you something—"

"No! FUCK YOU!" I scream, kicking my knee up and getting him in the groin. He lets me go, backing away as he holds himself, groaning out as I quickly grab my bags and turn back to him. "There is a part of me I can't get back. You took it and ruined that part of me but let me tell you something, you piece of shit, I may never be the same but you won't take anything else from me. I am taking back my life and there is nothing you can do about it. I hate you and you will never fucking hurt me again."

I turn and start for the door but suddenly he has me by my ankle, pulling me hard and causing me to fall face first onto my bags. I scream out, kicking my legs, hoping that one of my heels will hurt him but soon he is hovering over me. I cry out as he takes me by my hair, bending it back so he can look at my face.

"You aren't going anywhere," he said, his voice thick and dripping with menace. He lets go of my hair before slamming his hand to the back of my head. I scramble away, until I am up against the wall but he is right there, trying to grab me. I shield myself, while I try to kick him but then he kicks me in the gut, knocking the air out of me. Gasping for breath, I block my face as I slide up the wall so I can try to run but it's no use. His hand is around my neck within seconds, squeezing, and I can't breathe. I pull at his hands, I even smack his arms but it doesn't work. He is squeezing and I swear to God he is going to kill me. When I slam my fist against his face, his eyes go wide before he slams his fist into my face, getting me in my right eye. Lights go off and my face feels like it has exploded and I can't see to focus right.

"You are mine," he says, spitting in my face.

I am squirming, trying to get out of his grab but something isn't working, he is holding me in a way that I can't get away. I am at his mercy but then my hand falls onto something hard and I know it's his grandmother's ugly vase. Getting a grip on it, I raise it up and his eyes go wide in surprise but before he can move or even get out of the way, I slam it against the side of his head causing it to shatter. He falls to the ground and I drop the piece of the vase I am holding as my tears gush down my cheeks. He isn't moving. I killed him. Oh my God.

"Oh fuck," I say as I bend over to look at him. I fully expect him to pop up and hit me but he's out cold. His is breathing steady and that's all I need to know, as much as I want this man dead and out of my life, I can't go to jail. That's not the place I want to be at. I want to be with Tucker.

Quickly I rush to my bags but it's hard. I am stumbling because my eye is swelling and my head is aching but I make it and pick everything up. Going to the door, I open it and look back at where Rob is passed out on the floor.

"I belong to no one but myself."

Without another look back, I leave and promise to never come back.

Chapter
TWENTY-TWO

"What the hell happened to you?"
I close the SUV door and move my hair out of my face before looking up at Tucker. He is standing in the doorway of his condo with shock all over his face. He is wearing just a pair of sweats and a thin tee. His hair looks like he has been running his fingers through it the whole time I've been gone. Climbing up the steps, I stop in front of him and bite into my lip to hold back my sob. My face is aching. I can only see him through one eye and I'm afraid that Rob might have re-broken my nose. It feels off. I don't know, but I left.

I fucking left him.

I don't even think I could describe what I am feeling right now. I feel so free. As if everything that was holding me down is gone and now I have the world at my fingertips. I know once I see the Tennessee state sign in my rearview mirror, I'll feel even more advantageous. I am ready to rebuild my life and heal. I'm taking back my life and I couldn't be more excited about it.

Reaching out, I wrap my arms around Tucker's waist and softly lay my head against his chest as I take in a deep breath.

"I left," I whispered.

His arms come around me, holding me tightly but carefully as his lips dust the top of my head. "I'm so proud of you, but can you explain to me about your eye?"

"He showed up, but I got away. I left. I did it. I left him," I say, my voice hoarse from my crying and probably from Rob choking me.

Tucker's arms tighten around me as his lips rest on my neck. "I'm so proud of you. So proud."

I squeeze my eyes shut, taking in his masculine scent but I know I have to go. I'm not sure if Rob knows where Tucker lives but he could even drive by and see my SUV. Tucker lives on the main road, and I can't chance Rob seeing me with him.

"I never want to leave your arms, Tucker, but I have to. I have to go."

He pulls back, looking down at me as he nods. "Okay, let me grab my wallet."

He lets go of me, walking back into his condo as I ask, "What? Huh?"

"I'm coming with you," he proclaims. He says it like I should have known that but doesn't he know that he can't do that?

"No, I have to go by myself. I don't want anyone in my hometown to see you. I don't want anyone to know that you are a part of this."

He smiles. "I know I shouldn't be offended that you don't want to show me off, but that's fine. You can drop me off at the airport in Denver before you go to Loveland. No one will know, sweetheart. I can't let you drive nineteen hours by yourself and plus, if I'm not going to see you for a long time, I am going to cherish the little time I have with you."

I bite into my lip because I want to say yes, come with

me but I know he can't. He needs to stay here, but without realizing it, I'm nodding. "Okay, let's go."

As I go to my SUV, I hear him locking up and then he has fallen in step with me and reaches for my keys.

"Let me drive. We'll stop and get some peas for your face."

I agree because I really shouldn't be driving when I can't see out of one eye. Going around the SUV, I jump in as he starts the engine and then we're off. We ride in silence and, like always, my hand finds his before resting in his lap. When he pulls into the parking lot for the local Publix, I wait in the car as he goes in. It only takes a few minutes before he is back and we're back on the road, heading out of town. I don't think my heart has slowed down in speed since I went back home to pack. I still can't believe I did it. For so long I stayed and thought that it was what I supposed to do but that all changed when Tucker walked into my life. I glance over at him and smile.

I love this man. So much. And I think I always will.

I know I need to heal, I know I need time to myself, but I can't help but want to say fuck it all and ask him to stay. I want to start a life with him now. I want to love him for the rest of my life and never live another day without him. I've spent so long in such a dark place, that I want nothing more than to live in the light with this beautiful man.

"Say goodbye to Tennessee," he says and he smiles when he finds me looking at me. I turn back before looking out at the window, just in time to see the state sign. As I watch it pass by, a single tear rolls down my face as the biggest grin imaginable curves my lips.

"I did it."

"You did."

I look over at him. "I couldn't have done it without you."

Tucker smiles and shakes his head. "I did nothing more than be here for you."

"That's all I needed."

"Good because I will always be here for you."

"Hey, wake up sweetheart."

I open my eyes and look over into my savior's eyes. He smiles, moving a piece of hair out of my eyes before kissing my nose. I smile as I stretch and then I remember everything that happened. I don't know why I thought it was all a dream because if it hadn't have happened, I wouldn't be staring into the eyes of the most amazing man in the world. No, I'd be on the floor, bleeding and crying under Rob's fist. Tearing my eyes from his, I look at the clock and I am stunned. I don't know how Tucker drove seventeen hours straight but he did. I fell asleep somewhere between Missouri and Kansas and I'm not really sure where we are now.

"Where are we?"

"Aurora. I figured we'd get a hotel room and sleep a little before you take me to the airport later on tonight. I couldn't get a flight until eleven tonight."

"Oh, why didn't you wake me?" I ask sitting up.

"You needed to rest," he says before throwing open the door and getting out. I grab my purse before doing the same and following him to the door of our room. I always liked the hotels like this. No need to walk all the way to your car from nine stories up, nope, the car is right outside the door. When the door opens, Tucker waits for me to pass and then he follows me in, shutting the door behind us as I lay down my purse. "I know it's not much but I didn't want to go anywhere anyone would see us."

I smile over at him. "Thank you."

"Anytime, now go freshen up and you should probably call your mom and tell her you're coming."

I nod in agreement. "Yeah. I need to use the bathroom first."

"Okay," he says with a smile before falling on top of the

bed and pulling his phone out of his pocket. I watch him for only a second before turning and going into the bathroom. After cleaning up and using the bathroom, I head back out and go straight for my purse. When I turn it on, I realize that I have twenty missed calls from my mom and even more from Rob. There are even texts and when I open them, I cringe from all the angry texts, demanding that I answer his calls and texts.

"Crap," I mutter as I read each one.

"What?"

I look up to see that he is coming toward me. I hold out the phone and let Tucker see each message. Each one so mean and hateful that it gives me chills. When we get to the last one, I gasp.

> *Rob: I will find you and I will kill you for what you have done, you stupid cunt.*

I bite into my lip nervously before looking up at Tucker. He looks cool as a cucumber as he says, "Okay, no worries. He won't find you, sweetheart. I am going to take your phone back with me. We will stop in Denver and get you a new phone. I'm going to show this to my lawyer and get a restraining order filed. This will help the divorce proceedings. Don't worry though, everything is fine."

He wraps his arms around me. "You're safe, baby. Don't worry."

"I'm scared," I whispered as I reread the message.

"Don't be. I will make sure you're safe. Call your mom, I think y'all might need to move."

I nod. He's right. "I think my mom inherited my great grandpa's old house in Sterling. Maybe I can ask her if we can go there."

"Sounds good. Call her, and I'm going to call my lawyer."

"Okay. Thank you."

He smiles before pressing his lips to my forehead. "Anything for you."

When he pulls away and brings out his phone I want to slap it away and ask him to hold me. I know that I can't though. I need to call my mom. Getting out of my messages I go to my dialer and call my mom. She answers on the first ring.

"Oh, thank the sweet, gracious Lord, Violet, I thought he found you," she cries into the phone. "Are you okay, baby?"

"Yes, Mom. I'm a little bruised but I'm fine."

"Oh, thank you, Jesus, I've been so worried. Rob called cussing and blaming me for you leaving. He asked if you were here, he even sent his stupid friend from the hospital over here to check. I hate that asshole. Where are you?"

He sent someone to look for me? Dammit. "I'm so sorry, Mom. I'm in Aurora right now. I'll be home later on tonight and then we need to leave. Just in case."

"We will discuss that when you get here. Maybe we can go stay at the farm for a bit but why tonight? Why not now? Aurora is only an hour away."

I pause. Shit? What am I going to say? I glance up at Tucker and he smiles. "I have to drop someone off to the airport."

"Who?" she ask, her voice crazed. I know she is scared and worry. I am too but I can't ever tell her about Tucker. Not until everything is settled. I know my mom wouldn't ever rat me out but just in case Rob ever finds out that I am with her, I don't ever want Tucker's name to come up.

"A friend. Someone who I can't tell you about yet, but they are the reason I got out. They have helped me tremendously."

My mom pauses. "Tell this person that I owe them everything and that I hope I can meet them one day. Call me when you are on the way."

"I will. Can you start packing?"

"Absolutely. Be careful."

"I will. Call me if something happens. Love you."

"I will, love you more."

I hang up the phone and take in a deep breath. I knew this

would happen. See, this is why I needed more time but then I can honestly say I am glad I am away from him. Things may be a little crazy but I'll get them sorted. I'm going to be okay.

"Everything okay?"

I look over at Tucker and shrug my shoulders. "He sent someone to my mom's house. He's been threatening her and blaming her for what is going on."

He nods as he asks, "Is she willing to move? Maybe you should go straight to the other house."

"She is willing. She's going to start packing so we can go once I am there. I think I'm going to be okay."

He comes toward me and pulls me into him, sheltering me in his thick arms and broad chest. I go willingly, wrapping my arms around his waist as he envelops me in a tight hug where I feel completely safe.

"You will be. Maybe not today or even tomorrow, but soon. Soon you will be okay. Maybe even better than okay."

"Maybe," I say against his chest. "Once we can be together."

He pulls back, cupping my chin in his hands before nodding. His eyes bore into mine as he slowly and hypnotically runs his thumb along my jawline. I want nothing more than to go up on my tiptoes and press my lips to him but if I did, I would be at his complete mercy. I wouldn't stop and I'm not sure if that is something we should be doing. It's already going to be hard to walk away from him without begging him to stay with me, and giving into my desire will make it worse. But something is about to happen. I can feel it deep in the pit of my stomach, I can see it in his eyes. They're the warm color that always curls my toes. He keeps looking at my mouth, and I need to pull away but I can't. I can't move and then to my complete delight, his mouth comes crashing into mine.

Lifting me up into his arms, he devours my mouth, kissing me like it's the last time he'll ever taste my lips and shit, it is. I won't have this moment again for a long time so I'm going to make it worth it. Wrapping my arms around his neck, I move my tongue with his, biting and teasing as we get lost in our need for each other. When he pulls away, I whimper, trying to kiss him again but he presses his finger to my lips and whispers, "I know I said the next time I kiss you, you had to be completely mine, but I don't think I can leave you without reminding you of what you'll have once we can be together. Let me make love to you."

I don't even nod or answer for that matter, I just press my lips to his, running my fingers through his hair as he slowly lays me down in the bed. We slowly kiss and tease each other and my body is trembling with desire. Reaching for the hem of his shirt, I pull it up, revealing the exquisite body I never want to stop loving, touching. I reach up, kissing his chest above his heart before running my hands down his torso to the top of his sweats. He kisses down my throat as my hands slide into his sweats, gripping his butt. His mouth is hot against my skin and I gasp as he pulls my shirt up, kissing down the valley of my breasts.

Sitting up some, he removes the rest of my shirt before pulling my jeans down, too, along with my panties. I'm bare in front of him except for the yellow lace bra I am wearing. We're both breathing heavy and my eyes cloud with the lust for this man. When his eyes meet mine, I want to cry from the love I see in his eyes. God, he is hell on my heart. Closing my eyes when his lips met mine, he moves his body against mine, his hard length against my warm center.

Reaching up, I cup his face, kissing him as I slowly rub myself against him. His breath is choppy against my mouth, his hands shaking against my torso and I never want to leave this bed ever again. Tearing his mouth from mine, he kisses down my neck and my breasts, pulling my bra cups down to suck and bite my nipples in the most delectable way. Arching my body so I'm closer, he continues to consume my breasts. I am in heaven. Complete and utter heaven.

Replacing his mouth with his hand, he kisses down my

belly and my breathing hitches because I know what he is about to do. Kissing my hip bones, he runs his tongue down my left thigh as he pushes my right leg open so he has better access. I close my eyes tighter, my breathing so erratic that I'm gasping for air. His breath teases my soft, wet center, and I cry out. I arch up to meet his mouth, but he holds me down and when I look, he is smirking at me. The anticipation is killing me. I want to scream. I want to thrash. I just want this man, now.

"Now," I cry out. "Please." I am basically begging, and I am not one bit ashamed of it.

His eyes are dark as he nods and slowly lowers his mouth to me. I cry out as his tongue draws figure eights around my taut clit. My body is trembling and I swear everything feels so much different now. I feel like I am able to let go, that nothing can ever come between us. When he enters a finger in me, my legs start to shake as he continues to flick his tongue against my clit. My orgasm is building, my heart is pounding, and I feel like I can't breathe. Everything is so perfect.

Thrashing beneath his mouth, I cry out and then come undone. As I ride the most glorious release of my life, he softly kisses my thighs and my pussy before slowly trailing up my body. Giving love to my breast, he continues his journey until he is hovering over me, his eyes boring into mine.

"I love the way you taste."

Oh, come on, seriously? I think I just came again. I try to say something but my mouth is dry and I am still trying to catch my breath. He presses his lips to mine before rolling off of me. I watch as he pulls his sweats down, taking his wallet out for a condom. His eyes are on me as he slowly slides the condom down his engorged flesh. I want him. I do. But for some reason, I am nervous.

I know it worked last time but what if it doesn't this time? I want the connection. I want him inside me. As he crawls over me, he brings my legs up, hanging them over his arms, opening me even further for him. Looking up from where he is about to enter me, he looks into my eyes. A smile rests on his lips, but I think he sees that I'm nervous because his smile falters.

"I'll go slowly."

I nod and, as gently and slowly as he can, he tries to enter me but it isn't an easy fit. I want to cry but before my eyes can even fill with tears, his lips are hovering mine and he says, "Relax, baby, I won't hurt you."

And I know he won't. Closing my eyes, I take in a deep breath. He then covers my mouth with his own, kissing and teasing me as he slowly slides into me. When he is fully inside me, I groan out as my body squeezes his.

"There we go, that's right, baby. God, you're so perfect."

I am at the mercy of this man. He has my heart, my body and soul, and I don't ever want this to end. Opening my eyes, he is watching me with a satisfied smile on his face. Kissing my lips softly, he pulls away and then starts a rhythm that has both of us crying out in pleasure. His fingers dig into my thighs as his rhythm starts to pick up. I can feel that he is almost there and so am I. Dropping my legs, he takes my hips in his strong hands and angles me in the perfect position that has me coming in a matter of seconds. He comes quickly after I do before collapsing against my body.

Chest to chest, we both gasp for breath as I slowly run my fingers up and down his back while his face is in the nook of my neck. Holding himself up on his forearms, he looks down at me and I smile up at him. I want to say so many things. I want to beg him never to leave me. I want to thank him for changing my life completely. But before I can even say anything, his lips are on mine, moving ever so slowly as if he is savoring me. I know I'm savoring him, that's for sure, how could I not? When he rolls off me and gathers me in his arms, I close my eyes as my face rests on his strong, toned chest.

"If it's okay with you, I want to hold you until we have to leave."

This moment is everything I want, but it's bittersweet. Tears cloud my eyes and then they slowly roll down cheeks before gathering on his chest. He doesn't say anything; he doesn't even ask why I'm crying. I think he knows why. I think he is thinking the same thing I am:

How are we going to say goodbye to each other?

After picking me up a new cell phone and then taking pictures of my face for his lawyer, Tucker and I stand in front of the security checkpoint of the Denver airport. We stand in each other's arms, looking into each other's eyes as people move around us like this isn't the saddest moment of my life. Tears are making it hard to see his beautiful face. My heart feels like it's breaking because I don't want to say goodbye. I am scared. I'm sad and I don't know how I am going to watch him leave. I know this is for the best. I know that I have to protect him; I have to remember that I can't be with him until my divorce goes through. No matter how much I want to keep him and love him for the rest of my life, I have to let him go. I have to.

"No crying," he says with a small smile curving his lips. He catches one of my tears and wipes it away before cupping my jaw. "This isn't goodbye."

My lip wobbles and I take in a shuddering breath. "I can't even begin to tell you how much you've helped me."

"I won't stop until you tell me to. My lawyer will be in contact."

"I'll pay you back."

He shakes his head. "You don't have to."

"But I will."

He gives me a half grin before looking away. "Fine."

I bring his face back so I can see his eyes and I smile. "Thank you."

"Anytime," he says before leaning his forehead to mine. "Call me. Anytime. I want to hear from you. I want to know you're safe."

"I will," I promise. He nods before capturing my mouth. My eyes drift close as our mouths move together. When he pulls away, I bite into my lip to keep it from wobbling as he slowly backs away from me.

"I'll see you soon," he says, and it's like he is promising me that.

I can only nod as he gives me a small wave before turning to walk away. Tears rush down my face and then I yell out, "Don't."

He stops and then turns to look at me. "What?"

"Don't leave," I say closing the distance between us. "I know it is selfish of me to ask you to stay, but please. Don't leave. We can figure something out. I just don't want you to leave."

I should be embarrassed, ashamed even, but I don't know how to do this on my own. I've tried so hard to be strong but I can't watch him leave. I need him. I'm scared, terrified really, to face a day without him. This damn fear in me just won't go away. If it isn't Rob, it's the fear of being alone. When will it ever go away?

When his hands come up to cup my face, I close my eyes, feeling safe in his hands.

"Violet." He says my name as if it's his last breath. His breath tickles my face as he whispers, "As much as I want to stay here and be with you, I need you to love yourself before you can love me."

"But I—"

He shakes his head, covering my mouth with his own and stopping anything else from coming from my lips. He draws the kisses out of me, out of my soul. I never want it to end but it does. Looking up into his beautiful whiskey eyes that I am going to miss more than ever, I feel my lip wobble because I know he is leaving. I can see it in his eyes. As much as it pains him and I know he doesn't want it, he is leaving.

"No, don't say it. You need to grow, you need to heal, and you need to love yourself before you can ever love me. You need time for yourself and I know this. This is why I am walking away because I know that one day you'll come back to me."

A tear rolls down my face, my heart breaking as I whisper, "What if I'm too late though? What if you get tired of waiting for me?"

He smiles, his perfect mouth curving in a way that leaves me breathless. "Won't happen."

I take in a breath, biting on my lip to keep it still as I look up at him. I ask, "How do you know? How am I enough? I've done nothing to keep you. I don't believe I'm worth it."

His head falls to the side as he gathers me in his arms. "You're more than enough, but this is the reason you need time. You have to love yourself, Violet. You have to, or we will never last. I want a life with you and I have no problem waiting because I believe in you. I do."

I wish I believed in myself but all I can think is that when he walks away I'll be alone and have no one. I've never been alone. I've always had someone to fall back on and maybe that's the root of my fear. God, I am so fucked-up. It's scary, you know? Will I ever overcome this? Will I ever be the woman I want to be? Closing my eyes, tears leak down my cheeks as his lips dust my forehead.

"I'm just scared of it all. I don't ever want to lose you."

He nods, his face slowly touching mine as our eyes meet. "I understand that, but sweetheart, there is this huge universe, nine planets and two hundred and four counties and out of all that, I met you, I fell for you and have had the pleasure to feel your lips against mine. You are the piece of me that was missing. My heart and soul. Nothing will ever change that. My love will never fade because you have me. All of me."

He says it so confidently, so full of himself, as if he knows that it is the truth and I want to believe him. Maybe he is right. Maybe I need this time. I've wanted nothing more than to do this all myself and here I am, about to do it all and I am panicking. This is what I wanted. I wanted to be away from Rob. I want to heal. I want my life back so I need to stop this. I need to let him go because I know in my heart that one day he will be mine and we will be happy. Change is the scariest thing in the world. It is, but you know what is worse? Regret. And if I don't let this man go and I don't heal and love myself than he's right, we won't last and that can't happen.

I love him.

I have to let go and pray that one day his heart will lead him back to me.

Opening my eyes, I run my hands up his chest, up his neck to cup his face. I look into his eyes and know that this is going to be brutal but it has to happen. So with a nod, I press my lips to his as my tears roll down my face. Then I let go and slowly back away. He watches me and somehow, I muster up the strength to smile, to show him I got this even though inside I don't believe that at all. A smile curves his lips as he slowly waves.

He turns and I watch as he disappears into the crowd of people who are leaving. My heart is pounding; I feel like the biggest part of my soul is gone. I want to cry out for him, I want to give up, but instead, I turn and head out the airport thinking that I may not be okay right now and that's okay but I will be okay. I will succeed.

And I will love Tucker McCloud for the rest of my life.

Chapter
TWENTY-THREE

"It's been eight months since I left my husband and I have slowly but surely found myself again. It hasn't been easy. No. Not at all. I've cried, I've wanted to give up, and I've wanted to just scream but I'm still here. I'm me again."

A true smile rests on my lips as the woman I started this journey with looks at me with love in their eyes. There were only four of us when I started: Jenifer, Megan, Riley, and Amy, but today a beautiful girl with blond hair and blue eyes showed up with a busted lip. She reminds me of myself eight months ago and I want nothing more than for her to get out and leave. I can tell she is stronger than I was. She could only take a month of it before she was ready to go. The only problem is that she is pregnant and doesn't know what to do.

I'm thankful I was never in that position but there is no reason why she can't leave. For the first time since I came to this group, I'm introducing myself without even thinking twice about the words that are leaving my lips. I have never been so proud of myself in my life. I say the words about how I left, how I got away, and how I stayed away, so proudly. And I should say it that way. I should be proud of myself. I mean, look at me. I'm beautiful again. My eyes are actually sparkling. Can you believe it? Guess what? I love me. I do. I love the person I have grown into and even with all the drama Rob continues to put me through, I'm happy.

I have done it.

Judy, the group leader, sits in front of me, nodding her head as she smiles. "Any word on your divorce?"

Blah. I hate talking about this, but I know I have to. It helps.

"He still won't sign and now he is threating anyone who comes to his door. My lawyer wants to send a cop out there but the law enforcement won't get involved unless he does something to the people delivering the papers."

Judy nods. "But still no contact with you?"

I smile as I shake my head. "No, and I couldn't be happier. He has called my mom multiple times and I feel bad but she tells me she can handle it."

I know you are confused but after realizing that I am always depending on someone, I decided that I was going to move to my grandpa's house by myself. My mom and Tucker threw a fit but they understood and supported me. So now, I'm making a house my home and I love it. Before, though, I was scared out of my mind every second of the day, worried Rob would find me. But he hasn't. He went to my mom's house a week after I left, and my mom acted as if she didn't know where I was. He was livid but thankfully, my mom wasn't alone so he left and hasn't come back. It terrified me, though. I knew he would find me, somehow he would, but to my surprise Rob has never thought to look here. Now, I walk with no cares in the world. I wear what I want. I do what I want and I am happy.

I have my life back.

Well. Part of it, at least.

The other part is in Tennessee, over one thousand, two

hundred, and eighty-two miles away. I miss him, more than anything in the world, but not once have I regretted watching him walk away. It had to happen and it has paid off. I'm sitting so tall, I am proud of who I am, and it has everything to do with him. He helped me get away. He loaned me the strength I needed. He loved me when I didn't think I deserved it.

He saved me.

"Things are still good at work?" Judy asks me, and I nod.

"Yes. I love it there. I miss my old office but Dr. Fresh is a nice guy."

Judy continues to smile because she set me up with this guy and then Tucker talked to him. I got an interview and the next thing I know, I'm hired. It worked out because I needed money. The lawyer Tucker hired is not cheap. Thankfully, though, I'm making it. I'm going to be fine.

"This is true but I understand why you would miss your old office. The McClouds are good people."

It's a small world, you know? Judy is Tucker's mom's friend from college and they stay in contact regularly. Tucker is the one who found this group for me. It's forty minutes away but it's worth every minute it takes for me to get here. I just feel so complete when I leave these meetings and I know they have helped me learn to love myself again. Sometimes, when it's dark and I'm sitting on my porch enjoying the view from my grandpa's house, I think that it was all fate.

Brace yourself, but I've forgiven Rob.

I'm not saying I want to see him tomorrow, but I'm not scared of him anymore. He has no hold on my life. I have me back and nothing can ever hold me back. I know you probably think I'm nuts, and I understand that, but I had to forgive him to get me back. Thinking of him, giving in to my fear of him, gave him power—and I couldn't do it anymore. I have the power now. Now all I need is for him to sign these fucking papers so I can be completely rid of him.

"They are," I agree with a smile.

"I think it's easy to tell that we are all very proud of you, Violet," she says before turning to the new girl. "Jami, see it's possible. You can leave and not worry at all."

I watch as Jami slowly shakes her head and the tears roll down her face as she starts to sob in front of us. I feel horrible and as she goes into the reasons of why she can't leave — he'll find her, she's scared, he owns her — you know, it's the same shit I went through. I stand up and walk to her, surprising everyone. Bending down in front of her, I take her hands in mine as I look up into her beautiful blue eyes and I smile. Her eyes are sad, her soul is broken, and I feel it's my duty to do what was done for me. As much as I thank Tucker for what he has done, because obviously he's done more than any other man would have, I have to remember that it wasn't just him who helped me leave. It was Marci, my old group leader, too.

It's funny how different people help you in life. Tucker gave me the strength and the love I needed, while Marci gave me the knowledge and the kick I needed. Tucker tried so many times to tell me to leave, hell my mother did too, but it took six sentences to wake me the hell up. So looking up into this beautiful girl's eyes, I say, "We all want the same thing here, Jami. We want you to get away and be happy, like you want. But I'm telling you, you're never going to leave if you keep waiting until you're ready. Because, honestly, you'll never be ready. You have to just go. You have to do this. You're ready in our eyes. If you weren't you wouldn't be here. You can do this, Jami. You can leave. Just do it. Don't let him hold you back, go."

As the same words that I have written in various spots of my house leave my lips, my skin breaks out in goosebumps because I know it's scary and I know it hurts but she has to leave. If she doesn't listen to me then all I can do is support her and hope she makes the right choices. But there's a fight in her eyes, something fierce that I wished I had found in myself a long time ago. I believe in her.

She's got this.

"I think she is going to leave."

I can hear the excitement in my mom's voice as she says, "That's great, baby. I'm so proud of you."

I smile as I reach for the groceries out of the back of my car. I sold my SUV to a car dealership that guaranteed me they didn't need the title. Sketchy but I needed to get rid of it. I didn't want to be seen in it and plus, because of it, I got a great deal on my little Honda. "Thanks, Mom," I say as I walk toward the house.

"No baby, seriously. You've completely blown me away, you are back to the amazing woman I raised. I am so proud of you."

My face warms as I lay my bags on the counter. "Thank you, Mom, really. I couldn't have done any of it without you."

"Yes, you could have. You've done it all."

"Tucker helped."

"Yes, he did, and I am completely in debt to him. But it took your strong will and that helped you, too."

I know I had said that I didn't want anyone to know about me and Tucker's relationship through this whole thing, but one day I let his name slip and she questioned me until I told her. He wasn't mad; I really didn't expect him to be and he can't wait to meet my mom. He is really amazing and I can't wait until we can be together. I'm not sure when that will be, but I hope soon. I miss him. Desperately.

"Yeah," I agree as I walk from the house to the car. I always try to hold back my feelings for Tucker when I am talking to my mom. She wants me to be so happy, I know this, and if she knows that Tucker can make me happy, she'll start harassing me about him. She already wants me to go out and meet people but I've been able to dodge that because my divorce isn't final.

It takes three trips out to my car for my groceries and in that time, my mother has told me her whole itinerary for her Bible Retreat with her friends. I am glad she is going out of town for a couple days. She needs time to herself; she has been so worried about me that I think she forgets sometimes that she has a life, too. She has started to date one of the deacons at her church and I couldn't be happier. I want my mom to be happy and I hope this little trip out will help her relationship.

"Sounds great, Mom," I say as I put things away.

"I'm a little nervous, though. I don't want to leave you."

I knew she would say that. "Mom, you aren't leaving me. You're going out of town. It's no big deal. You act like we live together. We're fifteen minutes apart."

"I don't care. I worry."

"I know, but I am fine."

She pauses and I can tell she is holding something back. "What?"

"Nothing."

"Yes, it *is* something, what is going on?"

"Rob called yesterday, asking the same questions like always. I told him I had no clue. That you won't tell me but something seems off. He sounded a little crazed. He was screaming more than usual and calling me the most awful stuff, so I don't know. Maybe you could come with me?"

I shake my head. So he had a temper tantrum? I don't care. He won't find me. He can't find me. I am too close to being done with him. "Everything will be fine, Mom. Don't worry. I'll call Tucker and ask him to tell my lawyer that he called again. It's almost over. I'm almost completely done with him."

"Good, well, call me if you need anything. I'll only be an hour away."

I nod. "Thanks, Mom. Don't worry okay?"

"I'll try not to."

"Good. Bye, love you."

"Love you more, baby, bye."

Hanging up the phone, I lean against the counter and look at the time. It is too early for me to call Tucker because he is at work. Laying my phone down, I moved around the house, doing things that need to be done while trying to calm myself. Being on the phone with my mom, I hid the fact that I was scared out of my mind, but now that I'm alone, I'm freaking out. My hands are shaking but I don't know why. He can't find me. He won't. I'm safe. I'm not scared. I'm going to be fine.

Nodding to myself, I know I'm right. There is nothing to worry about.

Nothing.

Leaning back in my rocking chair, I let out a breath before bringing my sweet tea up to my lips. It's such a gorgeous night, not too cold so I'm able to sit outside. I throw my legs up on the banister and lean back, closing my eyes. I love it here, I do, but I miss Tennessee. I miss the beautiful trees, the weather, the kindness in the town. I miss how close everything was there; here it takes forever for me to do anything. I miss my job. My coworkers and even the work load, everything. I miss it. I mean don't get me wrong – I love working with Dr. Fresh, but he isn't Tucker.

Boy, do I miss Tucker.

When my phone starts to ring, I laugh when I see who it is. "I was just thinking of you."

"Well, that's nice to hear. What were you thinking?" he says in his low sexy way.

A shy smile rests on my lips as I say, "About how much I miss you."

I can hear the smile in his voice. "I miss you too, Violet. A lot."

Before I can say that I missed him more, he asks, "How did today go?"

"It went well. I went to work, then my self-defense class and then to group and guess what? I think I actually helped someone," I say with a big grin.

"That's amazing, Violet. What happened?"

I explain Jami's whole situation and tell him what I said and how I think that she will leave him. I'm still on a high from it. I feel so good, like I passed on the torch. Like Marci had done for me.

"That's awesome, I'm so proud of you."

I smile, biting into my lip. It's awesome to hear my mom say she is proud of me but when Tucker does it, I tend to get a little more giddy about it. "Thanks, it was an awesome moment and actually has me thinking."

"About?" he asks and I can't stop smiling.

"I think I want to go to school for social work. I want to help abused women. I want to make a difference; I want to be what Marci was to me. I want to be the strength for a woman like how you've been. Ack! I'm not sure if this is doable but I sure hope it is. I mean, don't get me wrong, I love working as an office manager and I know my goal was to be a CEO but maybe, this is something I should do. Maybe this is my calling."

When he goes silent, my heart drops and then I sit up, letting my legs hit the ground. Does he think it's stupid? Is it stupid? No, it can't be. I didn't go through all this shit for nothing. I went through it to grow and to also one day help a woman who is in the exact same position I was in. I completely believe that but I want Tucker to agree. I need him to agree because I want him to be there with me, every step of the way.

"Tucker?"

"I am completely stunned. Sweetheart, I think you would be the best counselor and I think it's your calling. You are sweet, caring, and kind-hearted. You are a natural helper and I think you would save a lot of women. It would be perfect for you."

"Ekk!" I giggle, and his laughter rings over the line, too. "I'm nervous but I think it's something I really want to do."

"That's great; I think you'll do wonderfully."

"Thank you."

"Anytime."

I smile as I fold my legs beneath me. I'm on a natural high and I feel amazing. I think that this is the right thing for me. I want to help people and what a better way than doing what someone had done for me? It will be perfect, especially with Tucker right there with me, every step of the way. Which reminds me! "Question?"

"Shoot."

"Why haven't you cashed my check?"

He laughs and I roll my eyes. This man is notorious for not cashing my checks for the lawyer. I don't understand, it's simple! "Tucker, just cash the damn thing."

"It's so pointless," he complains, and I can hear him moving through his condo. "I don't like taking your money."

"But it's my debt. Please cash it tomorrow and stop making me call and beg you to cash checks."

"Maybe I like it when you beg?"

A breathy laugh leaves my lips before I say, "Then make me beg for something better, not about a check."

He groans, and I laugh as I reach for my tea. "No fair."

"Cash my check and I wouldn't have to play dirty."

"Fine, I'll cash it tomorrow."

"Thank you."

"Sure."

I can tell he isn't happy about it but he never is and I'm okay with that. Since the check has been brought up, this is the perfect time to ask about my divorce. "So I left a message for the lawyer but haven't heard back. Have you? Do you know what is going on with the divorce? My mom says that Rob called her and it worried her. He's being more than his usually asshole self, apparently."

Tucker lets out a breath. "Yeah, he is. Dean says he's having problems with the judge just allowing the divorce. He wants one more attempt to get it signed. If that doesn't work, then they'll pursue a default case. Don't worry. It's almost over."

"Good, I'm tired of it all.'

"I know, sweetheart."

"I'm worried a divorce won't keep him away, though."

"Maybe not, but I will."

I roll my eyes. "Oh gosh, the caveman Tucker is coming out."

His low laughter tickles the pit of my stomach, sending heat straight between my legs. God, I miss him. Suddenly something makes a noise behind me, and I whip around to find that nothing is there. My heart is jackhammering against my chest but it must have been nothing. Maybe an animal or something. Shaking my head, I lean back and ask, "So anyways, how was your day?"

He scoffs. "It sucked."

"Blah, why?"

"Because I have a shitty office manager. I'm about to fire her and beg my mom to come back."

I hate that for him. I want him to be happy but me leaving has taken a toll on both of us. "That sucks."

"Yeah, I miss the office manager before her."

"Oh?" I say a grin pulling at my lips. "Was she good?"

"The best and gorgeous, too. She had to leave for a while, taking my heart with her, but that's okay because one day she'll come back to me, all ready for my love and then we'll be happy. She'll go to school to be this amazing counselor and I'll support and love her until she's done. Then she'll help people emotionally and I'll help them physically until it's time to come home and then I will love the hell out of her. For the rest of my life."

My cheeks redden and my heart speeds up. I want those things so bad. I want to feel his body in my hands, his lips against mine, his heart beating against my chest. I want to love him and be there for him. I don't need him anymore, but I sure as hell want him more than my next breath. I just don't understand why Rob can't just sign the fucking papers. Let me go. Leave me alone. Live his life and I'll live mine. Let me be happy.

Closing my eyes, I push away all thought of Rob and think of only Tucker. With a grin on my face, I play along by saying, "She sounds amazing."

"She is; she has my heart."

I bite into my lip and I can't take this anymore. "I want to come see you."

It's the first time I've said that and I can hear the shock in his voice when he asks, "What?"

"I want to come see you. I miss you so much it hurts and I'm tired of being apart."

"But, what? Wow, you've kind of stunned me there. I miss you more, baby, but is it a good idea? Don't you think we should wait? Maybe until the divorce? I just want you to be comfortable and completely mine."

"That's the thing, Tucker, I am completely yours."

"I've waited so long to hear you say that."

I hate that we're doing this on the phone, but I have to tell him. I can't hold it in anymore.

"I know but there is more."

"What?"

"I love you. So much more than I did when I was with you and I think that's because I learned to love myself. And now I want to love you completely. I want to be with you, I'm tired of being apart, and I never want to be apart again."

He doesn't say anything for a moment and my heart stops as I wait for his response. Finally, he says, "I want you to come home to me, now. I know you want to never be apart again, baby, but I really think we should wait until the divorce is final. Can you get away for a bit? Maybe just a weekend, until we figure out what we can do? Or maybe I'll come there. I can't describe the feelings that are coursing through me right now, but God, I want to see you, hold you. It's been eight months too long, and I've been waiting for the moment, but I want Rob completely gone first. What do you think? Do you want me to come there? I can leave Friday afternoon and stay till Monday, I don't know. I'll think of something, I just want to hold you."

I want that, too, and I know he is waiting for me to answer him but I am frozen in fear. My eyes are wide, my heart is pounding and I can't seem to catch my breath because a hand has come over my mouth. Finally my fear subsides and fight mode kicks in and I scream but then I watch as another hand takes my phone and slams it against the floor. I scream out again, slamming my elbows into the person's ribs, but it's as if it doesn't affect them at all. As I struggle against him, I slowly begin to freak out because I know the smell of the person who is holding me. I just can't bring myself to identify him because that means he has found me and I am more than likely about to be killed.

"Thought you could get away, huh?"

Panic fills me and I know there is no point in denying who it is, because Rob Moore is going to kill me, either way.

So why deny anything?

Chapter
TWENTY-FOUR

Slowly I blink my eyes, trying to focus. Lifting my head, I go to push my hair out of my face, but I can't move my hands. I am tied to the chair I am in. My body is covered with sweat and I feel like I can't breathe. Frantically, I look around the room and I think I'm at his house, but it's empty of our furniture. The only reason I know this is his house is the counter still has all my cookbooks on them. I pull at my ties again but I can't get my hands out and my heart is pounding so hard it hurts.

What the hell am I going to do?

Tears gather in my eyes and quickly roll down my cheeks and into my mouth. I am going through the options of getting out of this room while still pulling at the ties. I don't understand how I got here? What did he give me, what did he do to me? I hurt everywhere and I don't know why. I think that's the scariest part. I have to get out of here. I have to get away. I can't let this happen. Oh my God, I am so fucking scared.

When I hear a whimper, I turn my neck as far as I can to see that I'm not alone in this room. A woman, maybe my age, is in the corner with her dark hair covering her face. She is wearing a business suit but it is mostly covered with blood and when she looks up at me, I can see why. Her face is mangled. Oh god. Pulling at the ties harder, I get one of my hands free and I cry out in joy as I untie the other one. Quickly, I undo my legs and then I rush to the girl to help.

"It's okay, we're going to get out of here."

She is crying and can only nod as I work on the ties that are holding her arms and legs together in a hog tie. When I get one of her hands free, her arms falls to the side and I can see her nametag. She works for the law firm that Tucker has hired for me and instantly, I feel horrible. It's my fault she is here but why the hell would they send some girl to deliver papers to an abuser? They basically signed her death certificate!

I can't believe Rob did this. I don't know what has made him do this but this is crazy. He didn't love me. He didn't want me, I wasn't worth all this! Why hurt so many people? Why continue to hurt me? Why can't he just let go? I don't understand any of this and as this girl watches me untie her legs I feel horrible. I bet her mother is freaking out. She is probably calling everyone looking for her baby. How could this happen?

I shake my head as I quickly untie her legs. My hands are shaking so hard but I still manage to do it. I reach out, trying to get her but she is hardly responsive. She looks horrible but I have to get her out of here. We have to go. Have to. Reaching for her arm, she cries out and I cringe. I reach for her again but before I can move her anymore, an explosion goes off and blood splatters against my face.

I freeze.

Slowly I blink as I look down at where the girl I was just trying to help has half of her face missing. I can see the remnants of her brain, her empty eye sockets, pieces of her teeth and soon it is too much to take. I close my eyes as the nausea hits me and then I fall, my face hitting the ground hard before I succumb to the darkness.

My head is pounding right along with my heart. Everything is blurry as I open my eyes to find Rob watching me. He is covered in blood, his eyes dark and his mouth is set in a hard line. My breathing picks up and instantly I start to pull at the restraints he has me in but I know there is no use in struggling. He has me and there isn't a damn thing I can do about it. Taking in a strangled breath, a tear rolls down my face as I stay locked in his hate filled gaze. He lets out a long breath before running the tip of gun along his temple, still watching me.

How did I get involved with such a monster? I knew he was evil but I never expected him to be able to kill someone with no cares in the world. He is looking at me as if it's just another day, not as if he had just blown the head off some innocent girl. I know I'm next and I am freaking out. I can't get away. I'm going to die and there is nothing I can do about it. Nothing.

He drops the gun from his temple and lays it in his lap before slowly clapping. The sound startles me and I jump, feeling as if my heart just stopped. With heavy lidded dark eyes, he stares at me before slowly shaking his head.

"I applaud you for getting away and staying away for as long as you did."

I don't say anything but my traitorous lip starts to wobble and I try to hold in my sob but I'm not sure I can. I am scared, so fucking scared, and I don't know what to say or do. When he stands, I start to struggle more as he moves toward me. I watch as he tucks the gun in the waist of his jeans before leaning into me, bracing his hands on the top of the chair, looking deep into my eyes.

"But there is no use. You are mine, Violet. You aren't going anywhere unless I say you can."

"How did you find me?"

He smiles. "They sent that dumb bitch over and your address was on the paperwork. I had completely forgotten about your grandfather's house."

He looks at me, his head cock to the side as a sinister smile comes over his face. "Are you mad? Are you scared? Have anything to say?"

"Fuck you," I sneer.

He laughs before shaking his head. "You'd like that, huh? Or what? Are you fucking that doctor? The same doctor who has been making my life a fucking hell hole? The one who got me fired from my job, the one who thinks I don't know he is doing this all. The one keeping you away from me."

He looks at me for a moment as what he says registers in my head. Tucker got him fired? No wonder he looks like shit.

When I don't say anything, he screams, "He can't fucking have you!"

I know I shouldn't say anything, but I can't have him going after Tucker next. "I don't know what you are talking about."

"Oh really? I heard you talking to him. You love him, you want him, you two have waited so long to be together and now is the time. Fuck him; he'll get what is coming to him."

Panic fills me as my eyes go wide. "Rob, please, you have this all wrong. I left because you kept hurting me. I told you that. I don't want to be with you anymore. It has nothing to do with Tucker or anyone else for that matter."

"Oh, do you mean your mom?" he asks with his mouth curved up. His hands are shaking, his eyes look crazed, and I swear he looks so much different. Like he is on drugs or something. Something is off and it has me on edge. What if he has my mom or even Tucker? Is he going to kill us all? Oh, God.

"Rob, she didn't know where I was, I never told her."

"Yeah, okay, she is a fucking liar too, just like you, but

don't worry, I'll leave her alone 'cause she isn't the one who took you away for me."

"No one took me away from you; I left."

He nods. "Is that right? Hmm, okay," he says and then he quickly pulls back, crashing his fist in my nose. I scream out, closing my eyes tight as lights go off behind my eyes. Pain rips through my head and the room is spinning. What is going on? Why is he doing this?

"If you're going to kill me, do it already."

When I open my eyes, he is looking at me, in the same position he was in before he hit me. "I'm not going to kill you. I'm going to make you love me and make sure you don't go anywhere else. I will break you. You're mine and you will realize that."

"I won't ever love you, never again," I say as my blood drains down the back of my throat. Tears are rushing down my face, mixing with blood and ending up on my shirt and in my mouth but I don't care. I can't look away. He needs to know he can't do this. "Let me go. You're only going to make matters worse. Leave me alone, Rob, you don't love me."

"I do!" he screams before crashing his mouth to mine. I try to get away but he is holding the back of my head, so with no other option, I bite down as hard as I can until I taste blood, causing him to scream out before pulling away, holding his mouth. He glares, his hands shaking, but then he is swinging back and slamming his fist across the side of my face. My head whips to the side and I cry out as the pain shoots to the back of my head. As my head hangs to the side, I listen as he moves away from me, and I slowly close my eyes.

How am I going to get away?

I thought I had it all figured it out. I thought I was done with him but here I am, getting the shit beat out of me. I was so close. So close to having the life I wanted, but now that's over. Rob has taken it back and he is going to kill me. When he reaches for my face, he lifts it up to look at me.

"Do that again and I'll blow your fucking head off."

I want to say 'do it' but I figure that wouldn't be good. I also think that maybe I can get away but the chances of that happening are looking slim. My body is shaking and the pain is unbearable. I pull at the restraints again but he has made sure they're really tight this time. I pull harder but they aren't budging. My chest heaves and my tears roll faster down my cheeks as I continue to pull.

"Stop, you won't get out," he says. "Not till I let you go."

I look up at him with pleading eyes. "Please let me go, this is crazy, just let me go. I will go and you'll never see me again. I won't tell a soul about the girl you killed, nothing. Please, just let me go."

I'm lying but it's no use anyway, he laughs as he watches me.

"I don't care about that bitch and, hell no, you aren't going anywhere. When it's time to go, we'll go together."

He's delusional. That's the only explanation I can give right now.

Slowly, I shake my head. "Rob, I don't want to go anywhere with you."

"I don't care. You are mine and that's final."

"No," I say, tears gushing down my face. "I'm not, please let me go."

My wrists are burning from where I am trying to get them out of the restraints. It hurts so badly, but I can't give up. I have to get out of them, I have to get away.

"No. God, shut up, you aren't going anywhere."

I close my eyes and continue to try to get my hands out. I hear him moving so I look up and watch as he moves toward where the girl's body is slumped over. Tears cloud my vision. I hate what happened to her, and I blame myself completely, but the thing is, I don't want to fucking die. I need to get out. I had to. Cringing, I try to pull my hands out but when I hear a trash bag, I look up to see him stuffing her body into the bag. Ripping the bag and having to get another one to cover whatever part of her has torn the bag. It's disgusting and I am gagging on my sobs.

I don't want to be the next one in the bag. I want to leave. I want to be happy. I want to be with Tucker. I want to love him and continue to love myself. I was so close, and I have to keep fighting. I can't let him take anything else from me. Squeezing my eyes close tightly, I take in a deep breath and stop my movements. When the sounds of the bag being opened and closed stops, I open my eyes to see him looking at me.

Rob's eyes are dark as he watches me. I don't know what I'm doing but I have to do something. "Do you need help?"

He looks at me funny and shakes his head. "I'm done."

I nod as he walks to the sink to wash his hands. I continue to watch him as he cleans up and I hope what I'm about to do will work. When he reaches for a rag and wipes down his arms, I swallow loudly and then ask, "Rob, what do you want?"

He looks over at me with a confused look. "What do you mean?"

"Well, since I'm yours, I'm wondering what we're doing. Like why am I still in restraints?"

He scoffs. "'Cause you'll run."

"No, I won't. I'll stay for as long as you want me. Just please let me go, these things are hurting my wrist."

He laughs. "Do you think I'm stupid? Do you think I'll fall for that? Shut the fuck up, okay? I gotta figure out how to get this bitch out of my house."

"I can help," I say, trying anything to get out of these restraints. "Just untie me."

When he whips around, I cower back as much as I can in the chair as he screams, "No! Shut the fuck up!"

The tears that were clouding my vision soon fall in heaps and I don't know how the hell I'm going to get out of here alive. I watch as he stalks through the house, picking up things, and all I can do is cry and wait. What else am I supposed to do? My wrists are burning and my face is throbbing, but I know I can't just sit here and wait to die or whatever else he is going to do to me.

Even through the pain, I continue to work my wrist, hoping that something will give. It seems looser, but I'm not sure if it's actually working. I start doing the same with my feet, hoping to loosen something. Rob is paying me no attention as he moves through the house, doing whatever the hell he is doing. I have to get out.

I have to.

But before I can even try to do anything, a knock comes at the door and I freeze. Rob looks at the door and then at me, sliding his hand into his jeans to get his gun. Slowly, he walks to the door as the knocking continues. My heart is pounding just as hard as the person on the other side of the door is but I don't know if I should scream or not. He could flip and shoot me, or the innocent person who is knocking on the door. My breathing is erect as I shake my arms, trying to get them out. It's not working. All it's doing is burning me more but I can't give up.

I can do this. I can push through the pain.

Walking to the window, he looks out, and I watch as his eyes go wide. My stomach falls and my heart constricts because I'm pretty sure I know who is on the other side of that door. Rob cuts his gaze to mine, his eyes full of nothing but hate and anger. "It's that fucking doctor."

I start gasping for breath as I look at the door and then back at him. He holds the gun up and slowly cocks it before reaching for the door.

No. No. He can't do this. Oh my God. No. He can't kill Tucker.

"Tucker! He has a gun! RUN!" I scream.

Whipping his head back at me, he points the gun at me and yells, "You, stupid bitch!"

I know this is it. I close my eyes tight, expecting the explosion of the gun but it never comes. I hear something hit the floor and when I open my eyes Tucker has Rob on the ground. Shaking my body I try to get out of the ties as Tucker throws a punch but as soon as he lands one, Rob is right back at him and my heart stops. Blood is dripping from Tucker's mouth and the sight of his blood makes me weak. I am scared out of my mind, but I have to help, I have to do something. When I feel something pop at my feet, the tension from the ties is gone and I kick my legs out before standing up and bringing the chair with me. Running backwards, I slam myself into the wall and it doesn't do anything but send sharp pain up my arm.

"Dammit!" I cry out as I try it again, ignoring the pain, and this time it breaks. I cry out in relief as I detangle myself from the chair and see that my hand is turned in a way it shouldn't be, but I can't worry about that now. I have to help Tucker. When I turn, holding my wrist in my hand, I can't catch my breath at the sight I see. Rob has Tucker on the ground, holding him down with his hands at his neck and Tucker, my Tucker's face, is blue.

"No!" I scream and I start for him, but I trip over something, falling straight on my wrist and face. It doesn't stop me, though, I go to get up and notice that Rob's gun is right there by my face. Reaching for it with my right hand, I hold it up and squeeze the trigger without even thinking. The blast goes off, vibrating up my arm and I scream out.

Silence.

That's all I hear. Opening my eyes, I look to see Rob lying on top of Tucker, blood spinning out of his neck onto the man I love.

"No, Tucker. Tucker," I cry as I close the distance between us. Pushing Rob off of him, I reach for him, holding him in my arms, ignoring the pain that is burning on every inch of my body. I have to save him like he has saved me but he isn't breathing. I shake him, screaming out for help but no one is coming and he isn't waking up, he isn't looking at me. "Tucker, no," I sob as I lay him down, searching his pockets for his phone. When I finally find it, I dial 911 as I cry. My head is spinning, the pain I am feeling in ruthless but I don't care. I have to save him. He breathed new life into me when I thought no one could. He saved me. He loved me. Now I have to save him because I will never love anyone but him. I owe him everything.

When the operator comes on the line, I take in a shattered, hoarse breath, looking around the room at all the blood and death around me. I am so dizzy, I can't even catch my breath but I manage to say, "My husband killed the man I love."

And then everything goes black.

Everything is hazy.
And I hurt.
Everywhere.
There is a beeping sound.
Where am I?

Slowly, I blink my eyes open to find that I am in the hospital. My mom is sitting in corner, her face showing every bit of her fifty-two years and I can see that she is beside herself with worry. My mouth is dry as I try to say something but nothing comes out. She must have heard me or maybe she just knew, but she looks up at me and freezes.

"Oh my baby," she cries as she gets up and comes to my bedside. She wraps her arms around my pain filled body. I cringe, but I still hug my mom. I thought I was never going to see her again. I thought it was all over for me. She pulls back and softly dusts my face with kisses before looking down at me.

"Do you hurt? Do you need something?"

"Water," I croak out.

"Sure," she says, and I can feel her shaking as she reaches for the pitcher, pouring me a glass of water. Coming back to me, she holds it to my mouth and I slowly drink. The cold water soothes my throat and dry lips and when I look up at my mother, I want to cry. She looks so worried, so freaked out, and I want to reassure her that it's not her fault. "I'm okay."

"You were almost killed," she said, tears dripping down her face.

"I'm fine." If I don't reassure her, she'll continue to beat herself up. "It's not your fault."

She nods, cupping my face as she kisses me over and over again all over my face. I flinch from pain, but I can't bring myself to tell her to stop. All I can think of is that girl's mother, crying and beside herself because she doesn't have her daughter anymore. I couldn't imagine my mother going through that so if she wants to kiss me until she feels better then I'm going to let her. Thinking of her death makes me think of the sight I saw before I passed out. My heart feels empty as tears roll down the side of my face into my ear. She pulls back and I look up at her. I am scared to ask this question but I have to know. "Where is Tucker?"

She bites into her lip, and I know he's gone. I close my eyes tight and try to hold in my sob but I don't think I can. I have lost the one person who was a part of me. The person I knew I was going to love and will still love for the rest of my life. Right as I'm about to let it go and succumb myself to the most horrifying pain in the world, I hear, "Right here, sweetheart."

My eyes spring open and I look up into the face of the man I thought I lost. An uncontrollable sob leave my lips and I feel like my chest is caving in as our eyes meet. I choke on my tears as I take in every single inch of him. His eye is swollen, there is a cut is along his nose, and there are finger marks on his neck. But even with all that, his grin is still unstoppable. Taking my hand in his, he kisses each of my knuckles before softly placing his lips to mine. I feel like I'm hyperventilating as I wrap my good arm around his neck, pulling him closer and crashing my lips to his.

His mouth moves along mine, skillfully but cautiously. I want to tell him not to worry, that nothing could ever bring me down from the high I am feeling right now. I thought I had lost him. I thought the part of my life that included him was gone. I never want to feel like that again, I just want to love him.

Forever.

Resting his forehead to mine, I ask, "Are you okay?"

"Sure, just a little banged up."

"I'm so incredibly sorry," I say as my tears run into my mouth.

He shakes his head, running his nose along mine. "For what?"

"For everything."

"Always blaming yourself when in no way, shape, or form is this your fault," he says with a smile.

"It's Rob's fault but don't worry, you'll never have to see him again," my mother says and I turn to look at her.

"So I killed him?"

She looks sad as she says, "Yes, but honey he tried to kill you and he's hurt you so bad. We thought you weren't going to make it."

I'm not sure how I'm supposed to feel but I'm relieved. I don't ever have to worry about Rob coming after me again. I'll never have to look behind me and worry that he is behind me. I'll never have to feel the pain I did when I was with him. I am completely free from him. Remembering my mom just said they thought I wasn't going to make it, I ask, "What do you mean?"

"You had an infection and because of it, you had a really bad fever. They have it under control and I don't think I can describe how good it is to see you looking back at me," my mom says before she collapses against me, bawling her eyes out. I look over her shoulder at Tucker and he smiles. Reaching out, he cups my chin, running his thumb along my bottom lip.

"I love you," he says, so softly I almost don't hear him.

"I love you."

I watch as his face relaxes, his eyes bright as he reaches out to take my hand in his. I squeeze his hand as my mother says, "I love you too, baby."

Both Tucker and I grin as we hold each other's gaze. Rolling my eyes, I rub her back and then say, "I love you more, Mom."

As my mom pulls away, I look up into her smiling face and slowly wipe away her tears. "Mom, I'm fine."

"Okay, hush, let me just hold you."

I laugh as she continues to hold me like I'm only two instead of twenty-three. Deciding that she isn't going anywhere, I ask, "How did you know to come to his house?"

Tucker ran his hand through his hair before shrugging. "I called you over a hundred times and then I tried calling your mom but she wasn't answering because she was gone. I called the airline but they didn't have any flights going out that night so I had to wait till early that morning. Finally I get there and you were not there but I could see the evidence of a struggle, so I go back to the airport and fly back home for reasons I can't explain. I just figured he would bring you back here and he did."

Taking my hand in his, he squeezes it. "I thought he was going to kill you."

"I thought the same thing about you."

Tucker smiles, shaking his head. "He can't kill me."

"Oh gosh, here comes caveman Tucker."

He smirks at me before shaking his head. "The only thing that would have killed me was losing you, Violet."

I slowly nod my head, tears leaking out of my eyes as I look up at him. "I couldn't lose you either."

A pained look comes over his face as he slowly shakes his head. "It has been the longest four days of my life. I wasn't sure if you were going to make it and I was freaking out and my parents were freaking out with your mom and no one could give me an answer I liked. It was hard, Violet. It made me realize that this is it. You are it. You are my other half, and I can't live my life without you."

My heart explodes in my chest as I slowly nod my head. "Then, please, don't ever live another moment without me. I love you, Tucker, only you, and I want you in my life for the rest of my life."

"Then you have me, baby, all of me," he says opening my palm and kissing the inside. I cup my hand on the back of his neck and then I bring him down to me, crashing my lips to his. I know I shouldn't be kissing him when my mother is holding me but I can't help it. I don't ever want to live another second without kissing this man.

I guess my mom figured we weren't going to stop, and she slowly pulls away and sits up. "Okay, well, I'll be outside."

I part from Tucker's mouth and nod as she gets up and heads for the door. "Thanks, oh, wait, Mom," I say looking over at her.

She stops and smiles. I wonder if she sees that I have my happiness in my arms now. I wonder if she knows what this man has done for me. How this man made my life worth living for. Her content smile tells me she might, but I need her to know and accept him.

"Yes, baby?"

"Mom, this is Tucker McCloud," I say squeezing his hand. "A man who treats me the way a man should."

Tucker leans down and kisses my lips again before whispering, "And I always will."

My heart explodes in my chest as I whisper, "He loves me unconditionally and I love him the exact same way, maybe more."

He shakes his head, his nose rubbing mine. "Don't think so."

I grin as my mom says, "It's wonderful to meet you Tucker."

Tucker smiles over at her, holding me tightly in his arms. I know they have met but I don't care. I want her to know what he means to me.

"It is wonderful to meet you, too, Mrs. Brooks. I promise I will always love her and treat her in a way that would make you proud along with my family."

My mom smiles as she slowly nods. "I know you will. Now if you'll excuse me."

She leaves the room and I look back at him, my heart fluttering with love for this man. Kissing my nose, he whispers, "I mean what I say."

"I know."

"This is a forever kind of love."

"You're right."

"I'll never hurt you, only love you. For the rest of my life."

I nod as the tears gather in my eyes. "I know. That's why I'm not even the least bit scared to completely give myself to you."

As his mouth curves in a smile before crashing into mine, relief fills me to the brim. I thought I would be worried, I thought I would be scared to give myself to him. I know I wanted it but wanting and doing are two different things. But as I sit here, in the arms of my savior, my lips moving with his, there is no inkling of fear anywhere in me.

I feel safe.

Completely and utterly safe.

When a knock comes to the door, we pull apart as two uniformed men walk into my room. "Hello Mrs. Moore, we need to ask you a few questions about the death of your husband, Robert Moore."

I slowly nod before looking from the police up to Tucker. "I love you."

He nods and squeezes my hand. "And I love you. I'm right here and I always will be."

"Thank you."

With a grin I know I need in my life, he says, "Anytime, sweetheart, anytime."

Epilogue

"Savannah, please, just leave now. I'll set up a place for you to stay. No honey, he won't find you. I promise. I know you're scared. We all are, but you can do this. That's right honey. Okay, go and I'll meet you there."

Hanging up my cell phone, I let out a breath as I close my eyes. Savannah has been a client of mine for two years now, and she is finally leaving her abusive boyfriend. Her situation is so much like mine was. Her boyfriend is emotionally abusive, physically abusive, and he has even raped her. Every time we talked about her getting out, she reminds me so much of me and it brings me back to that moment in my life but she is leaving.

Leaving.

Thank God.

I feel like singing out in glee, dancing in the rain but instead, I head to the living room of my house. Tucker is lying on the floor while our daughter and son, Julia and Carter, climb all over him. I don't know how he does it. He works all day and then comes home to these two crazy kiddos and keeps at it, making sure to prove that he is the best father imaginable. At night, he is the most giving lover and the best husband a woman can get. I feel like a queen when I'm with him and it makes my head spin to think I thought I would never have all this. I watch them play for a moment, Carter pulling his ears while Julia tickles his neck, and Tucker is just laughing, enjoying the two people who were put on this earth for us to love and nurture.

It's just so crazy this thing called life, you know?

If you would have told me ten years ago that I would have to go through a trial to later be found not guilty for the death of my husband, I would have told you that you were nuts. I would never hurt anyone, but I had killed a man for trying to kill me and the man I love. Even though I thought I would never get out of it, I rose beyond it and even bettered myself. Since then, I have a husband who loves and treats me the way I yearned to be treated. I have a perfect set of eight-year-old twins who light up my day and the most gorgeous home in the best suburb in Tennessee. I got my degree in social services and then Dr. McCloud surprised me with the chance to host my own home for battered women.

I probably wouldn't have believed you if you would have told me this ten years ago when I was weak and thought my life was over but here I am, looking at my family with nothing but admiration in my eyes. Loving not only myself, but also them. Okay, love doesn't really express my feelings for them. No, I need them more than my next breath. Nothing could ever replace the feeling I have for these three people, these three parts of me, and I thank God every day for them. They are my salvation, my happiness, and my life is complete with them in it.

When Tucker sees me, he smiles as he stops, lying back on Carter, while putting Julia in a headlock before whispering, "Mommy is staring at us."

They laugh at their father, their sweet whiskey-colored

eyes meeting mine as I smile. "I am. I gotta go guys, give me sugars."

"Why do you have to leave?" Julia asks as she comes over and wraps her arms around my waist. "Who will read to me?"

"Daddy will," I answer kissing her sweet forehead. "I have to go help someone."

"Like Superwoman, huh, Momma?" Carter asks as he leans into me.

I smile. "That's right, baby, just like Superwoman."

I lean down kissing both their heads before they run off, leaving me alone with my amazing husband. "Make sure to read to them, please, and can you start a load of laundry? I don't know how long I will be."

He nods, wrapping his arms around me and pulling me close. "No problem, as long as you come home later and let me love you into the wee hours of the morning."

I giggle as I push him away but he doesn't move an inch. If anything he comes closer with a naughty grin on his face. "We will see."

He laughs. "Which means yes."

"Maybe," I say, even though we both know it's true.

"Who is it? Savannah?"

I nod my head. "She's leaving him."

He smiles as he nods. "Fantastic. Are you good, we can call your mom, have her come over and sit with the little bits while we go get her settled at the home."

I shake my head as a smile pulls at my lips. He amazes me every day and everyday it's like falling in love all over again with him. I couldn't do half of what I do without his support. Hell, his whole family. The McClouds have helped me every inch of the way. I couldn't be more thankful for them and I know you're wondering, but even Blaine and I are good. After finding out about what was going on, he apologized for being so hard on me. I didn't accept his apology because I deserved it. It doesn't matter now, though. My life is complete. We are good and Blaine even comes to cook for the shelter when he's in town.

Looking up at my husband, I smile. "It's fine. Marci is going to meet me and help me get her settled."

"Good. Have I told you I was proud of you lately?"

"Nope," I say with a teasing grin.

He smiles, leaning down and nipping at my bottom lip. "Well I am and I love you, too."

I close my eyes and go up on my tippy toes, kissing him long and hard, hoping he can feel how much I love him. When we part, I run my finger down his jawline and met his gaze with mine.

"I love you."

"I know you do," he says with a wink. He lets me go before playfully smacking my behind. When I smile up at him, he says, "Go save the world, Superwoman."

I nod my head because I intend to. No woman should take the abuse of any asshole and I don't care what I have to do—I am going to fight and make sure to help everyone woman I can. I know I can't save the world but I can't give up. I have to try. I have to fight, just like Tucker fought for me. No woman should feel like she isn't worth the love of a good man and if for some reason you hear my story and think you can't get out, let me tell you, you can. It won't be easy and you'll want to quit, but you can do it.

You can succeed.

Just believe in yourself.

Leave fear at the door and just jump in.

The world is at your fingertips and you deserve it.

You can be happy, you know?

Don't ever forget that.

Acknowledgements

When I wrote the first chapter of this book I sent it to my beta readers and one of them came back and said, "It's so real and I have to ask, is Michael beating you?"

I laughed. I thought it was the funniest thing in the world because my husband, Michael, would never ever do anything like that to me. All he knows how to do is love me. This has been a really tough couple months for me and like the champ he is, he has stood beside me and been the husband that I wish for everyone woman out there. Because of that, thank you, Michael. I love you.

My babies, Mikey and Alyssa, my life wouldn't be worth living it wasn't for you two. Thank you for being mommy's biggest fans.

Nick, I love you guy, so much and I thank you for being so supportive and helping me out so much.

Noey, wow, things suck so bad for us right now but I am thankful to have a brother that stands through thick and thin with me. I love you so much and don't you ever forget that.

Kristina, Dad, and Patsy, thank you for being there and loving me.

Nortis, what do you say to the bestest friend in the world. I love you and your family so much. Thank you so much for giving me a second family to love as much as my first.

Bobbie Jo, my Bobka, I couldn't have done these past few months without you. Thank you and I love you.

Heidi, my main chick, I love you girl and I couldn't thank you enough for your guidance, your advice and your love. I am so thankful to have you.

Jamie, I couldn't have written this book without you. Honestly. You knowledge and your heart helped me in every way. Thank you. I love you.

Fallon, this is our first editor/author dance together and I couldn't be more thankful for you. I have learned so much from these edits and I look forward to our future together. Thank you.

Toski, wow. What do I say to the person that listen to my vision and brought it to life? I am so thankful for not only your talent but also your friendship. This book couldn't have be complete without you so thank you. Thank you for bringing my book to life.

Sommer, just like Tosky this book wouldn't have been born without your creative decisions. Everything you have done has been golden and I couldn't thank you enough. I look forward to our future together and I thank you.

My main pimp, Jodi, you rock my world girl. I am so thankful to have you in my life. Thank you. And I love your flipping face!!!!

Beth, thank you for reading my book and bring the trailer to life. You are magical girl. Thank you.

My betas: Mary, Susie, Lisa, Althea, Jessica P, Jen Cola, and Julie P, thank you all for your time, your heart and your opinions. Let it be Me wouldn't be what it is without y'all. Thank you. Thank you so much.

Sue Grimshaw, thank you for believing in me.

And last but sure as hell not least, my fans. Thank you. From the bottom of my big ole heart. Thank you for taking the chance on this. I know this book is so much different than what I usually write. My best friend, Bobbie said that this is from my blue period and she is right. I wanted to send a message to women in this position to get the hell out. That they can do it. I know it is hard, I know it is scary but get help. Ask for someone to be your Tucker and get away from your abuser.

For more help please visit, http://www.joyfulheartfoundation.org or go to a meeting in your town or the next town over. There is so many outlets, so many people that want to help.

I believe in you. Now believe in yourself and live your dreams.

Thank you.

Books by Toni Aleo

The Assassins Series
Loveswept titlies:
Taking Shots
Trying to Score
Empty Net
Falling for the Backup
Laces and Lace (Due our November 2014)
A Very Merry Hockey Holiday (Due out December 2014)

The Bellevue Bullies Series
Boarded by Love
Clipped by Love (Early 2015)
Hooked by Love (Late 2015)

Standalone
Let it be Me

Taking Risks Series
The Whiskey Prince
Becoming the Whiskey Princess (Due out 2015)

And coming soon on December 9th, 2013
Blue Lines

About the Author

Toni Aleo is the author of the Nashville Assassins Series and Let it be Me. When not rooting for her beloved Nashville Predators, she's probably going to her husband's and son's hockey games and her daughter's dance competitions, taking pictures, scrapbooking, or reading the latest romance novel.

She lives in the Nashville area with her husband, two children, and a bulldog.

Read more about Toni at
http://www.tonialeo.com

Or connect with her:
Facebook: http://www.facebook.com/tonialeo1

Twitter: tonilovesweber6

This paperback interior was designed and formatted by

www.emtippettsbookdesigns.com

Artisan interiors for discerning authors and publishers.

www.ingramcontent.com/pod-product-compliance
Lightning Source LLC
Chambersburg PA
CBHW070656180626
46817CB00006B/2404